Praises for *Emerging Woman*

*The story of Emerging Woman stunned me into silence
(a very rare thing). The story is gripping with no slow points.
This is by far the best book on a woman's personal
journey to freedom that I have ever read.*

Pam Rousseau
MFT Marriage and Family Therapist

*Emerging Woman doesn't hold back anything, allowing the
reader to be intimate with the story. This is a book for anyone
who cares about women. And anyone who wants to know
MORE about life and truth. My favorite line is,
"Practice being still inside when the world
around you is in chaos."*

Brookelyn Sproviero
Professional Corporate Sales

*I am certain that this amazing and beautiful story of
Emerging Woman will resonate with anyone on a path of
spiritual growth and self-awareness. It reflects how we can
take each agonizing trauma and move beyond it. The
story is captivating right from the start.*

Carolyn Sell
Classical Cellist

More Praise for *Emerging Woman*

Emerging Woman walks the reader through the painstaking journey of spiritual awakening like no other book has done. For most of us on the path, we struggle alone in the dark. This book lets you know you can walk through the 'Dark Nights of The Soul' and not only survive, but be wiser and better for it. You can find peace and equanimity and a deeper connection to your own soul and to Source itself.

Sophia is a tenacious and committed spiritual warrioress. She has journeyed many times to the depths of despair, has been lost — adrift at sea without a compass — and has returned to land with all the gifts one finds in the 'Heroine's Journey.' For anyone one a path of spiritual awakening, this book will be a much-welcomed lifeline, guide, and companion for the journey.

Tina M. Benson, M.A.
Author of *A Woman Unto Herself:*
A Different Kind of Love Story
and
Soul Whisperings: Erotic and Devotional Love
Poems for an Outer or Inner Beloved

Emerging Woman

A Rite of Passage
from Shame to Freedom

Dear Shiri,
Together we Emerge
in the wholeness of Love
Kerani Marie
10-31-18

A novel by

Kerani Marie

Disclaimer

In *Emerging Woman*, a young boy finds a stone in a sacred canyon. He is encouraged to take it home with him and to honor it as a sacred talisman. At that time in the story, around 1974, there was little awareness of the importance of leaving artifacts and relics undisturbed in remote sacred places. The author encourages those who journey into the wilderness to leave sacred artifacts where they are found out of respect for the indigenous people.

This book is a work of fiction. However, it is based on women's real-life experiences fictionalized to develop the themes of transformation and spiritual growth. Names, characters, places, and incidences are the product of the author's imagination or used fictitiously. Any resemblance to actual persons, living or dead, other than historical public figures, events, or locales is entirely coincidental.

First Edition
Copyright © 2018 Kerani Marie

Edited by Alexa MacDonald
The Writer's Assistant

Front cover original artwork by Kerani Marie
Front cover artwork photographed by Tina Root McBride
Back cover photo by Noelle Gabermann Photography
Cover and interior design and layout Lucid Design Studios

SoWISE Creations
www.SoWISEcreations.com

ISBN: 0692099018
ISBN-13: 978-0692099018

PRINTED IN THE USA

*Emerging Woman is dedicated to
the soulful evolution of humanity,
and to my parents, who showed me how
to live from my heart and love more.*

Author's Reflections

Twenty years ago I was gifted a vision. As I sat in my candle-lit temple, I saw a red rock canyon. A hundred women were gathered to hear a story. Echoing off the canyon walls, I heard a voice speak to me, "This vision is your future. Call the women together and share their stories of emerging into wholeness. Share the journeys of women, their struggles, their triumphs, their initiations and rites of passage into new lives free from shame, fear, and doubt."

I listened to that call, and I began the 20-year journey of writing this mythic tale. The characters in *Emerging Woman* are a composite of all of us as we walk through this maze of life, tumbled and polished until our soulful light shines bright.

Each archetypal character in a myth lives within our collective psyche and informs us of deeper truths we all share. The characters in *Emerging Woman* took shape as archetypal reflections of our shared humanity and our particularly-feminine struggles in the pursuit of freedom.

This I know in my heart: The soulful stories of women must be heard. Only then will we be able to mourn our sisters' sorrows, understand their struggles, encourage their passionate creativity, and celebrate their triumphs and successes. Every woman has a story to tell, and every story contributes to our growing understanding of how to liberate ourselves from the cultural and societal restrictions that hold us back from being all that we can be.

Emerging Woman is for women who are walking the spiritual path, women who are embodying the Divine Feminine, women who are longing to connect with their souls, their voices, and their truth. And *Emerging Woman* is for those men who want to understand how to support the women in their lives and who long to better understand their own feminine natures.

May this story resonate at the deepest level of your soul. May it help you to emerge from the shadows of shame, doubt, and fear. May it help you to blossom into the fullness of soulful love, freedom, and joy as a sovereign woman.

Kerani Marie

Contents

And the end of all our exploring

Will be to arrive where we started

And know the place for the first time.

~ T.S. Eliot
from *Little Gidding*

Myth is a wild way of telling the truth.

~ Martin Shaw

Opening Ceremony

Grandmother Spirit

They call me Grandmother Spirit, the Soul Whisperer. I'm not sure when I got these names. At some point, this is who I became, and my old names dropped away. I am very old now, deep in the winter of my life, my hair as white as the snowcapped mountains.

It is quiet here in the lap of the Great Mother, in the spectacular red-rock canyons of southern Utah. As a younger woman I spent many days on vision quest here, guided by my teacher, learning to listen to my own inner wisdom. I have been here for three days, fasting and praying, preparing myself.

This is one of my favorite places, here beneath my old friend, Grandmother Juniper. This venerable old tree casts a welcoming shade and offers her berries to be sucked on. A cheerful stream laps at my feet. The colors of autumn are reflected in the sparkling waters like dancing red and golden butterflies. Old memories are awakening.

I was born in the autumn. This time in the cycle of the Earth awakens my deep connection with nature. I revel in the vivid colors of fall. I am inspired by the fearlessness of the foliage — letting go without regret, falling free, settling into slumber time. This is the time of year I choose to guide vision quests. In the autumn Mother Earth encourages us to trust, to let go, to nurture the seeds of our dreams, to prepare for winter's slumber, to rest, to turn inward.

For many years I have counseled women— challenging them, encouraging them to pay attention to their inner wisdom. I teach each woman how to listen to the unique voice of her own spirit as it whispers in her ear. I have guided many women on their vision quests over the years, and today I have called them all back here. I have a story I wish to share with them.

Four women have come early to help me prepare. They have cleared the circle and collected the stones and wood for the fire. They have built the Inipi, the sweat lodge that the ancestors of this land have generously blessed. Offerings were made as each stone and piece of wood was placed in the seven directions, giving thanks and asking for blessings from this fire, these stones and this lodge. The lodge is built in the Lakota tradition. It is Mother Earth's womb that we will all enter, naked and on our hands and knees, hiding nothing, ready to be reborn.

While they have been preparing for the Inipi, I have been preparing myself. I have performed my rituals and said my prayers. I am wearing my favorite ceremonial gown. My medicine bag holds my healing stone, sage, sweet grass, and tobacco. In these last moments before the women arrive, I close my eyes and go within. From the depths of my heart I pray for clear vision; I pray for the gift of powerful speech. May this story be of loving service to all and heal the hearts of many.

I hear murmuring voices in the distance, giggling, laughing, calling out joyful greetings. They are coming closer now, their voices drifting down the canyon. Then, gazing up, I see them – so many beautiful women! There must be more than a hundred of them! Bright splashes of color sway across the red rocks. I see women of every age, from the teenagers to the great-grandmothers. The younger ones offer a steadying hand to the elders as they move down the rocky trail. They have come. My heart is full of joy and gratitude.

Truly, this is an extraordinary collection of women! Each one of them has endured the fires of vision quest on her journey to understanding herself. Each one is deeply committed to her own soulful evolution through all of life's circumstances. Their lives are their promises to themselves to discover their own true natures.

We are all so happy to see one another! The women come one by one to greet me, and we share a heartfelt moment. In each woman's face I see the deepening of her soul's journey.

The women move off to find comfortable places on the red rocks around me and settle in. I beckon four women to come forward: a teenaged woman, a woman in her thirties, a woman in her sixties, and an elderly woman. They symbolize the four feminine life cycles: the Maiden, the Mother, the Matriarch, the Crone. They will help me with the opening rituals and will sit beside me as the story unfolds.

Together we prepare the offerings. We light the candles and the sage. We present our gifts of tobacco, sweet grass, and chocolate. Our altar to the Great Mother is a beautiful lichen-covered boulder; our temple is the magnificent landscape that surrounds us. All is still and quiet, as if the canyon itself is listening, waiting for the story to begin.

We light the fire. While I tell the story, it will heat the grandfather stones for the Inipi. The women will tend the fire and feed it so it stays strong, for it too will be a witness to the story.

I close my eyes. My hand wraps around the amulet resting on my heart. Everything becomes still. If I listen carefully I can hear Sophia's soul cry in the distance.

Help! I'm dying! Please, somebody help me! I am so afraid! This fear is a wild beast gnawing away at my insides! Am I going crazy? No one seems to know what's happening to me. I know I am dying!

Sophia's terror cracked her apart, and rising from the shattered pieces, she journeyed into the unknown to find her truth, her soul. Her journey was not an easy one. Again and again she touched the edge of life and felt the pull of death. But Sophia kept herself alive, holding on to a tiny thread, an instinctual knowing that all this pain and terror was essential.

Life gifted Sophia many opportunities to make new choices. Over and over again the thresholds appeared. Over and over again she opened the door and bravely stepped into the mystery. Immersed in the layers of multi-dimensional reality, Sophia chose to listen to her soul's cry for attention. She responded to that cry from within, and it altered her life forever; it helped her to heal her deepest wounds. I will tell Sophia's story, and my prayer is that those who hear will find solace and inspiration and hope.

When the time is right I begin to drum, softly, softly. The sound echoes off the canyon walls. When I stop, the drumbeats fade away. Then I speak.

Chapter One

Grandmother Spirit

Welcome my sisters! I am so happy to see all of you. I have asked you here to tell you a story. It is Sophia's story.

Many decades ago Sophia entered her vision quest journey right here where we are now sitting. Her heart was opening, and she was ready to create a deeper relationship with spirit. She could hear her soul's calling, and she longed to discover her true and authentic self.

She made many vision quests after that, and while it was true that Sophia learned from each one, she always came away from her quests with the feeling that there was more, something deeper she had once again failed to discover.

But Sophia was strong willed and determined. And finally, after many years of vision quests and spiritual practice, her prayers were answered. Here, in this very canyon, on the third day of Sophia's most difficult vision quest, the deepest secret, unknown even to her, was revealed. Her vision was shocking. It would change her life.

My sisters, there are many layers and dimensions of consciousness; there are many doorways that open up to the mystery. When you seek out one of those doorways, as Sophia did, and if you have the courage to walk through, you will find more than you have ever imagined.

Sophia's vision answered many questions that had plagued her throughout her adult life. Finally, she knew what she needed to do to further her own healing. However, there was a complication: her shocking vision had not just concerned her but also Anna, with whom Sophia had a complicated relationship.

They had been close since they were 18 years old, and Sophia understood how fragile Anna was, how dependent. Sophia knew with certainty that the gift of her vision was for both of them. She was determined that she would find a way to heal her own wounds and to help Anna find the peace that had always eluded her.

Sophia's grandparents came from Spain and settled in New Mexico, where Sophia grew up hiking the Sangre de Cristo Mountains and riding horseback along the Rio Grande with her friends. Albuquerque was a small city then, just beginning the sprawl that would eventually change its character and send it into a downward spiral of inner-city decay and racial unrest and crime.

Every month, from the time she was about ten, Sophia's mother drove her up from Albuquerque to

Santa Fe. They spent hours wandering the museums and art galleries, capping off their days out together with tea and treats at the legendary La Fonda Hotel with its mystery and magic. Sophia loved Santa Fe where so many artistic luminaries discovered their creative spirits. Sophia dreamed of being an artist one day.

Back home in Albuquerque, their lives revolved around the tight-knit Spanish-American community with its focus on the blessings and responsibilities of extended family and the moral dictates of the Catholic Church.

Sophia and Anna were very different. Anna always followed the rules, maintaining her good-girl image by actually being a good girl. Sophia, on the other hand, passionately longed to experience all the excitement that life had to offer. She was notorious for breaking the rules.

As an adult, Anna valued the security and the stability that comes from doing things "the right way." She was responsible and predictable, characteristics that Sophia, more bold and adventuresome, valued highly. Anna was kind and warm hearted, and Sophia loved her dearly. She was also well aware that Anna was emotionally immature, wounded, even fragile, hurt in a way that Sophia was only beginning to understand.

Sophia knew she was going to have to proceed very

carefully. How could she help her delicate friend heal from her great wound, even as she, Sophia, was doing? She prayed for guidance. She asked her friend and counselor, Perry, to help her, and together they came up with a plan.

* * * * *

Anna

The breeze feels good on my face. The fragrance of my jasmine tea is delightful. The woodpeckers are noisily poking holes in the ponderosa pines that frame our yard. It's a sweet yard. Overgrown bushes and flowers along the fence call out to be trimmed. Chirping birds flock to the feeder.

I'm sitting on the front-porch swing. I could be completely happy right now, but I am not. I'm beginning to worry about Sophia. I know she finished her vision quest almost a month ago, and I have not heard from her. She should have been home by now. When Sophia is away for too long I get jumpy, nervous. I start to lose my grip on my otherwise orderly life. Where is she?

I have heard people describe Sophia as mysterious. I see her as a woman of courage, integrity, and vision. Sophia has a passion for life! She is petite but full-bodied and strong with long, dark hair like mine. Sophia is full of energy. In some ways we are similar, and sometimes people think we are sisters. Her engaging smile and deep brown eyes seem to welcome you into her heart. She is my anchor. These thoughts sooth me, and soon, because I haven't been sleeping well lately, I am drifting off into a dream of ocean waves and seagulls.

I am startled out of my dream by a UPS truck screeching to a stop in front of our white picket fence. The driver hops out, barrels through the creaky gate and up to the porch stairs.

"Are you Anna?"

I nod.

"Sign here." Then he is gone.

I hold a package on my lap. It's big. And heavy. The return address is typed. It's my address. Does this have something to do with Sophia's unexplained absence?

This thought gets my mind spinning. I need to get this box open as quickly as possible. I grab Sophia's scissors and start working on the tape. Suddenly I'm not sure I want to see what's in here. Why? Am I afraid? Why should I be afraid of a cardboard box? I don't know, but I am. However, I am also curious and desperate for news from Sophia. My stomach does a flip-flop as I open the lid.

Nesting in the cardboard is a wooden box. It is golden brown with two ornate metal handles, one on each side. I recognize this box. It's Sophia's. It once belonged to Raven's great-grandmother. I lift it out of the shipping box and set it next to me on the bench where it seems to glow in some strange way.

I know I am supposed to open it. It was addressed to me, after all. But for a while I just look at it. Then my curiosity gets the better of me, and I slowly lift the lid and peer inside. On top is an envelope with my name clearly written in Sophia's hand. Under that, wrapped in a soft cloth, is an unusual stone; and under that, a stack of books.

The stone fits perfectly in my palm. It invites my fingers to close around it. It's warm. I enjoy the feel of it in my hand for a moment, but then — and I know this comes from the stone — I start to feel funny and a vision flashes across my mind. I see a group of women sitting in a circle around a fire. I drop the stone like a hot potato. It hits the floor and the vision fades. I am relieved to see that the stone is undamaged. Handling it gingerly, I set it aside and look again into the box.

I recognize those books. They are Sophia's journals. She has been keeping them since before we met. I have often seen her scribbling away at them, the stack of multi-colored bindings on her bookshelf growing taller as the years went by.

I stare at the envelope with my name on it. The air has gone very still, and the birds have stopped singing. Everything has become strangely silent. It occurs to me that I could just walk this box to the side of the house, open the trash, and drop it in. I could claim it never arrived … although there is the UPS tracking. Anyway, why am I having such disturbing thoughts? I take out the letter and read.

* * * * *

My Dear Anna,

Something extraordinary has happened to me. I've been troubled and confused for a long time about who I am. A voice from deep inside of me has been crying out, but I couldn't quite get the message. During my vision quest, I prayed for the gifts of my soul to be revealed to me. I prayed to heal whatever has prevented me from embracing my true self.

One thing that was revealed to me was that to live the truth of my soul, I must release my attachments to my old life and start building a new one. So I'm not coming back for a while. I'm going to take some time. I need to give myself space to integrate the information I've received. And I need to give you some time too.

Anna, I'm asking you to do something for me. I want you to read my journals. It's my hope that reading what I have written about my life will give you more insight into who I am, how important you are to me, and what brought us to this moment. I also hope it helps you to heal your heart.

I have entrusted you with a precious stone, a healing stone that was found in the Escalante River canyon when I was on pilgrimage many years ago. I love how it fits so perfectly in my hand and how it is shaped like an embryo. Over the years it has shown me visions and has spoken words of truth to me. Hold it in your hand as you read my journals. It will help you.

I am asking a lot of you, nothing less than witnessing my entire adult life. I suspect this will be difficult for you. But this request comes from my vision and it's important, maybe even a matter of life and death.

I really can't say more right now. Please do as I ask. Please trust me. Let Perry help you. Until we meet again!
I love you more,
Sophia

* * * * *

Anna

The porch swing has come to a halt; tears are running down my cheeks. A feeling of dread has descended on me. And other emotions too — a fear I can't explain and anger at Sophia for shaking up our cozy and comfortable life like this and for not being here to help me.

All the years I have known of these journals I have never, never had the slightest desire to read them. This is too much for me. No. No, no, no, no. I can't do this. I can't read them. I won't read them! I don't know why, but I am clear; I'm not going to read these damn things.

But how can I refuse Sophia, my closest friend – the one person who has always been there for me? What am I afraid of? We have known each other for nearly 50 years!

What could the journals reveal to me that I don't already know? Why do I feel so afraid? I am a mess of confusion. Sophia's absence is a hole in my chest. I feel so very alone.

As if on cue, my phone rings. I run to answer it.

"Sophia?"

"Anna?"

"Yes."

"This is Perry. You left a message asking for an appointment. I've had a cancellation this afternoon. Would you like to come in and see me?

I walk into Perry's office and it all pours out – how I miss Sophia, how I need her, the UPS truck, the journals and the stone, my inexplicable fear, my decision not to read them, and then my guilt and unhappiness at the thought of disappointing Sophia.

It's easy to open up to Perry. He's sensitive, direct, and understanding. Like most Jungian analysts, he is keenly insightful and an advocate for self-empowerment. Perry has a rugged, wise look about him. Brown eyes pierce through dark-rimmed glasses. He wears his long, white hair in a man bun. I can see that he recognizes how frightened I am.

He's sitting in his comfortable, overstuffed chair. Behind him, bookshelves are filled with miniature objects he uses for Sandplay therapy (which I hate). Masks from indigenous cultures stare down from the walls at the silent, waiting drums, the rattles and the shakers, leather and feathers. It's wild and primal in this room. Even so, I always feel safe here.

As soon as I stop talking, Perry says, "Sophia asked me to let you know that she came to see me last week. She asked me to assure you that she is safe."

At first I'm relieved. Then it hits me like a blow. She was here? "What did she say? Why did she come to see you and not me?" Even I can hear how timid and childlike my voice sounds.

Perry calmly says, "She said to tell you not to worry about her, and, when the time was right, she would return. She also asked me to encourage you to read her journals."

No longer timid, I roar, "That's not fair!" Suddenly filled with a frantic energy, I'm up and pacing the floor, even more confused than before. "I just don't get this. It's making me crazy!"

Perry's hand on my shoulder is gentle. "Sophia said she knew this would be hard for you, and she wants you to know that she will join you when the time is right."

I pull away and snap, "Why would she come and see you and not me? What does 'when the time is right' even mean? What are you guys up to?"

"Anna, I have known you and Sophia for a long time, and I promise you that if you are willing to trust and follow Sophia's lead and accept my guidance, you will find what you are looking for."

I yell at him, "I'm not looking for anything!" Perry is unshakable. His voice is always steady. "I want you to sit down and take a deep breath. Now, pay attention to what you feel in your body when you imagine yourself reading the journals and trusting the process."

So I think about it, and I check in with my body. We

have been working on this process for a long time. I know how to do this. I feel the sensations inside me as I ask myself the question. I'm surprised to find that, although the fear is still here, I feel gentle warmth, even a bit of excitement. There is uncertainty rising in my body, but my fears seem to have lessened some. Maybe I could look at this as an adventure. Maybe I will discover something, like hide and seek.

I nod. "Okay." I take another deep breath.

"Good. Now go inside again and see how it feels to choose not to read Sophia's journals."

I feel sad and empty, as if I was losing something very dear. After a few more minutes of silence, and from a still and potent place, I tell Perry, "It's clear. I know what to do." I immediately get up and head for the door.

"Anna! Are you going to tell me what you decided, or are you going to leave me wondering?"

I call over my shoulder, "I'm off to read the journals and find out what the hell this is all about. I'll see you soon. Thank you!"

Back home, as I step onto the porch, my eyes are drawn to the porch swing. Was it really only this morning that I sat there and had that vision? I feel both excited and apprehensive. I carry the journals back out to the porch and settle myself down on the swing. With some trepidation, I pick up Sophia's stone and hold it in my hand. No visions. The journals are numbered and dated. I open the first one.

Sophia is a woman who has faced crises and struggled with doubt. But she has always kept going. I am going to do my best to be like Sophia. A note is clipped to the outside cover of the first journal.

＊ ＊ ＊ ＊ ＊

Dear Anna,

Is this an illusion on my part to think that my life is important enough to write about? If so, it began long ago. I was just a mixed-up teenager when I began to write these journals. Only recently did I realize that all along I have been writing about my journey into consciousness — over and over again I have been forced to face my own unconscious patterns. I have come to a place where I can no longer indulge my doubts and fears. Nor can I ignore the gifts I have been given. To do either is to dishonor a sacred covenant, a vow I have made to my spirit, to life itself.

To really understand how I arrived where I am today, and in alignment with my vision, I am also reading through this record of my life, just as I am asking you to do.

These are the stories of my journey. They reveal how my humanness and my soulfulness dance together and sometimes struggle with each other.

They show how this journey pushed me beyond the conditioned structures of acceptable behavior present in so many families, certainly in mine! But you know, Anna, I am now and always have been a trailblazer, an initiator of change.

Each journal, obviously, reflects the energy and tone of the time when it was written. How the world has changed since we were teenagers! I too am reading the story of my life, and I can see my consciousness making incremental progress, even as I was experiencing the run-away evolution of the culture around me.

I have walked a difficult path, and I have learned, slowly, slowly, over the years to listen to something deeper than the voices of judgment and shame.

Anna, I hope the story of my life rocks your world. I am urging you to experience life in a whole new way, to awaken to new and extraordinary possibilities.
Loving you,
Sophia

* * * * *

Anna

I am so deeply touched I can't move – that is, until I see that my tears are falling on this precious letter. I dab at the wet spots. I sit for a moment, thinking of Sophia.

I have put my doubts and fears aside, and I am washed over by an instinctual knowing that it is all going to be okay. Just like Sophia, I can do no less than honor my inner guidance, face my fears, and do what I am being called to do.

* * * * *

Grandmother Spirit

Sophia's story begins over 50 years ago. Allow yourself to remember, or if you are too young for that, try to imagine how different the social norms of the day were. What is acceptable behavior now was completely taboo back then. What might today be considered a simple mistake was seen then to be a life-destroying devastation, an unrelenting source of shame.

I can see that my beautiful women of sprit are caught up in the story. This is gratifying!

Chapter Two

Anna

Sophia is and always has been a mystery to me. She is my closest friend and the person I love most in the entire world. When she is around, I feel somehow more complete. But I don't even pretend to understand her. I must admit, if I am being honest, that I have some feelings about Sophia's other worlds – her interests and her friends. I know about them, but I really can't relate. Like her constant spiritual seeking and her ability to bring about ease and healing in people just by putting her hands on them.

I understand what is happening here. She is asking me to open up to those other worlds. And I have agreed to do it. I have agreed because she asked me, not because I have any desire or inclination to explore what I have always thought of as Sophia's Magic. As a matter of fact, in all honesty, I am dreading this. I barely slept again last night.

Now it is morning and I have made tea and watered the garden and folded yesterday's laundry. I even cleaned out the refrigerator. I have no more chores or excuses.

I hold the first journal in my hands. Folded sheets of paper have been stuffed here and there between the pages, each one with my name on it. The first one is just inside the cover.

* * * * *

Dear Anna,

I know you are worried about me. And yes, things are not easy for me right now. Something happened to me a long time ago, right around the time that we met, and I am having to go back and unravel all the tangled threads of that time and all that led up to it. I am so grateful that you have agreed to be a part of this exploration.

In my vision quest I was given a different way to understand what happened to me. My prayer is that you too will come to understand your own experiences in a different way.

Here's the thing, Anna: I was seventeen, a smart and pretty girl, devoted to my Catholic faith, adored by my family, secure in my community. But there was another aspect to who I was, an aspect that I didn't even know existed — the part of me that was curious enough to go exploring where I was forbidden to go and rebellious enough to throw caution to the wind and forsake all that careful training. I made some very poor choices, and my secure little world and all the plans that had been made for me came crashing down, and I was wrenched out of one life and thrown into another.

Love you,
Sophia

* * * * *

Grandmother Spirit

In spite of her fears, Anna begins to read the first journal. It is dated October 31, 1958, Sophia's birthday. She just turned 15 years old. It was her *Quinceanera,* and everyone was preparing for the big celebration that marks a girl's transition into adulthood on her 15th birthday.

Sophia's birthday was an auspicious time of mixed cultures and traditions. It was Halloween, and it was the beginning of the three-day celebration of *Día de los Muertos,* or Day of the Dead, a time to celebrate the ancestors. And it was the eve of the two-day Christian celebration of All Saint's Day — November 1st for those in heaven, and All Soul's Day, November 2nd, for all who have died.

Sophia carried all these traditions in her heart and celebrated them in her unique way. She always felt deeply connected to her ancestors — it was something that was born into her.

* * * * *

November 1, 1958

Yesterday we celebrated my *Quinceanera.* Mom and

Dad gave me this beautiful leather-bound journal. All these clean, blank pages are so inviting! So this is my first entry. I want to write in it every day.

We got up early for a special holiday service, then there was a dedication mass. There were festivities all day long with music and parades and then at night there was a big dance.

At the dance, Mom and Dad gave me a bouquet of red roses. Dad danced the first dance with me to celebrate my coming into womanhood while the musicians played just for us and everyone watched us. Then Dad had them play *My Special Angel* and he sang it to me. I keep going over it again and again in my mind:

> You are my special angel, sent from up above.

> The Lord smiled down on me, and sent an angel to love.

He sang those words to me with so much love, and they landed right in my heart. Dad is the best dad in the world! For the rest of my life I want to remember how I felt last night — special, wrapped up in love.

Then, after all of that, Conchetta and Maria and I put on our costumes and went out trick or treating! I am so exhausted!

September 10, 1959

I'm not very happy with myself. It's been almost a year since Mom and Dad gave me this journal, and this is only my second entry! Oh, well. No sense getting down on myself about it. But over the last year I have had a lot of good thoughts that I wish I had written down. I'm going to do better. I'm making a commitment to myself that I will write in my journal every day, even if I only write a sentence or two.

Now to the good stuff! I'm going to have a birthday-Halloween party. I just asked my parents and they said yes! YAY! Conchetta and Maria said they would help me decorate the rumpus room. I want to hire the band I heard about at school. Some of the boys in the band went to AHS.

This is going to be fun!

October 31, 1959

I am so tired and excited at the same time. My party was a huge success. There were some amazing costumes! And everybody danced like crazy! The band was fantastic.

They played Special Angel and the drummer sang lead on that song. He looked right at me! Did he know? How could he know? He was staring straight at me. Our eyes locked and I couldn't look away.

He is really cute. His name is Kevin and he has grabbed my attention in a way I can't begin to explain. I guess he graduated from AHS last year, but I had never seen him before.

Kevin has lovely red-brown hair and gorgeous blue eyes. He's tall and built like a football player. He goes to UNM and wants to be a lawyer.

I think I'm in love. Have other girls felt like this before? It feels like I am the only one who has ever known this feeling.

December 8, 1959,

I overheard a conversation about Kevin at school. Some girls were talking and they said he had a bad reputation and that he fooled around with a lot of girls. Then I heard a voice inside my head. *Don't go out with him*, it said. *Don't get involved with that boy!* It just makes me long for him more. I think his bad reputation is exaggerated! Even if it was true once, I'm sure he has changed. They are not being fair to him!

But what if I'm wrong?

* * * * *

Dear Anna,

How naïve I was! I must tell you, it's a little strange to read what I wrote so long ago. My diary entries are so innocent, so simply written – and with so many exclamation points!!

I fell hard for Kevin. Now, of course, I realize that this happens to a million teenagers every day. But back then my womanhood was awakening inside of me, and it brought with it a longing like nothing I had ever known.

At first, in spite of my obsession with him, I decided to pay attention to what the voice said to me. I begged my mom not to let me go out with Kevin, only to find myself eight months later begging her to please ignore my previous request.

This was the first time the voice of my soul spoke to me, but I didn't pay attention. It has been one of the challenges of my life to learn to trust it and to act on this advice.

Love,

Sophia

* * * * *

Anna

Sophia definitely was caught up in the net of first love. She wrote on and on about her awakening feelings for Kevin. He had been calling her and trying to get her to go out with him. I have to smile at Sophia's teenage ramblings. I have a sense that I have experienced something like this, but I can't quite remember when.

I open up her journal to where I left off last and find another letter.

* * * * *

Dear Anna,

I didn't wonder much about my future at that age. My future was already clearly laid out before me. I would go out on a few dates, graduate from high school, find a good Catholic boy to marry, have a huge church wedding, have babies and raise a family. Marriage came after courtship. Sex came only after marriage. I would be a virgin on my wedding night.

We all knew girls who had to drop out of school because they got pregnant, but they were not like us. They were bad girls. Disgraced. Tarnished. I, on the other hand, was a good girl, and my parents did everything they could think of to keep it that way. On my first date with Kevin, I had to take my younger brother with me to ensure there was no fooling around! Imagine how a girl today would react to that.

Love,

Sophia

* * * * *

September 26, 1960

I am so excited I can hardly stand it! I am going to be a Homecoming Queen!! And Kevin is coming to the game and then his band is playing for the dance. So many amazing things are happening all at the same time!

September 27, 1960

Today I got to go and pick out my gown for Homecoming. I looked through hundreds of fabulous dresses. It was so much fun! I chose a beautiful blue gown that pushes my breasts up really high and has a very tight waist and long, full skirt. I've got the figure for this dress, and when I have it on I feel like a queen!

* * * * *

Dear Anna,
Isn't it interesting how we play out our roles in life? After being treated like a princess all my life, I was actually crowned Homecoming Queen!
Love,
Sophia

* * * * *

October 1, 1960

I don't think I had ever been so tired in my whole life. This whole week has been non-stop celebrations. It was a blast! There were Homecoming breakfasts, luncheons and photo shoots. Then last night was the main celebration with the parade and the game (which, of course, we won!) and the dance.

Kevin came to the game with my family and then took

me to the dance. He was playing drums most of the time, so I danced with other boys and some of my girlfriends. But I couldn't stop looking at him.

When the night was almost over, we had the last dance together. Halfway through the song he pulled me into a back room where we could be alone together. He brought me up close and opened his hand. He had a jeweler's box. He opened it for me to see. Inside were his-and-hers, matching heart-love pendants. They were beautiful! I separated the two pieces, and he put mine around my neck while I put the other around his neck. Then we kissed! I will never take this off!

He kept telling me how beautiful I was and said we were now going steady. I love listening to him talk that way. Later, exhausted, I lay in bed before I fell asleep. I could hear his voice saying sweet things to me over and over again in my mind.

* * * * *

Anna

Almost in spite of myself, I am fascinated by Sophia's story. I find myself reading sections of her diary over and over again. I can feel the excitement she felt when she got her driver's license. She wrote about her high school prom, dances, parties, football games, and homework.

Sophia was head over heels in love with Kevin. Day

after day her journal entries are filled with her dreams of love and marriage. She couldn't wait to finish high school so they could begin their life together.

Kevin studied hard, played in the band, and still found time to be with Sophia. He surprised her when he moved out of his parents' house and into an apartment close to the university. It was a run-down, shabby place — all he could afford on a student budget.

* * * * *

Dear Anna,

I started my senior year feeling like I was living a dream. I had one year of school left and Kevin had two years before he started law school. We were deeply in love, and I felt like I was really getting to know him. Certainly we were becoming more intimate.

We had not made love yet, but as the year progressed we began to talk about it more. As my last Homecoming approached, we were not just talking about making love but planning how we would make it happen.

I still had conflicting voices in my head. One very loud voice was warning me of potential trouble. But an equally loud voice was singing a song of first love and adventure and fairytales that come true. My body yearned for him. One little lie to my parents and we found ourselves together for the whole night after the Homecoming dance.

We started drinking. Alcohol was new to me. Even now I don't drink much because I get drunk very easily. And when I do, I get very excited sexually. I was drinking the vodka straight from the bottle! After a few drinks, it just tasted like water. Then our clothes were off and our excitement took us away. At some point, we ran out of condoms and, not caring, we made love all night long.

Loving you,

Sophia

* * * * *

September 22, 1961

It's morning and I'm sick. I can't write much. Last night I got drunk on Vodka and had sex with Kevin. What was I thinking? I wasn't thinking!

Oh, my GOD! I'm not a virgin! Even though I said yes, I really didn't want it to happen this way. What's wrong with me? Since I first learned about sex, I have had fantasies about what my first time would be like. It would be so romantic! There would be flowers and soft lights, music, and a commitment of his love. It would be my wedding night. Instead I got drunk, and now I am really sick and my head aches. And oh, my God! We ran out of condoms! No! Please God! Now I'm scared. I wish I could live yesterday all over again.

* * * * *

Dear Anna,

I vividly remember the feelings that flooded through me that morning – fear, remorse, but most of all, shame. I couldn't look at myself in the mirror. Good girls didn't get drunk and have sex with boys in sleazy apartments. And I was a good girl, wasn't I? I had always been the good girl. I hated getting in trouble. What kind of trouble would I be in if my period didn't come? As the next two weeks went by, I was terrified, remorseful, anguished, nervous.

Early October 1961, I missed my period. I didn't know what to do. When I told Kevin, he said I couldn't be pregnant because no one got pregnant the very first time. But when two more weeks passed and my period didn't come, he had to accept that it was true.

It's hard for me to explain just how shocked and devastated I was when Kevin said the only solution was to get an abortion. I wouldn't have come up with that as a "solution" in a million years. I was a Catholic, and I believed as a Catholic. If I were to have an abortion, I would be killing a child that God had placed in my womb.

But if I didn't, my whole life would be ruined. I knew about girls who got pregnant in high school. I had heard the stories of their sad, hopeless lives. And what would it do to my parents to have to bear this shame?

Finally, in a state of utter despair, I told Kevin I would do it. He made the arrangements.

Love,

Sophia

* * * * *

October 20, 1961

We went to a doctor's office in a part of town where I had never been before. It was run down and dirty. We sat in the waiting room for an hour with a woman who was there to pick up a friend who was in with the doctor.

When the treatment-room door opened and a girl not much older than me staggered out, I was horrified. She was deathly pale and could barely walk. With her friend helping her, she made it out the door which shut behind her with a finalizing click. I felt trapped. I was terrified. Ten minutes later, the doctor called me. In a trance, I got up and went into the treatment room, the door closing behind me with another ominous click.

Suddenly, I snapped out of my trance. This was wrong — oh, so very wrong on so many levels. I couldn't, shouldn't, wouldn't do this! No! I ran out of the treatment room, right through the waiting room, down the hall, and out onto the street with Kevin in pursuit. I was sobbing.

He tried to calm me down. He tried to coax me back into the doctor's office. Finally he understood. I was not going through with this. I could tell he was not happy. I knew he had already paid the doctor. This whole thing was a complication that was going to make everything more difficult for him. How could he finish working his way through school with a family to support? But he too grew up a Catholic, and he must have had his own conflicts over this, though he never spoke to me about them. He sighed and held me close for a moment. "Okay," he said. "I guess we're going to have to get married."

October 25, 1961

It has been so scary not knowing what to do, but Kevin and I finally have a plan to run away and get married. Then I can tell my parents that I got pregnant the first night we were married.

We have been carefully planning how to do this. We will go on the day of my 18th birthday so I will be old enough to be married by a Justice of the Peace. We will go to Las Cruces where we'll be less likely to run into anyone we know. After we are married we're going down to El Paso to celebrate Día de los Muertos. I'm so, so scared.

What if they find out I'm pregnant already? It would destroy them. What if they catch me trying to run away? I feel so ashamed. I just want to die. I can't look Mom or Dad in the face because I am sure they will see what is happening and what I am planning to do.

I've been gathering some of Mom's kitchen things for the home Kevin and I will make together when we return. I took some utensils, a pot and a skillet and a pair of scissors. I found some old bedding that I hope Mom won't miss. There is nothing in Kevin's apartment. I hope we don't have to stay in that horrible place for very long after we are married. I even took some of the green stamps Mom collects when she buys groceries, and I turned them in for silverware and dishes.

October 31, 1961

My parents went out for the night. That gave me a chance to get my things together. I told them I was going to a Halloween party with Kevin and some friends. After they were gone, I asked my brother Mateo to watch my little sister Serena. I didn't want her to walk in while I was packing. Mateo wanted to know what I was doing, so I told him. He got really upset. He said I couldn't do that! He yelled at me that I would be in big trouble. I told him I knew what I was doing. But I was lying. I don't have a clue what I'm doing. But I'm doing it anyway. I don't have any choice.

All the way to Las Cruces I was looking out the back window of the car, expecting my parents or the police to pull us over. There is a part of me that wishes they would find me. I wish they would rescue me, but they won't. They don't have any idea where I am. If they did, they would be horrified.

We're in a creepy, dirty motel in Las Cruces. For the first time we can be with each other all night long, something I had really looked forward to. But instead of a beautiful, romantic night together, we quarreled. Now Kevin is asleep. This is the night before my marriage, and I am so unhappy.

November 1, 1961

Today is All Saints' Day and Día de los Muertos. All day I have been praying to the saints and ancestors to help me through this mess. After we saw the Justice of the Peace and had our marriage license signed, we spent all day in downtown El Paso where it was like one big party with music and dancing and ceremonies and festivities going on everywhere. Finally, late in the day, we drove home to Albuquerque.

I am feeling pretty miserable. I left home yesterday without telling Mom and Dad anything about where I was going. They probably spent a horrible night worrying about me. I should call them right now and put their minds at ease. But I'm terrified to tell them what we have done, and I feel so ashamed. I am so bad. The thought of seeing the pain in Mom and Dad's eyes feels worse than death. I'm sure people can see just by looking at me that I am a girl who has let everyone around her down.

KERANI MARIE

November 2, 1961

This morning Kevin and I decided we had to call our parents. There's nothing else to do. We have to face them. And we have to face the consequences of what we have done.

His parents are used to him disappearing from time to time, but I have never spent the night away from home before without permission, and I can only imagine how upset my parents are. Putting it off will only make it worse.

We will ask all the parents to come over to the apartment, and we will tell them all at the same time. Our plan is to tell them how much we love each other and how we wanted to get married on my birthday. I don't want to tell them I'm pregnant yet. I'll tell them later and pretend that it happened on the night we got married.

November 3, 1961

The meeting with our parents was horrible. We told them we got married because we just couldn't wait. We were in love and wanted to get married now. I will never forget my father's fury and bewilderment. "Why did you do this? Why didn't you tell us? This marriage is not sanctioned by the Church. You, Sophia, are coming home with us until you are married properly in the Catholic Church! If you don't come home with us now, we will not honor this marriage and you will receive no support from us. Come home, and we will figure this out." I didn't want to go. But Kevin took my hand and told me to do as my father said.

* * * * *

Dear Anna,

I ended up going home with them. I was ashamed for lying; I was ashamed for being pregnant; I was ashamed for the anguish I saw on my parents' faces. I missed Kevin. I did not miss the shabby apartment.

We knew we would eventually have to tell them about the baby. Mom noticed that I didn't use any tampons that month and asked if I was pregnant. I said, "I don't know. Maybe I got pregnant the night we got married." She asked me why I had sex. I was shocked. What do you say to your mother when she asks this kind of question. I just said, "I wanted to."

I will always regret how I hurt Mom. I adored her. Lying to her was the hardest thing I had ever done.
Love,
Sophia

* * * * *

December 5, 1961

Kevin and I went to the doctor today and got a urine test that confirms what we already know. I am pregnant. Part of me was clinging to some hope that it wasn't true.

So now I have no choice but to tell Mom and Dad. Of course, we will stick with the story that I got pregnant on the night we were married. Maybe now they will let us live together.

December 6, 1961

Tonight we told our parents. We said that I must have gotten pregnant the night we eloped. Mom is really upset because I went to the doctor without her. I keep hurting her over and over again.

I'm still living at home, but now they are in a hurry for the Church wedding. And they don't even know that I'm a month farther along than they think. I feel so ashamed. I am such a liar.

* * * * *

Dear Anna,

Serena told me that the morning after we ran away, when I had stayed out all night and didn't come home, Mom lay down on my bed and sobbed while my Dad tried to comfort her. This is horrifying to me.

Also, even after all these years, I remember how awful I felt when a friend told me that my Dad had started crying at work. I had wounded my poor parents deeply and left them in a terrible position. How could they hold within themselves both the shame I had brought down on all of us and the vast ocean of love that they had for me. I was their beloved child; I was in deep trouble; I had done a terrible thing.

They had no way of knowing that I was just a little early in my sexual awakening. A few years later everyone would be talking about "free love." Reliable contraception would change the way young lovers behaved and give them the freedom to explore their sexuality. The occasional accidental pregnancies would soften old-world mores. Everything was about to start changing very fast. But not yet, not in my parents' world.
Loving you,
Sophia

* * * * *

December 19, 1961

Mom and I went to see the priest yesterday to set a date for the wedding. He said he didn't want to marry us because we are so young. So Mom went ahead and told him I'm pregnant. I could have died. Now the priest needs to get a special dispensation from the bishop to marry us. And he insisted Kevin and I have to get counseling from him about relationship and marriage. I cried all the way home.

But even that's not the worst of it. Mom says I can't wear a white wedding dress because I am not a virgin anymore and white signifies the purity of a virgin. I am going to have to wear a pink dress! Pink! After Mom told me this, I went to my room and sobbed for a long time. I wish I had never been born.

January 5,1962

I can't believe my Mother has to be so honest and tell the people at my school I'm pregnant. Lots of girls at school are pregnant and the principal doesn't know. Now I have to leave school. This isn't fair. I only have four more months to graduation. Now I have to be home-schooled for one class. It isn't fair.

* * * * *

Anna

I feel wrung out. Exhausted. As if I had been crying for hours like Sophia. It's cold outside, and the wind is howling. It just seems to make everything worse. I consider cancelling my appointment with Perry.

Perry, as usual, is warm and welcoming. But by the time I get to his office, my agitation had turned to anger. I spend at least ten minutes ranting about how unfairly Sophia was treated by her church, by her school, and even by her family.

"It's like a nightmare that Sophia can't wake up from," I say. "Her whole culture is condemning her. And shaming her! They keep telling her she has sinned in the eyes of the Church. Where's the forgiveness? Where's the compassion?"

"Didn't you know about this?" Perry asks. "You two have been friends for a long time."

It's true. But for some reason, we have never talked about this. I am lost for a moment in wondering why.

Perry startles me out of my thoughts. "How about we try Sandplay today?"

Sandplay therapy makes use of a sandbox, toy figures, and sometimes water, to create scenes of miniature worlds that reflect a person's inner thoughts, struggles, and concerns. It always makes me feel uncomfortable.

"Really, you know I don't like doing the Sandplay. I don't get much out of it." I was hoping he would go along with me. But he gently insists, "This is the perfect time. Go over to the shelves and pick your objects. And remember, don't think about it too much. Just let yourself be guided by your inner knowing about which objects to pick. All the emotions that you are feeling, let them guide you."

Reluctantly, I pick up a dark shadowy figure, a baby, and a masked woman. But before I can even turn around, I am overwhelmed with feelings. I walk toward the small sandbox on his table and start to place them in the sand. Then I just have to stop. "This really scares me. I don't want to do this."

"Okay, Anna. Come over here and sit down." Perry takes my arm and helps me. "You are in a deep process. Something is emerging in you. I know it's frightening, but if you are willing to step through your fears, you will gain a new sense of self-empowerment.

"Anna, do you remember the Rumi poem about not going back to sleep? Close your eyes and take a deep breath. I'm going to read it to you. I want you to imagine this poem is sinking into the deep, hidden parts of your heart and your soul.

The breezes at dawn have secrets to tell you.
Don't go back to sleep!
You must ask for what you really want.
Don't go back to sleep!
People are going back and forth
across the doorsill where the two worlds touch,
The door is round and open.
Don't go back to sleep!

"What does this have to do with me?" I am angry.

"Anna, your resistance tells me that reading Sophia's journals is opening up something in you that you don't want to see or feel. Rumi's poem speaks to not going back to sleep when something is awakening in you. I want you to read this poem when you feel yourself resist and remind yourself not to go back to sleep. And like I told you last time, I want you to pay close attention to your dreams so we can see what's going on inside."

"I just want to go home," I say, and I jump up and leave.

I am so angry, I feel like I'm going to explode. I'm angry at Perry. I'm angry at Sophia. I just want to forget it all – my promise to Sophia and all the things I am learning about her past. I want to forget all of it and go back to how things were before this started. I want Sophia to come home, and

I don't ever want to talk about any of this ever again. I just want to forget it all. Damn!

* * * * *

February 20, 1961

So now I am a married woman. My wedding day was hard. It certainly wasn't what I had dreamed it would be.

I woke up yesterday morning and opened my eyes to see the pink dress hanging on the back of my bedroom door. I felt sick to my stomach. That dress was a symbol of my downfall. But I had no choice. I bathed and dressed, putting on the pink dress of shame.

Later I was in Mom's bedroom just minutes before the photographer took over the whole house with his equipment and his bossy instructions. I was looking at myself in the ornate oval mirror of Mom's vanity when she walked in and said, "Hold your stomach in." I was stunned. I'm almost five months pregnant! How can I hold my stomach in?

But, of course, she doesn't know that I am that far along. It makes me feel lonely and miserable to keep secrets from my Mom on my wedding day. I just stood there, confused and ashamed, trying not to cry. Then I was called in to pose for the photographs. I'm not looking forward to seeing my own wedding pictures. I bet I look terrible.

When it was time to leave for the church, my Grandpa Alejandro drove me in his big white Cadillac. I love him so much. And I know he loves me, but whenever I look at him, I feel ashamed that I let him down. My Dad hugged me on the steps of the church and gave me his arm. I kept thinking, why is this happening to me? This is my wedding day. I should be joyful and full of love and hope. Instead I'm struggling to hold back tears. I said a prayer as we climbed the steps and entered the church. In the entrance hall, I caught a reflection of myself in the window. I looked tortured. I couldn't meet my Dad's eyes as we waited together for the first notes of the bridal procession.

How I dreaded the next few minutes. I knew that when I walked through that beautiful archway into the nave, everyone would turn and look at me. Everyone would see that I was wearing a pink dress, not the white one they expect. It was as if I had to walk down the aisle wearing a sign that said I AM NOT A VIRGIN. I AM A BAD GIRL. Inside my head I was screaming, *I am not a bad girl! I am the same girl you have always loved! You have known me since I was a baby. I was the little princess who grew up to be a homecoming queen, so full of promise.*

But from now on, that is not how they will see me. Now and forever, I will be the girl who got into trouble and got married because she "had to," wearing a pink wedding dress because she didn't deserve to wear a white one.

The walk down the aisle was endless. I kept thinking I don't know who I am anymore.

* * * * *

Dear Anna,

When I walked down that aisle, I was lost in a fog of shame and remorse. I still don't remember much of my own wedding ceremony. But I do remember one part. When we got to the place in the ceremony where I was to lay a bouquet of roses at the feet of the statue of the Virgin Mother, I looked up and she was peering into me with eyes as alive as yours or mine. It seemed to me at the time that she was scolding me. Her eyes glared, "Shame on you!"

Suddenly I was faint, disoriented. An usher came to help me. For a moment I couldn't move except for my eyes that frantically darted over the concerned faces of the people sitting behind my parents. I don't know what I was looking for — some miracle to save me maybe. I couldn't bear to look at Mom and Dad.

I saw a woman I did not know, also dressed in pink, though her choice was probably made for a different reason. Was she standing next to me up by the altar? No, that didn't make sense. She was there, sitting in the third row. She must be a relative of Kevin's or a guest of a guest, I thought.

She looked at me with an intense gaze filled with concern and pity. Our eyes locked for just a moment, and I felt a surging wave of recognition and loss. This, dear Anna, is how you first appeared in my life. Do you remember?
Love you,
Sophia

* * * * *

Anna

I remember her wedding, though I don't remember how I got there or why I was there at all. But this is how I met Sophia. I felt so sorry for her! How did she get through it all with those thoughts and feelings rushing through her? I can't imagine being in her place. I think I would rather die than endure that awful well of shame.

Knowing the details of her story opens a door in my heart, and I am overwhelmed for a moment by a wave of empathy like I have never known before. It takes me a moment to come back to myself, sitting there with Sophia's diaries and letters before me. I don't know why I never asked Sophia about the pink dress.

* * * * *

Grandmother Spirit

For good or for bad, your mother will shape your journey through life. Nothing is more foundational in a woman's experience than her relationship with her mother.

We humans are complicated creatures. We carry not just the scars and lesions of our personal wounds, but also the inherited traumas and unconscious patterns of our mothers and fathers, our grandparents and our great-grandparents — generation after generation passing on to their sons and daughters whatever has not been healed.

For women, our mothers model our feminine nature. By example, they teach us how to nurture, how to be creative, how to be in relationship with the masculine energies in the world, how to understand our sexuality, how to navigate our complicated lives.

Some mothers do this so beautifully. They gift their daughters with an example to follow, a way to decide for themselves what is true and real. Other mothers model only neglect and unconscious self-centeredness.

Most mothers fall somewhere in between. They do the best they can, feeding their daughters a mixture of devoted love, expectations of perfection, unique family histories, and a dash of ancestral shame. These become woven into the fabric of the daughter's mind, body, and psyche, causing her to see what she expects to see.

In the eyes of the Virgin Mother, Sophia saw disappointment and the stern, shaming look of disapproval. At that moment, with her emotions flaring, Sophia saw the projection of her own feelings. The blessed, archetypal Great Mother does not shame her children. She stands only in the heart of compassion and love.

In time, through her own healing, Sophia will come to understand this, and it too will become a part of her legacy, for whatever healing a woman can manage for herself will pass to her daughters and granddaughters. And in this way, she can make the world a better place for generations to come.

Sophia's mother was a paradigm of goodness, but she, like all women, carried the burdens passed on to her by the generations of women before her. She had her own personal trials and tragedies. Her life was built on a foundation anchored in restrictive cultural and religious traditions.

Sophia's mother had no intention of wounding her. She wanted only to support her daughter, to help her through a difficult time. On the morning of Sophia's wedding, when her mother told her to hold in her stomach, a deep and ancient wound became activated. Sophia had no idea how much this moment would inform her future.

Chapter Three

Anna

I take my morning tea and the journal I am reading out to the porch swing. I have been trying all morning to sort out my feelings about Sophia's past. Even though she wants me to read all of this, I still have a nagging feeling that I'm peeking into something private I'm not supposed to see.

Sometimes I feel like I am drowning in deep feelings of empathy for Sophia — I feel really angry, just as Sophia must have sometimes felt. Other times, I feel her confusion. Sometimes I am overwhelmed with a feeling of being completely lost.

This morning I am well rested and, for once, I feel ready to read on even though I know it means embarking on another rollercoaster of emotions. I am going to get through this thing, whatever it is. I really want to figure out why Sophia is so insistent on me knowing all about her past; why she is staying away, why she wants me to do this.

* * * * *

May 2, 1961

Kevin came home last night really late, smelling of alcohol and in a mean mood. When I asked him where he had been, he yelled at me to mind my own business. Why does it have to be this way? Here I am, getting bigger every day, trying my best to please him. But nothing about me pleases him right now, not even carrying his child. If he is this thoughtless of me and my needs now, what will it be like after the baby comes?

* * * * *

Dear Anna,

My dad is such a sweet and wonderful man. My water broke when he and I were out looking at model homes. I had just walked into the bedroom when I felt warm liquid going down my legs. When I told Dad what was happening, he led me to the closet where there was a shelf I could sit down on. He eased me down onto it and told me to stay right there, he would be right back. He went to the car and got some newspapers.

I felt embarrassed, but he was just calm and easy with it all. So reassuring. Of course, this was nothing new to him. He had been through this three times!

I was glad we were looking at a house with concrete floors and not carpeting! When we got to my parents' home, Mom was happy and excited, but also obviously concerned that this baby was coming early. She cooked a wonderful dinner for us. After we ate, she told me to go home and rest. "When your contractions get hard," she said, "call me."

I was excited too, but also afraid. In addition to my fear and anxiety about what was about to happen to me, I was also worried about the timing. Would they be able to tell by looking at the baby that it had not come early? Would they guess that we had lied to them?

I realize now that they probably had figured it out long ago. They just wanted to support me, but I didn't even know how to accept their help.

Love,

Sophia

* * * * *

June 12, 1962

All evening I have been waiting for the contractions to get harder. So far, I am just having little ones. I don't really know what to expect or when to go to the hospital. It's almost midnight, and Kevin is asleep. I called the doctor and told him my contractions were three to four minutes apart, and he said to go to the hospital. But I still wonder if I should go yet because the pain isn't bad. I guess I should do what the doctor says.

I just woke Kevin up, and he called his mom to come with us. He didn't call my parents, but I didn't say anything. I just don't want to fight right now. It's all happening too fast, and I need to set everything aside and focus on this baby. Here we go!

* * * * *

Dear Anna,

They took me to a tiny little room and did a pelvic exam. They said I was not dilated much, but since it was midnight I might as well stay because I would pay for the whole day even if I came in ten hours later. They said they would put me in a labor room and watch me. I asked if Kevin could come with me, but they said no, no one was allowed in the room with me.

Anna, when I read these journal entries and remember that day, I feel waves of compassion for my younger self. I was so compliant, so unable to speak up for myself. I should have said no, I want to go home. Instead, feeling afraid and alone, I hugged Kevin and asked him to call my Mom and Dad; then the nurse wheeled me away.

She took me down the hall and put me in a private room. She told me she was going to shave me and give me an enema. This was a shock. I didn't know they did that! After that ordeal, they left me alone, and I was able to call the hospital lobby and talk to Kevin. But I still felt alone and afraid.

I liked my first nurse, but she was busy and only came now and then to check on my progress. A few times she rubbed my back when the contractions got harder. She was kind.

In the early morning, when my contractions were getting really hard, there was a shift change and another nurse came on duty. This one came up to my bed while I was in deep hard labor and in a really sharp, scolding voice she said, "What are you doing moving your bowels in bed? What's the matter with you?" I had no idea I had done that. I couldn't feel it with all the pain. To this day I remember my feelings of shame and helplessness. She changed my bed with obvious disgust and then left me alone. I was glad she went away so I could be alone to cry. No one could hear me. There were women in other rooms screaming.

At 1:00 the doctor came in. He checked me and said he was going to take me in to deliver the baby. I had been in that labor room for 13 hours, alone, in pain, and scared. It seemed like forever.
Love,
Sophia

* * * * *

June 13, 1962

When they took me to the delivery room they put me on a big steel table with a little padding on top. The lights were really bright, and the doctor and nurses were all wearing masks. The doctor said he was going to give me a shot in my spine to numb me, and I needed to hold very still. I told him I could feel the baby's head coming, but he just told me to hold still. I didn't understand why I needed the shot when the baby was coming.

After the shot they laid me down and put my legs in stirrups. There was a mirror there, and I wanted to see my baby being born, but it was angled wrong and I couldn't see anything. I didn't even think to ask them to move the mirror. Because of the shot, the contractions slowed down. I felt numb, so when they said to push, it was hard to know if I was really doing it.

Then they said it was taking too long so they cut me and used forceps to pull my baby out. It felt like a big whoosh, and there he was! I saw the doctor hold him up by his little feet and slap his tiny butt. He began to cry, and the doctor said, "It's a boy." I barely got a glimpse of him before they took him away. I delivered the placenta, and they sewed me up.

I was longing to see him, to hold him, but nobody brought him to me. Soon they took me to an empty room and I waited. What about my baby? What about Kevin? I was left alone and no one told me what was going on. Was there something wrong with him? Where was he? I was impatient. I wanted to hold my baby. After a really long time, Kevin came in, and soon after they brought my beautiful baby boy to me.

There's no way I can describe what it felt like to hold him for the first time. It was magic! I have never felt so much love for anything or anyone before in my life. I held him in my arms and kissed his sweet little face and touched his perfect little fingers and toes. I'm in LOVE! We have decided to name him Sebastian after my grandfather.

They only let me have him for a short time, and then they took him away again. Then Mom and Dad and Kevin's parents and some friends came in.

Mom is hurt because I didn't call her when I went to the hospital. I feel ashamed of myself for hurting her again. I love her so much, and yet I keep doing things that hurt her.

Later they brought Sebastian back to me and showed me how to breastfeed him. I can't wait to go home and be a family.

* * * * *

Anna

I remember Sebastian's birth because I was there that day. But I didn't know anything about what Sophia was really going through. Reading this is pretty upsetting. I guess the barbaric way they treated mothers back then was just considered normal.

But there were good moments too. In spite of all she had been through, Sophia was radiant! She was a mother! I knew she was going to be a good one.

* * * * *

Grandmother Spirit

How is it possible that the most extraordinary act a human being can accomplish — that is, to give birth to new life — became so disrespected, even by women themselves? When giving birth became a medical procedure and moved from the home into the hospital, we entered a dark age of childbirth.

Now, finally, we are beginning to emerge from that darkness. We are remembering that giving birth is a sacred process. We are awakening to the importance of showing respect for women, for the birth process, and for the very Earth we are all entirely dependent upon! For she is a woman also, constantly giving birth to new life and nurturing that life by producing the sustenance her children need to thrive.

In the native tradition the creation of a new person is witnessed and honored in sacred ceremony. A

Blessing Way welcomes the new life that is coming and blesses the woman's journey of giving birth and becoming a mother. She is surrounded by those who love and honor her. Offerings are made to the spirits, and gifts are given to the new one who is coming.

This understanding of how to honor the sacredness of birth was unknown to Sophia. Nor was it taught to her mother, much less to the men in her culture or the doctors who were almost all men at that time.

As Sophia experienced, a laboring woman's needs and instincts were dismissed by hospital staff for the sake of protocol and expediency. Labor was believed to be simply a painful process that must be endured. But labor is so much more than just pain! It is a powerful, natural upheaval, full of dynamic impulses, intelligence, and grace. It is primal and raw. A laboring woman is a sacred vessel holding an amazing and courageous being who is working very hard to move from one world into another.

* * * * *

June 15, 1962

I am home, and it is amazing to care for my precious little boy. I have a baby boy!!! It's a miracle. When I hold him in my arms I feel my heart bursting with love. He is so incredible! So tiny, soft, and precious. I have never felt anything like this before. There is more joy and love inside of me than I could ever have imagined. I am flying higher than a kite! Everything is going to be better now. I just feel it. Kevin and I will be okay now. We will be a loving family together. I feel my worries melting away.

July 15, 1962

I'm not making enough milk, and I am going to have to put Sebastian on formula. This is so hard. I have loved holding him to my breast and knowing that I was giving him everything he needed. But, just like Mom, I am not able to produce enough milk.

Here's the other thing: Part of me wants to stop nursing him. I'm tired of getting up in the middle of the night and washing my breasts as I am supposed to do before feeding him. And the one time I didn't do it, he got thrush mouth. I'm ashamed of myself for being lazy.

The doctor prescribed some pills to dry me up, and tonight I ran out of them. I had asked Kevin to get the prescription refilled for me, but for some reason he didn't do it, and now my breasts are really painful from the buildup of milk. We had an argument about it. He said I would be fine. But I wasn't fine! I couldn't seem to make him understand that I was in terrible pain and needed his help. I finally asked my Mom to get the pills for me. I don't understand him. I feel so sad. I wish I had my own money and a car.

August 18, 1962

Kevin has been even more horrible than usual this week. He yelled at me last night that it was my fault that he was going to have to drop out of school and get a job. His dream of being a lawyer is dead, and he is blaming me and Sebastian. He is enrolled in a course to get his license as a private investigator. Maybe when he has a job and is bringing in some money he will not be so angry.

* * * * *

Grandmother Spirit

For thousands of years, goddesses and archetypes of the feminine have held significant meaning as reflections of the Great Mother. Traditionally a woman's journey through this life has been seen as progressing through three stages: the Maiden, the Mother, and the Crone. This concept came out of the triple goddess worshipped in many ancient cultures. Now we are coming to realize that we, like the moon, have four phases.

When we are Maidens we are young and fresh, innocent and expansive. We grow through childhood and begin to learn what it is to be in the world as adult women. We are open to bold ideas and intense desires. We are impatient, full of potential, seeking new beginnings, and open to infinite possibilities.

When we are Mothers we are sensuality, fertility, strength. We bloom like flowers. We are the irresistible candle flame, the reflective power of the moon, attracting to ourselves the energies we need to create life. We draw them in; they flock to us like bees. Like Spider-Woman, we weave our ideas, dreams, and desires into being.

In these childbearing years, like females of every species, we are the most creative creatures in this physical world, for only we can give birth. We are alchemists; we create new life. And when we have created it, we nurture it until our children are strong and independent, able to move off into the world and fend for themselves.

Then we enter our power years. With the wisdom of experience and the knowledge we have gained through trial and tragedy, love and devotion, we become the Matriarch. Still active and vital, our passion for life is potent, surging through us. We are whole unto ourselves. We have freed ourselves from the burdens of our former insecurities and complexes; we have draped ourselves with new garments of grace and ease; we are able to create with immense power; we can effect great change in the world.

Was this most-powerful phase of womanhood repressed and ignored by a culture intent on minimizing all feminine influence? There is probably some truth to that. Also there is the simple fact that we live longer than we used to. We have the luxury of time to develop this potent aspect of ourselves and to bring ourselves into balance with the Earth and her cycles, the four phases of the moon, the vast cosmic cycles.

As Crones we embody transformation and transcendent wisdom. We see far beyond the mundane, far beyond the physical world and the business of living. We recognize that death is a transformation and that beyond it is life in a new form. Here in the fourth and final phase of life, we see and embody the complete arc; all the phases of womanhood live on within the Crone. She has nurtured a deep relationship with her divine inner light, and she shines for anyone with the eyes to recognize her radiance. Honored in her culture and content within herself, she is free to give of herself as she pleases and to ready herself for her next great transition.

* * * * *

Anna

I have read up to 1963 in Sophia's journals. Sebastian was six months old, and the stresses of the marriage and the baby were creating problems for Sophia and Kevin. He was mean and inconsiderate! I feel for Sophia – she tried so hard to make her marriage work!

I'm sitting inside today, wrapped in a blanket, sipping hot tea. I feel like I have to fortify myself before I sit down to read. Every time, I feel all that Sophia went through as if it were happening to me. Weird.

* * * * *

March 12, 1963

Last night Kevin got really angry while we were sitting together watching TV. I was asking him some questions, just trying to understand some of his behaviors. He hauled off and slugged me on my thigh! I was shocked – this was a level of violence I have never seen in him before. And it really hurt! But what hurt most was inside, in my heart. I don't understand why he hit me! Is it the stress of work, school, and the baby? Did I do something wrong? I was never afraid of him before. Now I am.

* * * * *

Dear Anna,

My mother once told me that she would never leave my father unless he cheated on her or hit her. I guess this had become my guideline too because when this happened I left Kevin for the first time.

Later Kevin came to find me at my parents' house.

He apologized and said he would never hit me again. He was just upset, he said. He gave me a hug, and we kissed. It felt good to be wanted and to be in his arms. I didn't believe he meant to hurt me, so I forgave him and let him take me home.

How did I allow myself to be manipulated so easily? I just didn't know any better at the time. When Kevin apologized to me – and this happened over and over again – I thought it meant he loved me. Each time this happened, I saw it as another chance for everything to change and get better between us.

Also, I was very confused at that time about what it meant to be good and to do the right thing. I thought he hit me because I had done something wrong. In some way, I thought, it must have been my fault.

Although I had no idea what I had done wrong, I was determined to do anything I could to heal this marriage. I decided having another baby would bring us closer together and create the family I so desperately wanted.

Love,
Sophia

* * * * *

Anna

Sophia wrote of her shock and distress over John F. Kennedy's assassination. She was in her kitchen, preparing a snack for Sebastian when she heard it on the TV. The news hit Sophia like a blow, just as it did the rest of the country — stunned by how everything can change in a moment. For Sophia, it was another reason to do whatever it took to keep her family together.

When Sophia decided that having another baby was the way to heal her marriage it didn't make any sense to me. I'm guessing the president's death influenced her in some way, reinforcing her belief that what was really important in life was love and family.

But how in the world was having another child supposed to make things better? Sophia carefully planned how she would get pregnant. On the night she conceived, she prayed to have a girl. I didn't see how having another baby would help anything. To me, it was obvious it would only make things worse.

＊ ＊ ＊ ＊ ＊

Dear Anna,

I was devastated when I miscarried. I was lost in sadness for months — no, that's not accurate. I was lost in sadness for years. Kevin was probably hurting too. But we didn't go through it together, comforting

66

each other. Instead he was angry and explosive.

And poor Sebastian! He has always been sensitive to the feelings of people around him. I know he felt all of our turmoil and sorrow. Once he put his little hand on my cheek and said, "It's okay, Mama. I'm still here."

Over time, Kevin got worse and worse. He was not just physically abusive, he was mentally and emotionally abusive too. Even after he had found work as a private investigator and was making money, he wouldn't give any to me even for things that Sebastian needed. I didn't even have a car. I walked everywhere, sometimes long distances.

Kevin went through periods of being on his best behavior. Then, without warning, his anger would erupt – he would yell or throw things or say something cruel. When he drank it got worse.

Several times I left him, but I always went back. This went on for years. I felt defeated, angry, and unappreciated. Sebastian was my solace and my joy. He was the center of my life and I adored him!
Love,
Sophia

* * * * *

November 3, 1964

I love being a mother! I have been helping Sebastian's

teachers in the classroom. It's amazing how much I am learning about encouraging individuality in children and how to raise them with respect, honoring their differences and not imposing outdated ideas on them about their genders. This is most important for Sebastian who is an exceptionally sensitive child who will, to Kevin's consternation, as happily play with a doll as with a truck.

I have been reading books about psychology, and I love it! It's helping me to understand Sebastian and myself. My Dad and Kevin say it is all bunk. But I think it's fascinating!

March 7, 1965

I'm so upset I don't know what to do. I take good care of Sebastian. I clean the house. I cook. I do laundry. I wash dishes. I volunteer at the preschool. I make sure Sebastian is clean, and I look nice when Kevin comes home. But it's never enough.

Today, he came home and wiped his finger on the top of the door jam and found dust on it. He looked at it and asked, "What have you been doing all day?" I just don't get it. I'm doing everything I know to be a good wife and mother. Why is he like this?

September 2, 1965

Yesterday I was sitting at the kitchen table with Kevin. I had just made a fresh pot of coffee. We were talking, and there was some money on the table. I was feeling seductive and playful so I picked up the money like I was going to take it. He told me to put it back. I put it in my bra and said, "Come and get it!" He stood up, knocking his chair over backwards and yelled, "Give it to me!" So I took the money out of my bra and threw it on the table and walked away.

The next thing I knew, he picked up the pot of hot coffee and threw it at me. It hit my back and legs. My clothes clung to my skin, burning. I screamed and ran to the bathroom, undressed, and got into some cool water. I couldn't stop crying, more from the hurt of what he had done than the pain of the burn. I was really scared.

Kevin kept saying he was sorry and that he didn't mean it. I told him to go away. I didn't even want to see him. After I stopped crying I got dressed and left. I walked down the street to Mom and Dad's house. Dad said he would go and talk with Kevin while Mom was telling me to forgive him. When Dad came back he said Kevin didn't mean to hurt me and he was sorry. Of course, later that night I reluctantly went back again, hoping things would change for the better.

This morning I went to the doctor for the burns, and when I told him what had happened, he said that Kevin needed to get help. I left the doctor's office feeling better. He seemed to understand what was going on. When I got home I asked Kevin if he would please see someone to help him with his anger. He said he would think about it.

* * * * *

Dear Anna,

When I started taking classes in child psychology, it was as if a whole new world opened up for me! I started to learn how to think for myself. I got a job, and the new friends I met there were like a breath of fresh air! I hadn't realized before just how constricted my life had been. My family, the Church, our close-knit community — these had made up my world. Now, at work and in my college classes, I was getting to know people whose lives and cultures were entirely different – people who were open to new ways of thinking.

I met Dara at work. She was not like anyone I had ever met before. Not only did she exude an aura of peace and contentment, she was very open about the fact that she was gay. In my sheltered life, I wasn't aware of ever knowing anyone who was homosexual. I had been taught by the Church how wrong it was, depraved and sinful.

But my new friend just seemed like a nice, normal woman in every way except that she was very open about her sexual leanings. She asked me once if I had ever had a sexual relationship with a woman. I was shocked! But it got me thinking. I wondered what that would be like. Certainly I no longer felt any sexual attraction to Kevin. He had destroyed that.

All my new, expansive thinking wasn't helping our

relationship. In fact, Kevin got upset when I tried to do things differently, to incorporate into our lives the things I was learning. I was excited about these new ideas and wanted to apply what I was learning to how we handled Sebastian and how we communicated with each other. It felt natural for me. But Kevin fought me at every turn.

Love,

Sophia

✳ ✳ ✳ ✳ ✳

October 16, 1967

I'm not sure what to do. Clearly it would be a disaster to have any more children. All my life the Church and my family have drummed into me that using birth control is a sin. Kevin and I don't make love much anymore. He drinks a lot, and I am often afraid to even speak to him. But sometimes he wants to have sex, and so we have sex. But I can't let myself get pregnant again!

Last week I went to get some counsel from Father David. He married us, and I like him. He is young and a good listener. I told him how difficult it has been, how I have been trying so hard to make this marriage work and how Kevin seems to be doing everything he can to make life miserable. He listened to what I told him and then said, "Considering the situation, using birth control would not be committing a sin." I was surprised that he said that, but it was a huge relief.

October 18, 1967

Well, that didn't last long. At church last Sunday the older priest got up in the pulpit and said, "Those of you who think you can break the rules of the Pope are sinners. If you are using birth control you are committing a sin." These words hit me hard. I sat through the rest of mass feeling completely discouraged and hopeless. Where did that leave me? What was I supposed to do?

After mass I was sitting in the choir loft looking down at the altar when something changed in me. I think this is what they call an epiphany. I thought, *that's it! From now on it's between God and me. No more going through someone else to know the truth of what I should do. I'm going to make up my own mind about what's right and wrong.* I felt the light of grace enter my heart. Since this happened, I have been feeling free!

October 22, 1967

I had a doctor's appointment today, so Kevin picked up Sebastian from preschool. That was a big mistake on my part. When he got to the school he found Sebastian sitting with two little girls playing with dolls.

Kevin exploded when he got home. He wants to move him out of his school! He said he will not tolerate having his son turned into a pansy at some liberal new age school. He was yelling at me. He said it was my fault that Sebastian was such a sensitive child. He needed to toughen up. This is ridiculous. Sebastian is only five years old!

September 26, 1969

I'm taking two more college classes so I can work at the school as a teacher's aid. For now, I volunteer whenever I can. I love being with the children, and I feel valued for what I do there.

I don't care so much anymore what other people think. And Kevin's overbearing need to control everything doesn't have as much of an effect on me. What matters to me is that I listen to the inner voice that is coming alive in me! A voice that says I can't live this way any longer. There is more to life! The way we have been living is unhealthy for all of us. I haven't thought about it this way before, but I have allowed myself to be mistreated in this relationship. Yes, Kevin needs professional help, but so do I.

October 15, 1969

Janice from work recommended her family counselor to me, and I went to see her last week and then again today. I've never been to a therapist before. At first I was nervous. Thea is big and strong, but very gentle. She is wonderful! From the moment I walked into her office I felt safe and supported. I believe she hears and understands my thoughts and feelings. She is helping me learn how to be true to myself.

Also, I am starting to understand more about the dynamics of my family patterns and how deeply I have taken them on. And I'm starting to see how my reactions automatically come from those patterns. Most important, I am learning that I can make a different choice! Maybe, just maybe, there is a way out.

October 22, 1969

Today, in my session with Thea, for the first time I was able to open up and talk about Sebastian. I am beginning to suspect that he might grow up to be gay. If this is so, I'm okay with it. But Kevin definitely would not be. He keeps pushing Sebastian to "be a man!" and "quit being so sensitive!"

When an older boy started picking on him, Sebastian came home in tears. Kevin wanted him to fight back and was trying to teach him how to hit the other boy. But that is not Sebastian's way. My sweet little boy has no interest in the things that Kevin wants him to be into, like sports and boxing. He likes to draw and read, and he still loves to cuddle with me, which I love. Now, when Kevin is around, Sebastian just gets quiet or goes off to his room.

Of course, none of this necessarily means he is gay. It's far too early to know. But when Kevin yells at him, "Don't be a pansy!" it worries me that poor Sebastian is being belittled for just being who he is.

November 5, 1970

Things are changing for me! I'm learning so much every day – about child psychology and education, and about honoring my own feelings and making new choices.

But it seems that my feeling better about myself does not make Kevin happy. I have been growing and changing, and we have been growing farther apart. He is sullen and difficult, and every day is stressful. He has not even tried to find some help for himself to deal with his anger. My work with Thea has only angered and upset him. I don't think I can stay with him any longer. I can't imagine what else I could possibly do to make this marriage work.

March 9, 1971

I have left Kevin! I need some time to figure things out. I have been praying for guidance, and I heard a very clear voice in my head saying that I needed to take care of myself. So I packed up a few things for Sebastian and myself and went back to my parents' house. At least here is an atmosphere of love.

Dad, who is so kind and dear to me, voiced his opinion about the situation when he said, "If you had stayed home and not gone to work you would still be in your marriage." I felt his words begin to wrap around me like an old, familiar cocoon. But then something different happened. Because of my work with Thea, I actually saw this for what it was! This is huge. Maybe now I will be able to break out of these old limitations.

* * * * *

Dear Anna,

For the first time in my life I was completely responsible for myself. I was taking classes, taking care of Sebastian, and I had a job! Do you know what the biggest thrill of all was? I had my own checkbook and my own bank account! By April, Sebastian and I had moved into our own apartment.

Kevin tried over and over again to convince me to go back to him and give our marriage one more chance. He apologized; he threatened; he pleaded. But all the new ideas I was learning about were empowering me to stand up for myself.

And I had another new source of strength: I was forging my own personal relationship with God, with no one else to intercede and tell me what He wanted me to do.

Love,
Sophia

* * * * *

Anna

I am late for my appointment with Perry. Just five minutes late, but when I arrive I feel frazzled and exhausted. Perry suggests that my tiredness may be coming from emotions not being fully felt and processed or expressed. This makes me mad, and it takes Perry quite a while to calm me down. We did some breathing exercises.

I tell him about what has been going on for me – how I just seem to lose it sometimes, overwhelmed with feeling all the emotions. Too many feelings to process; too many images and impressions to deal with. I feel like I am getting to know Sophia better, and that's good. But most of the time it's hard.

Perry says, "Let's try a little experiment. I want you to feel into being Sophia. Feel what it's like to be her, and ask if she can help you."

I close my eyes. "Okay. I can feel her. When I ask, she smiles and reaches for my hand."

"Stay with it awhile and listen with new ears."

I hear Sophia say, "Please trust me. It will be okay if you just keep going. Don't give up.'"

* * * * *

Grandmother Spirit

Om Tara Tu Tara Tura Soha! The goddess Tara is within all of us, speaking her words of wisdom and showing us the full range of her expression, from the beloved embodiment of compassion to the agent of wrathful destruction. For our protection, she cuts through the false cultural ego and reveals the truth.

Do you know what it feels like to be a woman unto herself, a woman fully initiated and wise, a sovereign woman? She is a woman who doesn't let her fears decide her fate. She does not let her culture determine her actions. She is complete unto herself, capable of making clear decisions. She understands the importance of loving and nurturing herself. She does not jeopardize her own safety for the sake of her desires or how she is seen. She listens to the guidance that whispers in her ear. She does not sacrifice her needs. She celebrates her divine feminine nature and sexuality.

How does a woman become sovereign? It can be a long and difficult journey if, like Sophia, she has grown up in a culture that does not honor independence in women, where every woman is expected to be a perfect wife, a perfect mother, to obey her husband, to do everything in her power to keep her family together for the sake of the children, to put everyone else's needs ahead of her own. Sophia's difficult journey is just beginning.

Anna is taking in Sophia's life and feeling everything that Sophia felt. Sophia, as a young woman, is awakening to a new way of understanding the world. She is beginning her journey to become a sovereign woman. And Sophia, as an older woman, is looking back on her earlier life with the wisdom of age, for she has made great progress on her journey.

Do we ever fully arrive? To that I can only answer, everything is a process.

Chapter Four

Dear Anna,

The years between 1968 and 1973 are a blur in my memory. But there were a few significant events that stand out. Big things were happening in the world — Martin Luther King was assassinated, the Watergate scandal and President Nixon's resignation, Neil Armstrong walked on the moon, and Roe vs. Wade finally gave women the right to control their own bodies and their destinies.

Sebastian was growing up. I finished taking the courses I needed to work as a teacher's aide, and I got a job in the same high school I had attended. I left Kevin many times over the course of these years, and many times I went back to him. But eventually I gained enough strength to stand on my own and to not cave in to his bullying.

As you know from reading these journals, there were many times when Kevin threatened me, intimidated me, belittled me, then begged me to go back to him. He simply would not accept that I had left him for good and I was not going back.

My friendship with Dara changed my life. She was different from anyone I had ever known. She was at peace with herself. She was so beautiful.

It didn't take me long to realize that I wanted what she had! A desire was awakened in me, and for the first time I looked at what my life had become, so full of struggle and shame and discord, and I considered that maybe it didn't need to be that way. Maybe there was a way for me to find peace too, in spite of everything.

I cornered her at work one day and asked, "What makes you so different?" I begged her to tell me her secret.

She asked, "Do you really want to know? Do you really want to go there?" Yes, I did!

Love,

Sophia

* * * * *

January 10, 1973

I love the books Dara gave me. *As a Man Thinketh* is a beautiful little blue book that slides into its own pocket-like sleeve. This book is tiny, but powerful! The author says everything you think determines the way you see and experience life. I've never heard of such a thing! Every now and then, while I am reading, I get a little glimpse of what it actually means to have your life created from your thoughts. If this is true, the implications are huge!

Another book is by Edgar Cayce and this one really blows me away. He is a psychic who writes about healing techniques, Karma, the Akashic Records, and reincarnation.

Dara also introduced me to the teachings of Theosophy, which means "knowledge of the divine." This is the name Madam Blavatsky gave to the knowledge she brought to the world from the ascended masters.

I have never heard of any of this before, but deep inside me, pulsing through my blood, I have known all along that there exists a deep ocean of spiritual knowledge; beyond anything I could conceive of, waiting to be discovered.

April 2, 1973

It's been a month now since I got those books, and I have been reading them in every spare moment. Every day at work I find a way to be alone with Dara, and I pour out my questions. I must have asked her a hundred questions. She's been really kind and patient with me, and she seems to genuinely like me. Today she asked if I would like to meet her spiritual teachers. Yes! Yes! Yes! I can't wait!

Dara has been attending classes at The Center for Divine Union. Her spiritual teachers are Raven, who is considered a Shaman or Priestess, and Yogi Sitananda. Strange names! Dara said they teach a blended philosophy that includes the Goddess teachings, Native

American spiritualism and eastern religions like Buddhism and Hinduism.

Just two years ago I would have run screaming from this – pagans and heretics! But the Catholic Church has let me down, and since my epiphany I'm no longer horrified by the thought of learning about other spiritual practices and religions or even trying out their practices. As a matter of fact, I am consumed with my need to learn more!

Also, if I'm being honest, I would go anywhere with Dara just to be around her.

April 4, 1973

Last night I had a really mysterious dream.

I saw a foggy glow, and in the middle of it was a little book with a bright light shining on it. Or was the light coming from the book? On the simple cream-colored cover was written Raja Yoga, foreign words I had never seen before. They meant nothing to me.

All day those words haunted me.

* * * * *

Dear Anna,

On April 5, 1973, my life's path veered off into a new direction when I met the teachers and students at The Center for Divine Union.

The ashram was an older house set back from the street with lovely arches over the driveway. As we entered the house the smell of incense was unfamiliar but soothing.

On a shelf in the entryway there was a little book with a light shining on it. When I saw the title I was stunned! On the cover it said Raja Yoga.

I'm sure my mouth fell open in amazement. Raja Yoga was the title of the book in my dream. How was this possible? But at the same time something in me knew the unusual is really quite natural. How did I know this? I just did. In that instant it felt like the world I knew was crumbling, and a new world was opening to me.

We waited in the entryway with about 20 people. Everyone was laughing and talking. One of the monks, Jahi, was carrying on a conversation with another man. They were talking passionately about philosophy and spirituality like I had never heard anyone speak before.

When it was time to enter the temple, Jahi opened the big double doors for us. The smell of incense was stronger, and the candle-lit room had a mysterious feel to it. There were cushions neatly placed around the room. On the back wall was a lovely altar with tiered shelves holding candles, pictures, and flowers. There was a beautiful Om sign that looked to me like a fancy number three – I didn't have a clue what it was! The walls on the sides of the room held smaller altars with pictures of beings I didn't know. Jesus was the only one I recognized. Later, I learned that the others were Ramakrishna, Vivikenanda, Kahlil Gibran, Rabindranath Tagore, Gandhi, Mirabai, Tara, Inana, and Lakshmi – saints and sages who, in the years to come, would be my companions and my teachers. We sat in the dark and waited in silence. A few minutes later I heard the door open behind us.

I turned around and saw Raven and Yogi Sitananda for the first time. She wore a long white dress, a red shawl draped around her shoulders. Her black hair made a thick braid that fell all the way down her back. She carried a pipe with a long handle. Peace and joy radiated from her body. Yogi Sitananda's hair and beard were long and white. He wasn't a big man, but his presence seemed to fill the space. They were unlike any man or woman I had ever seen before in my life.

They walked down the middle of the room and stopped in front of the altar where they bowed their heads with their hands in prayer position. Then she placed her pipe on the altar, and he placed a flower.

As they sat down they took their shawls from around their shoulders and placed them over their heads, and we all sat together in silence for a time. The room became luminous.

Swami Sitananda removed his saffron shawl from his head and looked at us with a soft smile and said,

"Good evening." His words felt like a gentle breeze that reached inside my heart and filled it with light. His eyes were gentle. His hands moved like someone reaching to touch a newborn baby. I was so altered from the book/dream incident and all the new sights and smells, that adding this magnificent human being to the mix was lifting me higher than I had ever been before.

Raven looked at us with a beautiful smile and said, "We welcome you and your beautiful hearts." Then Sitananda began to speak.

His speech was slow and deliberate. "Tonight we will begin studying from the book Raja Yoga or Conquering the Internal Nature, by Swami Vivekananda. The first line in the book is, 'Each soul is potentially divine. The goal is to manifest this divinity within nature, external and internal.'"

I was a dry sponge that had fallen into a pool of liquid light. I soaked it all in. I felt free, alive, ecstatic. My prayers had been answered, and the spiritual teachings to create a new life were now available to me. The walls of my cocoon cracked open, and I could suddenly see a whole new life of possibilities stretching out before me. It was unlike anything I could have imagined.
Love,
Sophia

* * * * *

Anna

Last night Sophia came to me in my dream. This is the first time that I have dreamed of Sophia. Can that be true, after knowing her for all these years? It must be. I can't remember ever dreaming of her before, and until this moment, I never realized how strange that is.

In my dream Sophia was sitting here at the kitchen table and talking to me about her dream so many years ago. She said the dream was an opening for her into the spirit world. It was a bridging of the physical and spiritual, and Sitananda and Raven were able to communicate to her through the spirit world in her dream. I don't remember what else she said. The rest of it was more like a feeling that if she listens to these messages she will never be led astray.

When I called Perry today and told him about my dream he reminded me how important it is for me to remember and write down my dreams. He said, "They are a way of communicating and acquainting yourself with the unconscious. Dreams are not attempts to conceal your true feelings from your waking mind; they are a window that allows you to see into to your unconscious. They can guide your waking self to achieve wholeness and offer solutions to problems you might be facing in your waking life." Perry has studied dreams for a long time, and I could tell he loved that I had a dream about a dream!

* * * * *

Grandmother Spirit

Divine grace, karma, dependent arising – there are many ways of contemplating why we are sometimes blessed to be in the right place at the right time to receive a precious gift. Sophia knew right away these teachings were the answer to her prayers. And the elation that she felt? It was the ecstatic experience and expression of her soul's authentic journey. It was a direct connection to her true nature.

* * * * *

Dear Anna,

Raven and Sitananda were extraordinary teachers. As you continue to read these journals you will learn more about them.

They traveled together when they were younger. All around the world they visited sacred sites and sat at the feet of sages and gurus and priests and priestesses.

In the early 1950s, they came back to the States from India, and Raven took Sitananda to her village on the Lakota reservation. She wanted to share the creation stories she had learned in India, which were so similar to the ones her grandmother had told her. She also wanted Sitananda to meet her family.

They stayed with the Lakota people for some months, and one day Raven found herself in the back of a pickup truck with three of the elders. They drove out across the desert plateau. When the truck stopped, she could smell smoke and sage. Drumbeats and songs filled her ears.

She was told to take off her clothes and told to wrap herself in her red shawl. They passed around the pipe and offered prayers. Then they gave her the plant medicine to drink. She was lead into the Inipi, the sweat lodge. The drumming continued as they prayed to Wakan Tanka, the great mystery.

With each round, more of the fiery red grandfather stones were brought into the Inipi. The heat grew hotter and hotter, and the steam from the water blessing became more and more dense. Raven lost track of time and space and had visions of times long passed and far away. The next thing she remembers is being handed a blanket and a jar of water and told she was safe.

Three days had passed since the Inipi ceremony. This was her vision quest initiation. She shared that White Buffalo Woman had come to her. This is when the elders knew it was time for her to receive her sacred pipe.

Sitananda and Raven then went to visit the Hopi reservation where they shared the stories and were invited by the Hopi people to share in their ceremonies. It was unusual for outsiders to be accepted into these ceremonies. It seemed that the radiance of their characters and the sincerity of their hearts had bypassed the concerns of the Hopi.

Over time, I would learn from them about the eastern religions, karma and reincarnation, the oneness of all life. They shared with me the Native American ceremonies and traditions, sweat lodges, medicine wheels, animal spirits, and kachinas. And I was introduced to the way of the divine feminine as the alchemist in all her varied forms.

As I share this with you now, I am reminded of the magnitude of my blessings. I am grounded in deepest gratitude.

Loving you,
Sophia

* * * * *

June 28, 1973

Twice a week I go to the Center to receive more teachings. I love learning about different spiritual traditions and practices from the East and West. I love the ceremonies and rituals.

The book *Raja Yoga* is full of practices to expand my

consciousness and to awaken to my true nature, and I am working with these practices every day. Raven and Sitananda take turns teaching from this book by having us read a few lines or a paragraph. Then they give us a commentary on the meaning and an opportunity to ask questions on how to apply this to our lives. What I like best is the way they weave in other spiritual traditions, particularly the Native American teachings. They teach a philosophy of unity within diversity and a blending of eastern and western spiritual practices. This is all new to me, yet somehow so familiar, like being awakened from a dream. Each teaching closes with a powerful chant sung by Raven or Sitananda. The chant transports me into the realm of the divine – *Om, Shanti Shanti Shanti.* Peace, peace, peace be unto us and through us to all beings.

June 30, 1973

At the ashram everyone is talking about the next pilgrimage. Once a year Raven and Sitananda lead a three-week journey into the sacred lands of the Native Americans. I would love to go, but can't imagine taking three or four weeks off from work to do such a thing. But the more I hear about it, the more I want to go. At the Center everyone is talking about nothing else, and I'm so jealous! When I talked to Sitananda about not being able to take off from work he said, "Why are you letting others rule your life?" I am determined to do it differently next year. Next year I am going.

August 21, 1973

They are all on fire when they return from the pilgrimage. Their excitement and wonder are contagious. Jahi brought me a special stone he found in the canyon. When I touched it, it felt alive. It carries the energies of the Escalante River canyon. I keep it where I can see it as a reminder to myself that I will find the courage to go next year. I need this magic in my life.

* * * * *

Dear Anna,

I had been open with my family about my involvement with the Center. Staunch Catholics that they were, I was afraid that they would reject me because of my new-found spiritual path. And, to be honest, I was afraid that they would be angry at me as well for leaving the Church and finding my spiritual fulfillment in religions and practices that were considered by the Church to be ignorant, blasphemous, and heretical.

However, they surprised me with their acceptance. I think they followed Mom's lead. Mom always understood me better than anyone else, and I guess she realized I was going to go my own way regardless of their advice or their beliefs.

Mateo, Serena, and Sebastian were all coming to

the Soyal Ceremony at the Center, and I really wanted Mom to come too. But I didn't think she would.

As she has done over and over again throughout my life, she surprised me. She accepted my invitation and came to the ceremony with an open mind, an open heart, and a big platter of bunuelos de vientos (light-as-air fritters). Of course, everyone loved them! And, of course, everyone loved Mom — how could they not?

Love,

Sophia

❋ ❋ ❋ ❋ ❋

November 17, 1973

Last night everyone gathered at the Center for Soyal, a Hopi ceremony in celebration of the harvest and preparation for winter solstice.

The whole ashram, including the temple, was transformed into a lovely autumn scene with red sand from the Escalante River canyon and corn stalks and multicolored ears of corn surrounding a Hopi mudhead kachina. I didn't know what kachinas were, but I learned they are symbols of the different energies of life. Resting against the center of the altar was a small wooden ladder made from tree branches. Colorful Native American rugs covered the floors. It was beautiful!

We gathered together, and Sitananda shared the story of this ancient ceremony. He taught us the rituals that were part of the ceremony, and as the story progressed I was transported to another time and place. I cried through the whole thing. I realized that before that night I had never understood the real meaning of Thanksgiving — the giving of thanks.

When it was time for the feast, Jahi carried a platter of food offerings into the temple and placed it on the altar. Then Sitananda broke the bread and invited us to share in the blessings of this delicious food and to celebrate in our thanksgiving.

Two amazing things happened. First, Mom came to the ceremony! This made me really happy. Then, while we were gathering together, Dara came to find me and stood next to me. She took my hand. Surrounded by my family, we sat next to each other through the ceremony, holding hands and feeling love all around us and coursing back and forth between us. She is so beautiful and so dear to me.

* * * * *

Anna

My time with Perry this week is spent talking about marriage. I tell him about how disappointed, how crushed I had felt when Sophia couldn't make her marriage work, even for Sebastian's sake. I guess I've always believed that a divorce is a failure, though I don't think I ever put it in those words. Yes, I tell him in answer to his question, I can see that sometimes getting a divorce can be a sign of success, not failure. Oh, Sophia, all these years I have judged you so harshly.

* * * * *

February 13, 1974

I really like the people I have met at the ashram. They are all kind and accepting. I am developing a friendship with Jahi, the monk who escorted us into the temple that first night. He's very talkative and well versed in all things spiritual. His eyes are deep and intense. I didn't like him much at first, but he is growing on me. And he seems to like me. He finds excuses to be close to me and watches me all the time.

I have a new life and a new sense of myself. I'm so grateful for Raven and Sitananda. Life is hard right now, and the Center is my saving grace.

Kevin continues to harass me and make things hard. He just wants to cause trouble. I think he followed me to the Center one night because the next day he yelled at me about the "creepy people I was hanging out with." He said he is investigating those "weird spiritual leaders" and was "going to find out what was really going on there."

July 4, 1974

Tomorrow morning we leave on pilgrimage! There are 12 of us going. Raven is taking us into the same holy lands where she was initiated, and she is going to teach us the ways of the ancient ones. The prospect of carrying a backpack with food for three weeks is scary. Dara's children are coming, and so is Sebastian! He will have to carry a heavy pack, and that makes me a little nervous. But mostly I am excited! I am about to go on a journey into nature, and this is something I have never done before. And Sebastian will be having his first experience of being in nature overnight. He has developed a friendship with Dara's son, Micah, and I'm happy to see them playing together. They are both sensitive boys, and they seem to find comfort in each other's company.

* * * * *

Dear Anna,

To get to that magnificent canyon we traveled across the desert of southern Utah to a place near Escalante. We drove for 45 minutes on the Hole-in-the-Rock Road, a bumpy dirt track. That night we camped on the rim. The next morning we started our decent into the sacred canyon.

It was hot and dry, and the beauty of the place took my breath away. From that first morning, the

Escalante River canyon enchanted me with its high red sandstone walls reaching to the sky. On that pilgrimage I discovered that I had a relationship with nature! I learned that it would speak to me if I would listen. Since that time, Nature has been one of my greatest teachers.

Sebastian was 12 years old, and he did fine with his pack. Raven is in her 60s, and I was 31. I could hardly keep up with her. I learned very quickly that if I walked behind her, her energy would carry me along. She was steadfast and consistent with her pace.

Raven was our guide, spiritual teacher, and storyteller. At every campsite, each one named after a particular teacher or legend, Raven shared a story and taught us chants and practices of the ancient people of this land. I particularly loved the Spider Woman and Butterfly Maiden stories. She also taught us about the native plants – which ones could be eaten or used as medicine.

One day Sebastian came running to show me something. It was a beautiful stone he found inside a cavern full of pictographs that were teachings about conception and childbirth. Raven said to Sebastian, "This is a healing, teaching stone. Listen and it will teach you many things."

In that sacred river canyon I found pieces of myself I didn't know existed. For the first time, I saw and experienced the felt sense of myself as a Native

American woman who had lived in this canyon in a past life. And one day I saw, as if watching on a screen, Jahi and me as young lovers living there in that canyon. It was as natural to see and know the truth of reincarnation in that moment, as it was to breathe. I could see a knowing in Jahi's face. In my vision, our eyes locked in silence as we drifted in and out of present time. I didn't speak of this for years afterward, but when I did, Jahi told me that he had experienced the same thing.

I don't think I had ever been so happy. Dara and I slept close together, our friendship growing deeper and more profound. There were times when I was overtaken by an impulse to jump into the water and play like a child, only to realize I had done this before right here as a little girl. That journey awakened a new way of being and a new way of seeing the world. I was transformed.
Love,
Sophia

* * * * *

October 7, 1974

I came back from the pilgrimage feeling so full of gratitude I thought I might burst! I just want this to keep going! I want to learn more. I want to have more experiences that leave me feeling so alive!

October 10, 1974

Now things are getting really crazy. Kevin is spying on me. He calls all the time or just shows up at my door wanting to know who I am seeing, who I am sleeping with. Where does he get this? I am not sleeping with anyone! If he's such a good investigator he should be able to figure that out. This is ridiculous. It feels awful, but I don't know what to do about it.

October 18, 1974

It's late, but I can't sleep. I am in shock, and I can't stop crying. Tonight I went to a special meeting at the Temple. Raven told us that the Ashram is moving out of state. She said, "In order to create a place in nature where people can learn to live in harmony with the annual cycle of life, we need to buy some land. We will be looking in Utah and Colorado."

Sitananda has not been well, and he is not going to move with the ashram. Buying land is a wonderful idea, but I am being abandoned. How will I live without them in my life?

October 19, 1974

Just as I was waking up this morning, I heard a voice inside me say, *Why don't you go with them?* Then I saw a vision of what my life might be like if I quit my job and devoted myself to the work of The Center for Divine Union. For the last year and a half, I have been absorbing the teachings and going through my personal struggles and triumphs putting those teachings into practice. The practices have opened my eyes to a new world. It's all part of me now. My psyche and my spirit have come alive, and a door has opened allowing me to peek into the mysteries of life. I am just beginning this journey! I can't shut the door! I can't allow it to be shut by circumstance! I think it would kill me. I have to call Dara!

October 20, 1974

Dara wants to go too! First we have to talk to Raven to see if it's okay. Then I will have to think about quitting my job. My mind is going a hundred miles an hour – planning and daydreaming about what it will be like. I know I'm getting ahead of myself here. They haven't even found the property yet!

October 29, 1974

I saw Raven today, and I told her I want to dedicate my life to serving the Temple and the teachings. I want to move with them and help in any way I can. She was very welcoming and encouraging. She could tell I really meant it. I'm so grateful! I told her I would like to go with them when they look for property. Now, instead of feeling abandoned and sad, I am feeling elated and full of possibilities.

* * * * *

Dear Anna,

Dara and I went with Raven and Jahi to look at property. I had never been to either state before, and I loved the open spaces and the mountains covered with giant red rock formations. We looked for several days in Colorado, but we didn't find anything we liked that we could afford. Then we moved on to Utah and eventually we found ourselves in the little town of St. George in southwestern Utah. Nearby there are state parks, dunes, and red sandstone cliffs. Zion National Park, with its spectacular canyons, is just a bit northeast.

Not far from town we found a place that had a feel about it that made us all think of the Escalante River canyon country. It was a very large home on 15 beautiful acres strewn with clusters of massive boulders. We all loved it. This would be the new home of The Center for Divine Union. We headed home to take care of business. We had a lot of work to do to make this happen.

That night we stopped at a motel for the night. Dara and I were sharing a room, talking about our plans and sharing our excitement about the new place. Then something happened. She told me that she was in love with me. Hearing her say that opened up my heart in a way I had never before experienced. We held each other and laughed and cried and kissed. Then we made love, and I knew that what I had experienced with Kevin was not love at all.

Anna, it felt so natural! Even so, my mind wanted to try and make it go away. How could this be? I have been attracted to men all my life. I even married one! And now this? What did it mean? Was I a lesbian? But Dara was wise and kind and encouraged me not to worry about it. She said, "Just enjoy, and let love be love."

All the way back to Albuquerque we were making plans. I had such a good feeling inside, a warm mix of happiness and excitement that I don't think I had felt since childhood. And I felt scared about what would happen if people found out about Dara and me. But Dara was not a worrier. She very gently touched my cheek and said, "Sophia, there's nothing wrong with what we are doing. We're just two people loving each other. How can that be wrong?"

I hadn't been home more than a day or two when all those good feelings came crashing to the ground like a ton of bricks. Kevin was still stalking me – calling me all the time, showing up at odd hours, begging me to go back to him, and then, when I refused, becoming violent. He threatened my counselor. He threatened Sitananda and Raven, which was bad enough, but when he heard from someone — I'm still not sure who — that the Temple was moving out of state and I was planning

to go too, all hell broke loose.
*   That's when he showed up with the gun.*
Love,
Sophia

* * * * *

November 25, 1974

I remember exactly what he said when he pointed that gun at me. "If you don't come back to me, I swear I will kill both of us."

I couldn't run. There was nowhere to go in my tiny kitchen and no way to get past him. My heart was pounding, and I was shaking with fear. Then the most amazing thing happened. Everything came together – our shared history, all the trauma and fear, the spiritual teachings I had been studying, my awakening awareness of the power of love. Grace.

Something inside directed me to hold him in my heart as a good man. I knew I needed to reflect the best in him even while I was scared to death. I surrounded him with love and repeated to myself, "He has a good heart, and he is spirit." I did my very best to be present with strength and clarity even though I was trembling and terrified. How was I able to do that?

Even with a gun pointed at me, I was able to say clearly and calmly, "I am not going back to you." I trusted that, if I could hold my focus, keep it in the realm of love, he would have to feel it, and love would guide his actions.

The standoff lasted about an hour. For the entire time I was holding on to the thread connecting our hearts. Finally, after he had exhausted his arguments, pleas, tears, and threats, he surrendered to his spirit, and put the gun down.

This was the most challenging day of my life, and something miraculous happened. I'm so grateful this day is over and I'm still alive.

* * * * *

Dear Anna,

I still don't understand what informed me and held me in such impeccable clarity. I was able to hold on to my truth, trusting in something greater than myself. Even though I was terrified, I was guided to see him in the light of love, and by some miracle I was able to stay in spirit. I will never forget that day for the rest of my life. My authentic truth was loud and clear and guided my actions. I stood steadfast in that space with my heart wide open.
Love,
Sophia

* * * * *

Anna

I'm glad Perry is able to see me on such short notice. I'm sitting in his waiting room in a state of shock. All those years ago I knew that Kevin had threatened Sophia with a gun. But now, oh, my God! I am feeling it all as if it is happening right now – as if I was just mugged while on my way to this appointment!

It's beyond me how Sophia managed to find the courage and strength to stay so clear. She wrote that she was able to do that because she called on resources she was learning in her spiritual practice. I only know I couldn't do that. I feel shaken to the core.

Perry calls me into his office. I'm a wreck, but Perry is his normal calm, kind self. The contrast somehow makes me feel worse. I plead with him, "Perry, I need help! I feel like I'm living Sophia's life all over again, and it's overwhelming me. I feel like I'm splitting apart at the seams!"

Perry takes a moment, thinking, then says, "Tell me what you mean by 'splitting apart at the seams."

I can't stop crying. I try to explain the feeling: I'm cracking open, my insides are coming out, and I can't stop it, something is wrong with me. I go on for a long time. Finally I say, "I feel like I am losing something of myself, and Sophia's life is becoming bigger than mine." We both think about that for a while.

Perry sends me home with an assignment. I am to get clear with what I feel I am losing. Also, I am to think about what it is I think I need. Always before, when asked that question by Perry, I knew immediately that what I needed was for Sophia to come home and for life to go back to the way it was. But now, for the first time, I am thinking that maybe there is something else I need. I need to know why Sophia is doing this. And there is only one way I am going to find out.

* * * * *

December 3, 1974

Just when I think things could not get worse with Kevin, something happens and, sure enough, it gets worse. Every time I speak with him he yells at me that he will not let me take Sebastian with me. If I want to move away that's up to me, but he will not let Sebastian go with me.

And then, late last night, when Dara had been over for dinner, we kissed goodbye on my front porch, and damned if Kevin had not been sitting in his car spying on me. When he saw us kissing he jumped out of his car screaming about how I was an unfit mother. He called me a pervert and yelled that he would take Sebastian away from me, and I would never see him again. Oh, God, why is this happening to me?

December 6, 1974

I told my parents and siblings about Dara. I knew it

would not be good if they heard it from Kevin. I wanted them to hear my heart. They were pretty shocked. Dad looked like I just told him I was from Mars. He yelled at me, "God made you a woman not a man!" Serena was gentle and asked me to say more. Mateo was pretty awful about it. He said it disgusted him to think of me being with a woman. Mom cried.

I told them I loved her and it was natural to become sexual when you loved someone whether they are male or female. I asked them to please consider our relationship as being a good thing.

I can see this is going to take time; there's a lot of healing that needs to happen here. I hope they can find their way.

December 15, 1974

Kevin has filed a lawsuit for custody of Sebastian claiming I am a lesbian. It's amazing that being homosexual is illegal in New Mexico, but it's true. I can't believe this is happening.

Today I hired a lawyer. I also filed for a restraining order because he is becoming more aggressive – he is stalking me! He calls constantly and just shows up at my place yelling and threatening me. Why does everything have to be so hard? I'm angry at him for all of this, but I feel confident the truth will win. Clearly it is better for Sebastian to be with me.

February 27, 1975

For a month we worked on strategies for this hearing. I was determined to do this right. But today I went to court and had a rude awakening when the judge said he wanted everyone in my life and in Sebastian's life to be interviewed. This means his school, his friends, teachers, my friends, family, and the teachers and students of The Center for Divine Union will all be scrutinized. Then, when the judge has all the information, he will decide if Kevin should have sole custody of Sebastian because I am having a relationship with a woman.

This is totally bizarre to me. What just happened? What am I going to do? I'm going to see Raven tomorrow. I asked if I could have a private meeting with her. Maybe she can help me find some clarity in this mess.

March 3, 1975

I told Raven the whole story. I told her about the violence and threats and about what the judge said. She was very kind and listened to my whole story. Very softly she said, "Considering all the problems you have had with Kevin, if it was me, I would leave Sebastian with him. Remember what Gibran said about children: They come through you and are not of you."

Her words shake me to the core. Leave Sebastian? How can that be the best thing to do? I keep thinking there must be some other way, but as many times as I go over and over Raven's words, I can't see an alternative. Either I leave Sebastian, or I stay and my spiritual community leaves me. My heart feels like it is suffocating. There has to be another way. Please, God, help me find another way!

March 4, 1975

Raven's words weighed heavily on me last night. I lay awake most of the night. They are all leaving, and if I stay I will be left here without the support of my spiritual community. Even though this is where I grew up and where my family and many of my friends are, the thought makes me feel very alone. If I stay here I'll have to deal with Kevin's rage and abuse over and over again without their help and support. All I can see, when I contemplate that future, is how I could end up badly beaten or dead, and Kevin could end up in jail. How can I do that to my son?

I am in agony. There is nowhere to stand in this that doesn't feel awful. How can I leave Sebastian with him? Kevin has never hit him, but he does demean him. Another thought – if I pass up this chance to follow my soul's direction, and instead stay here and subject myself to abuse and danger, what kind of example am I setting for Sebastian?

March 11, 1975

After a week of anguish, a week of looking at this

from every conceivable angle, I have decided maybe the best thing to do is to leave without Sebastian for now. This doesn't feel good, but the other options feel worse. My leaving would be less traumatic, even if Sebastian doesn't understand right now. Sebastian and I are so close he will probably put up such a fuss that Kevin will send him to me after a few weeks. And the worst-case scenario, if Kevin insists on keeping him, Sebastian will be 16 in a few years, and he can decide for himself where he wants to live.

This feels like that morning in church when I said no! It stops here! I decided that from then on my decisions would be my own, just between me and God, not based on any advice I got from two priests who can't even agree. Again I am saying no! I will not let a judge tell me what I can and cannot do with my life. I will not let this happen. I will not allow all my friends, family, Sebastian's teachers, and all of the people at Center for Divine Union to be subjected to the scrutiny and the whims of the legal system with all of its biased values and ideals.

Sebastian and his dad will be living with Kevin's older sister Kelly. She keeps Kevin in line, and she loves and understands Sebastian. Knowing her love for my son is my one thread of comfort.

I can hardly bear the pain of having made this decision. But at the same time I have an underlying feeling of empowerment. I am taking my life in my own hands, trusting that my love and good intentions will serve us all and it will all work out okay. Dear God, please let it all be okay!

* * * * *

Dear Anna,
    The choice to move away without Sebastian was the hardest decision I had ever had to make in my whole life. And I didn't get much support for my decision from anyone except my friends at the Center. My family even held an intervention where they all took turns telling me why I shouldn't go. With each argument they presented, I defended and explained my decision. My father said, "You're going to end up alone and lonely when you're old." By the end, at least Serena and Mateo could see both sides.
    The ordeal did not cause me to change my mind, but it did make me feel worse. For years I had been shadowed by the guilt I felt for having been a bad girl. Had I now become a bad mother?
Love,
Sophia

* * * * *

March 22, 1975
    I called my lawyer today. He is going to make the

arrangements for Kevin to have custody of Sebastian. When I hung up I felt numb.

This evening I sat down with Sebastian and explained everything I could about my decision. I was very careful not to make his father out to be the bad guy. I told him how much I love him and how I want us to be together as often as possible. I told him he could come and stay with me any time. He didn't say much. He just acknowledged what I said. He is very wise, my boy. I think he understands.

April 5, 1975

On Saturday I took Sebastian out to lunch at his favorite restaurant. We had a wonderful talk and came to an understanding. I felt we were deeply connected and were experiencing our love for each other. We came home feeling good, close, connected. I hope this is the feeling we can keep between us in spite of what happened later.

That evening, as arranged, Kevin came to pick up Sebastian and his things. Because he is Kevin, of course he couldn't let pass an opportunity for a final assault. After yelling and calling me names he grabbed me and shook me. Then he threw me across the room, all the while yelling profanities. Poor Sebastian! He cowered in a corner and yelled for his father to stop. I tried to sooth him, but when they finally left he was still upset. Kevin was telling him to quit crying and stop acting like a girl.

Then I called the police. This turned out to be another

of many futile attempts to hold him accountable for what he had been doing to me. The police couldn't do anything except tell me to call the courts and set up a time to hold him in contempt of court for not honoring the restraining order. I am leaving in two days, so that isn't going to happen.

April 8, 1975

Everything about this move is devastating. I remind myself it requires courage and fortitude to walk into the light of God. I am standing at a threshold, and if I keep going, I will be catapulted out of my ignorance and self-clinging into the mystery. This is the big picture I do my best to hold on to. At the same time I live each day in the pain of my guilt, grief, and loss.

April 12, 1975

Finally, we are on the road. We have three trucks filled with our belongings. Mateo is driving my overloaded car. Mom came to see us off this morning even though I had asked her not to. I love her so much, but when I'm with her I am aware of her sadness and her disappointment. Her belief that I am making a mistake makes me question my decision. I am trying to be brave and to hold on to the reasons I am doing this. I'm feeling like a bad girl, again.

Well, it's done now, and I'm on my way. I know this is the right thing, but I have an empty, sad feeling in my heart. I am sitting in the passenger seat of the truck, with Serena at the wheel, as we drive on and on through the desert. Under my shirt, next to my heart, I have a letter I wrote to Sebastian. I will put it in the first mailbox I see in Utah.

* * * * *

Anna

Hours ago, I brought the current journal and a thermos of tea down to the creek. I have been totally absorbed in this part of Sophia's story. I am sitting on a blanket under a towering ponderosa pine. The whole time I have been reading, I have been vaguely aware of the creek gurgling and singing softly in the background. Now I stop and just listen. I use some of what I have been learning from Perry. I let the sound of the water sooth my battered emotions.

Sophia broke all the rules. She got pregnant before marriage, then she got divorced. She claimed her sovereign right to make decisions based on her own ethics and her personal relationship to God. She got involved in esoteric spiritual practices. She had a love affair with a woman. Now she was leaving her son and her family.

As always happens, I have been feeling what Sophia felt. She wrote about her churning, conflicting emotions – grief, excitement, and yes, relief. Because, as hard as it was to leave Sebastian, she was liberating herself from

Kevin's immediate presence in her life – Kevin who made everything difficult, yelled and screamed, physically hurt her, and threatened her at gunpoint! But it broke her heart to leave her son.

* * * * *

Grandmother Spirit

People ask me what the purpose of life is. What a question! One thing I do know is that life is a glorious initiation. It challenges us to be present and to remain centered even as it bumps us up and down, batters us and celebrates us, gifts us with treasures and snatches from us what we hold dear. When Sophia sacrificed what she held dearest of all, her son, she was focused on the bigger picture — her soul's journey.

Like Sophia, we are challenged to see that bigger picture. We can surrender to despair, or we can gather the gems of wisdom embedded in the human experience. We are all tested by life. Are we able to hear the message of the Gods in the most difficult times as well as the times of grace? Are we able to see how they are one and the same?

Chapter Five

Dear Anna,

For the next three years, from 1975 to 1978, we lived in that beautiful house in the red rocks. At first, Dara and I were ecstatically happy together, but as the years went by we started to drift apart. We still loved each other, but something had changed, and I could tell she was getting restless.

As my relationship with Dara was drawing to a close, I struggled with questions about my sexual orientation. Was I a lesbian? Would I have relationships only with women from now on? Was I bisexual? Dara, still my wise friend, encouraged me to be relaxed about it, to let my love-life unfold as it would, but I wanted to be able to define myself, to know who I was.

During that time, Kevin intercepted every call I made to Sebastian and returned to me every gift and letter I sent to him. I saw him only twice, each time a burst of joy followed by gut-wrenching separation.

I was in a torture of ambiguity—loving so many things about my new life in Utah, and plagued by shame, guilt, and longing. I had to learn how to live

*in that heartache. Sometimes I thought my sadness
would crush my heart.
Love,
Sophia*

* * * * *

Anna

Again, I feel like I'm being punched in the stomach. This feels like more than just sympathy for what a friend experienced. Sometimes it literally makes me feel sick. Sophia found some comfort from the support of the other people living with her. But for me, I would have hated living with a group of people who meditated every day and did ceremonies all the time and used their belief that "everything has a bigger purpose" to justify anything and everything.

I have always wanted a simple, clear-cut, right-and-wrong kind of life I could navigate with certainty. Intense emotions have always been hard for me to deal with, and aberrant sexual behavior is distasteful to me. Sometimes Sophia's inclinations, like her choice to become sexually involved with a woman, make me feel isolated and separated from her even though these events in her life happened long ago. When I shared all of this with Perry at our last session, he encouraged me to be present with all those feelings and not run away.

* * * * *

July 4, 1975

Today I was ordained as a priestess. I am now a spiritual teacher of The Center for Divine Union, ordained to teach and to perform ceremonies including marriages and death services.

Honestly, this is a miracle! Four years ago I was spiritually lost. I was longing for a path to follow that would bring me comfort when I was in pain and help me understand this amazing, beautiful world that is sometimes so cruel. I wonder what I did to deserve this great gift. My intention is to become a teacher and to pass on to others what Raven has taught me. I want to help other people learn how we can live better, fuller lives by honoring all beings and the natural world around us.

The ceremony involved an initiation through communion with Nature. For the past week I have been preparing my body and mind for my initiation. I have collected things from nature that represent my new commitment: feather, charcoal, and vines. Today I sat in one place outdoors all day, praying and making a staff. I chose a limb and asked the tree for permission to take it. I promised the tree that this staff would always be used with great respect and only for good. And then the most amazing thing happened. I felt the tree give me permission — clear as anything I've ever felt! So I sat under the tree and embellished the staff, carving into it the images that held my intention.

The main image is of the divine masculine and feminine energies emerging from Mother Earth. My carving represents all human beings walking the Earth, with our feet on the ground and our heads in the heavens, bridging the two as we spread the seeds of creativity. Today, I make a commitment that I am going to walk this Earth spreading the seeds of love and creativity.

Another image I put on my staff was the Om symbol, the first thing I noticed when I walked into the temple at the Center in 1973. Its energy imprinted itself on my being with a power beyond anything I knew at the time. From the top of the staff I hung a feather to represent my connection to the winged spirits and a piece of charcoal as a symbol of the transformation through fire I had gone through to get to this moment.

This was a powerful process for me! I was shown a vision of myself as an artist bringing forth the Divine Feminine. Today I am full to the brim with hope and promise and potential!

As the sun was going down, the other initiates and I were called to the temple where Raven officiated over the ordination ceremony. We repeated vows and spoke aloud our personal intentions.

Being ordained reinforces my commitment to the path of consciousness and unconditional love. I see myself differently now — married to the Divine with a clear and powerful path to follow. I am so grateful.

* * * * *

Dear Anna,

Raven wrote volumes of teachings and practices every year. I had the privilege, although sometimes tedious, to sit with her and Jahi to edit her writings. She was methodical and very clear about what she would and wouldn't change. Patience became my practice during those times. It was rewarding and exciting that Raven's writings were being published as lessons and were being read by people all over the world.

And there was something else beginning to happen. Sebastian was now 15, and as he got older he would call me and I could call him. I had only been able to see him about twice a year, but now we could communicate without his father's interference. He had reached an age where he could speak for himself. The wound of our separation was beginning to heal.
Love,
Sophia

* * * * *

Grandmother Spirit

Since the beginning of human history we have recognized that there is something greater than ourselves — something that makes the sun come up and the thunder roar, the lightning crackle and the rain fall from the sky, something that informs the seed to sprout and guides it to reach for the sky. We have seen how new life is born and how spirit leaves a body. Through communing with nature, watching and listening, our ancestors came to understand the seasons, the cycles of the year and the cycles of life, and they sought ways to be in relationship with the natural world. They became aware of the unseen forces at work beyond what they could observe in the physical world around them — the Great Spirit, the Gods and Goddesses.

Humans have an insatiable yearning to know the Divine, and with our great imaginations we have created whole philosophies to explain and describe our relationship to the gods. But religions and philosophies differ from one another, even contradict one another. So how are you to know what to believe?

This is the truth that Raven taught: respect all traditions and take as your own those beliefs that speak clearly to your heart and soul. Do not be fooled by dogma. Truth is not constricting. Truth is liberating.

* * * * *

July 16, 1978

For years I have been telling Sebastian that when he turned 16, if he wanted, he could come and live with me. His father couldn't stop him if that's what he chose to do. And I expected him to want to come. So today, I called him and asked what he wanted to do.

Sebastian was very quiet for a long while. And then he told me he wanted to stay in Albuquerque. I knew he was not happy living with his dad, so I asked him to explain why this was what he wanted. After another long silence, he told me he was in love with a boy named Seth. They had been together for the last year, and he didn't want to leave him. In a small voice he asked, "Is that okay, Mom? I know you want me to come." "Of course," I told him, "you can do whatever feels like the right thing for you. I'm glad you found someone you love. If this changes, you can always come to me wherever I am."

Sebastian was so relieved. And now that he had broken the ice and told me about Seth, he started chattering on and on about him and all the things they had in common and how they helped each other. When I hung up, I was full of sweet sadness. My little boy is growing up.

* * * *

Dear Anna,

In August of 1978, Dara told us she was going to move her family to California. I knew I would miss her terribly. We had gone through so much together. She had been there for me when my world was falling apart, and she had held my hand as I left my son behind to follow the calling of my soul. We would now need to sell the house and property as there was no way we could afford this huge place without her support.

So the woman I had loved more than anyone before was leaving. And my son was not coming to live with me.

But my sadness was soon forgotten as Raven suggested that after the house sold it would be a good time to travel. She and Jahi and I would take a trip around the world! She wanted us to experience the richness and diversity of the world's religious traditions first hand. She was to be our guide and our trip historian. I can still clearly remember how excited I was! In many ways I had led a sheltered life. I had never traveled anywhere beyond the American southwest!

Love,

Sophia

* * * * *

September 20, 1978

I just got back from Albuquerque where I visited Sebastian and the rest of the family and shared with them my excitement about our pilgrimage.

Mom knows how deeply touched and inspired I am by Mother Teresa's work. When I told her I was hoping to meet Mother Teresa in India, she was concerned I would stay there and not come home. I assured her I would be coming back.

October 18, 1978

I am excited in every cell of my body! First we are going to Japan, then on to Thailand, Singapore, Hong Kong, Taiwan, Malaysia, Indonesia, India, Sri Lanka, and then to Europe. Is this real? Is this really happening to me? I never even dreamed that something like this was possible for me. I can't sleep!

※ ※ ※ ※ ※

Dear Anna,

Our journey was far and away beyond anything I could have imagined —cultures, foods, spiritual practices, temples and shrines, customs, languages, ways of dressing and ways of experiencing the world.

India was rich and evocative, full of visual delights and steeped in history. I felt like an ancient part of me was awakened while I was there. In some ways it was like coming home to a place I had never been before. I understood the culture in ways that didn't make sense, knowing my limited life experiences. The old temples felt familiar. Modern India is a paradox, a democracy that embraces the new even as it clings to the remnants of an ancient past. The wealth inequality was striking and disturbing. The plight of the poor and the beggars on the streets made my heart hurt.

Raven had traveled the world several times before, and we benefited from her abundance of knowledge and experience. Our focus was to touch the heart and soul of all the different spiritual traditions and to experience how the people in each of these varied cultures found their connection to spirit and how they expressed it in their rituals and their practices. Did this journey open my eyes and my mind and my heart? Oh, yes, it did! It showed me how people around the world live and work and pray in ways that were unimaginable to a middle-class girl from Albuquerque!
Love,
Sophia

* * * * *

November 17, 1978
   We are in India! Raven lived here for a long time

when she was a young woman, and it is wonderful to see her so happy to be here again. When she lived here, she was friends with Rabindranath Tagore, the Nobel-prize-winning poet and spiritual teacher.

Today we are at Tagore's home, a place called Shantiniketan (The Abode of Peace). He founded a school here and taught children using the natural world as his classroom. He said children learn more through nature than through books.

Even though Tagore has been dead now for over 20 years, I can feel his warmth and energy here. The house he built is a stone bungalow with rich rugs and simple decor. I feel very at home here.

Jahi and I are falling in love. It seems crazy, but maybe not when I recall my vision of us as lovers in a previous life. For years now we have been good friends, though he tells me now he has been waiting for me to recognize how we are good for each other in other ways and should be together. We are going to find a way to sleep together tonight. I feel like a teenager sneaking around! But it feels good and feels right. He is a good man. He understands me, and I feel safe with him.

December 4, 1978

Raven met Mahatma Gandhi through Tagore. She spent nine years traveling with Gandhi, working by his side and learning. Today she told me, "Gandhi was connected to his soul's purpose. He had nothing to lose because he had it all. He lived in the heart of his compassion and truth to the point that no one could move or sway him from that focus. He could look his assassin in the eye and say to him, 'You are God'."

Raven was with Gandhi when he was assassinated. She took us to the place where he was shot. There is a little house where Gandhi waited on that fateful day before he entered the courtyard. It is now a museum, and on the wall is a picture of a young Raven with Gandhi. We entered the courtyard together and walked the path Gandhi had walked to his death. It was surreal and deeply moving.

* * * * *

Dear Anna,

Learning to hear the call of my soul has been a hit and miss process. And the results of listening or not listening to the whispers of my soul have played out like reading a good or a bad novel. I know my soul will always urge me to listen and to hear the words of grace and wisdom available right there in every life experience. The question is, will I listen? Will I hear my soul when it calls to me?

While in India the one most important thing for me was to meet Mother Teresa and offer my help. I knew she traveled a lot and might not be there. I was deeply touched, as I still am today, by her unselfish generosity of heart as she helped the poor and orphaned children.

At our hotel, I looked in the phone book for the number for the Sisters of Charity convent. I called, and a woman answered. I told her we were from the United States, and we wanted to make a donation to the orphanage and, if possible, visit with Mother Teresa. The voice on the other end of the phone said, "I am here now. Come." It was Mother Teresa. I was stunned. I ran to tell the others, and soon we were on our way.

When we arrived at the Sisters of Charity building, there were hundreds of people waiting in line for donations of food and clothing. I donated all my western clothes from my suitcase and gave them some money. I chose to only wear saris while in India.

We were given a tour with our last stop at the children's orphanage. My heart was so moved by these precious little ones and how the sisters cared for them. We were then led upstairs onto an outdoor corridor. On the way we passed a room with an altar where some of the nuns were praying. We were invited to have a seat on a stone bench outside of this room. Down the corridor, I saw a small figure in nun's clothing walking toward us. It was Mother Teresa.

What an honor that she took the time to speak with us. Listening to her, I was struck with the power of this tiny woman. Her beautiful heart and soul shone from her face, permeating the atmosphere around her. Her quest was to bring love to every being she touched. When I asked her what I could do to help, she said, "I don't need your help! Go home and do your part. If each of us does our part where we live we can make a difference. People in your country are so lonely. This is a serious problem."

My ego had a moment of shock — she didn't need my help? But it had been my dream to help her! Those thoughts and feelings quickly changed, and I began to look at how I could help others at home.

Mother Teresa's words have lived in my heart since 1978. Not only was Mother Teresa committed to those she worked with in her own country, her heart stretched across the ocean, and she understood the pain in our country. That meeting changed my life in ways that I am still discovering. At every retreat I have led, I use her example of how to do our part where we live.

I was also blessed with the chance to meet Krishnamurti in Sri Lanka. His words of wisdom seeped into my heart and soul like warm, melted chocolate, dripping with sweetness.

There are those who could take issue with each of these extraordinary people. But no one could ever say they didn't live their souls' purpose. They had not only been touched by grace but lived in it and graciously bestowed it upon others. I asked Raven what makes

enlightened people different. She said, "They live their humanness."
Love,
Sophia

* * * * *

February 3, 1979

We are in London, and we just got engaged! When we arrive home, Raven will marry us. She is very happy and has given us her blessing. Jahi and I decided that if we could be together 24/7 for these last five months and still like each other, we could be happy being married to each other. We have so much in common and so much respect for each other.

May 19, 1979

Raven performed our marriage ceremony with our families and friends here to witness our love. I am so happy! This marriage is nothing like my first marriage, so constricted, so full of fear and pain and conflict. Jahi and I laugh and play together and are very much in love.

We have both found new jobs, and we all are beginning our search for a new piece of land for our spiritual center. I have never been so happy! Every day is a new adventure with our future stretching out before us, full of unimaginable possibilities!

* * * * *

Anna

I guess I have made some progress, but I feel like I'm moving at a snail's pace. Perry says to keep paying attention to my dreams and feelings. This is still really frustrating for me. I am reading about Sophia's amazing and crazy journey, and I can see how life keeps providing her with opportunities and changes and revelations.

Me, on the other hand, I could live the rest of my life just like it is and be perfectly happy. Except, I'm not happy now. Sophia's story is rattling me to the bone, shaking up my certainties, haunting me with some presence I can't put my finger on. It's like something keeps scratching at the window for my attention, but when I turn to look there is nothing there.

* * * * *

February 12, 1980

Yesterday we were driving through a beautiful little valley just outside of town. We passed a piece of land with a For Sale sign out front. Jahi told me that he and Raven had already considered this land and rejected it for various reasons. But I had a strong feeling about it and insisted that we stop and walk around. So we climbed under the barbed wire fence and proceeded up the rocky mountainside. When we reached the top we stood together in silence, awed by the beauty. The view was spectacular! We looked down the canyon slope to a sweet little running stream. We decided if the stream was part of the land we would buy it. Today we found out the stream is on the property! We have found our new home!

Our intention on this land is to show others how to live in harmony with the annual cycles of life, blending the wisdom of spiritual teachings from the East and the West.

June 16, 1980

Sebastian has been looking at colleges and universities. Today he called and told me he has decided to go to Berkeley. He said life is easier for gay people in California. I'm happy for him. He will be able live his life in the open. I love him so much.

August 13, 1980

It's been magical how all the pieces came together! In just six months we were able to close escrow on our new home and move our spiritual center onto 40 acres of sacred land. We are only 20 minutes outside of St. George, so getting to work hasn't been a problem.

Over the last six months we have walked the land every weekend, dreaming and making plans. We also had a lot to do, cleaning out two old shacks on the property that people had used as a dump. In this process I found the statue head of a Buddha and later I found the body. I cleaned it and glued it back together. This Buddha will be placed at our first shrine.

* * * * *

Dear Anna,

Over the years we created miles of paths and over thirty shrines scattered in the boulders reaching up the mountain and down to the stream below. Raven did the bulk of the work while Jahi and I worked in town. Each night when we arrived home we climbed up the mountain to see what new pathway or shrine had been developed. It felt like walking into a new mystery every evening. On the weekends, we all worked together forging new trails, moving stone and dedicating shrines.

The local people referred to Raven as Hawk Woman. From the road below they could see her on the mountain-top with the hawks soaring above her. She does have a way with animals. Once while on her hands and knees working on the path, she felt something at her feet. When she turned it was a baby javelina!

We built the temple ourselves using existing wood from old buildings on the property that we dismantled. Raven not only taught me how to build a relationship with the Divine, but how to build a temple!
Love,
Sophia

* * * * *

August 3, 1981

Kevin is dead. Sebastian called to tell me Kevin was in a horrible car accident. I'm in shock. Sebastian is in shock. He is on his way to Albuquerque. I'll go tomorrow to be with him.

My life with Kevin flashes before of me — the drinking, the abuse, the whole complicated emotional mess. I feel sad it wasn't different.

We had lived in our family constellation with Kevin as the central energy. He embodied the shadow – the unpredictable abuser who staked his identity on our confusion and fear. Sebastian and I learned to navigate around this center.

When I was able to really accept the fact of his death, I saw a vision of a mandala with the central pole collapsing, and I energetically felt our family constellation reorganize. Liberation and sorrow are both swirling around inside of me.

I'm grateful for Kevin's part in bringing Sebastian into this world and how our time together pushed me to grow. Oh, my dear Sebastian. You are strong. You will be okay. We will be okay.

November 6,1981

Today Raven said she had something to show us. Jahi and I followed her up the mountain to a place where we have created a shrine called the Blessing Way. Raven had found a petroglyph of Kokopelli! This is a gift of great magnitude. We found a Buddha the first year we were here, now several years later the flute-player petroglyph reveals itself to us. The blending of the East and the West is already here. We are the stewards of the land, bringing its spirit into manifestation.

The Center for Divine Union honors the heart of all traditions, providing a place for people to come and be in communion with their internal nature and the reflected outdoor nature. The shrines are made from the rocks and trees with a focal point where we place a candle or picture. Each shrine has a name, either to a teacher, a tradition, or an aspect of nature. For example, there is a shrine to Mother Teresa, Gandhi, the Great Mother Goddess, Jesus, and Buddha. There are shrines created by the Bahai community, and a place where fire ceremonies have been performed by a Tibetan Llama. Honoring Nature, we have shrines to the marriage of the earth spirits, a Soyal cave, and a cave to the North Wind. We provide teachings, meditations, and ceremonies in harmony with the Cycles of Life.

This was my dream when I chose to leave Albuquerque. Now I am living it. Here on this land with Raven and Jahi, I am learning to trust life and walk toward my soul. As time passes I can hear and respond to the transcendent with greater ease as the land speaks to me.

* * * * *

Dear Anna,

One beautiful fall day I was walking along the trails of our sanctuary. I reached the top of the mountain overlooking the canyon where I could hear the running water below and be at eye level with the turkey vultures that soared so close I could hear the wind against their wings. On this day I was called to go to one of our outdoor shrines dedicated to the Great Mother right near the Marriage-of-the-Earth-Spirits shrine.

I was walking slowly, as Raven had taught me, not in a hurry to get anywhere, wrapped in the knowledge that the here and now is filled with everything — there is nothing lacking.

Raven always walked these paths with such presence and no hurry to get anywhere, showing me how mindfulness connects us with divine expression. All we have to do is show up and be aware.

On this day I was walking in that rhythm, and as I entered the shrine my eyes were drawn to a slight imprint in the earth. At first I thought it was a shoe print, but as I bent down and brushed away the dirt a beautiful stone amulet revealed itself to me. I picked it up and was jettisoned into a space so sacred I fell to my knees and sobbed.

As I held it close to my heart I was infused with its magic, its history, its power. I have no idea how long I stayed in the grips of this awe-inspiring connection. In ways that were not cognitive but deeply felt in every cell of my being, I was filled with the power of the memories the amulet carried. I was being blessed, taken into another time and place, and given a precious gift. My vision blurred with tears, I tried not to stumble as I ran down the mountain trail to show Raven. Her kind response was so Raven — no surprise that such a magical object would reveal itself to me. This was just a reminder to listen to the stone's messages.

As the years have passed, I have consulted the stone amulet over and over again. I listen, and it speaks its messages to me. I wear it when I teach, for ceremony, and when I take people on retreat. When it isn't being worn, it hangs on the Native American altar.
Love,
Sophia

* * * * *

March 27, 1986

It's been five years since Kevin died. Sebastian just graduated with honors and has a loving partner whom he hopes to marry when the laws change. I am so proud of him.

When I visited Sebastian last week, I gave him all the

letters and gifts that his father had returned to me over many years. It was a wonderful opportunity for more healing between us. It gave us the chance to talk about how we felt during those years. I was able to express to him the deep attachment I had for him, the pain I had experienced, and how the choice I made has tempered me. I have a deeper understanding of loss, shame, and guilt. I also have grown to appreciate that each of us comes into this world with a personal path, even our children.

Perhaps, if I had given him these letters before his father died, Sebastian might have talked to him about these feelings as well. So much for "could haves."

Sebastian is leading programs to increase awareness of health issues for gay men and is serving on the board of an organization that promotes sex education for young people around the world. I am so proud of him. Slowly, slowly, I am finding I can let go of guilt and just love him and myself for our humanness. The shame continues to let me know it is there. I feel it in my body. I still don't want to be seen as a bad person or a bad parent...but it is better. I am getting better.

* * * * *

Dear Anna,
Something happened to me in 1988 that rocked

*my world. It all started with such an ordinary event —
I went, on a friend's recommendation, to receive a
bodywork session. That's how I met Karin, and meeting
her changed everything. I know I have said that often,
but it is true. Each time it feels like another layer of
consciousness and aliveness is gifted to me.*

*And this is how I took my first steps on the long
journey of healing myself — a journey I am still on and,
I have come to realize, I will be on until the day I die! I
came to the miraculous realization that not only could
I heal from my wounds, but I could learn how to help
other people heal from their wounds too.*

*I confess I had no idea how long a journey this
would be or how many obstacles and tragedies would
present themselves. I didn't know the pathway to
healing can sometimes lead us through treacherous
territories. All of that would reveal itself in time. But
when this world of healing began to open up to me, it
gave me hope, and it gave me purpose. And it gave me
another great gift, because as I began to heal, I realized
if I found good teachers, starting with Karin, and if I
studied diligently, I could make a living doing
something that filled me with joy — helping other
people to heal.*

Love,

Sophia

* * * * *

March 13, 1988

Karin is very sharp with her insights and has a straightforward way of communicating. The work I'm doing with her is opening up new worlds for me! The first time I saw her, she told me that emotions are held, locked up in our tissues. Of course, it didn't take long before I had the direct experience of my emotions being released as Karin worked my muscles. I am really into this! I have been seeing Karin every week for months. Today she agreed to teach me the work! This is a new opportunity for me to integrate my spirituality and the healing of my body.

June 5, 1988

Since I began working with Karin, I am realizing that there are times when I don't remember what happened the day before or even a few hours earlier. I feel a void sort of like sleeping without dreaming. I worry a little about this. Maybe I should tell someone.

November 26, 1988

I want to try to write down what I'm learning: emotional traumas are held in the cells and tissues of our bodies; it is possible for me to heal my past traumas; and — another amazing part — I could learn how to help other people to do the same! This is opening up a whole new way of understanding the world and my place in it. I'm studying Reiki, and Karin is teaching me about the amazing work that I have been receiving from her. At first, I didn't even know how to be in my body at all. Through my work with Raven, learning to be present in the here and now, and my work with Karin, I am learning to inhabit my own body.

Jahi and I have been in a committed relationship now for 10 years and our wonderful connection has grown while at the same time it has suffered from the challenges inevitable when two people live and work together over time, especially in a spiritual community. We need more privacy, more time alone together for communication and intimacy. What I'm learning is serving our relationship in a good way. Karin and her husband have become very good friends.

May 6, 1989

I love working with people! I have been seeing people at the Center, and I have a small office in town. I look forward to when I can stop working for others in the business world and have more time for this body of work. I call my work Soulful Touch.

September 18, 1990

After working in town for the corporate and nonprofit world for the past 15 years, we are finally in a position that I can leave my job and dedicate all my time and energy to the growth of our spiritual center and my own healing practice. I have set up programs to host guest meditation teachers, llamas, tai chi and chi gong teachers, and much more. Each year more blessings reveal themselves. My teachings are becoming alive! I am taking classes and going on retreats. Great Spirit is manifesting more and more through my work. I am feeling empowered.

November 26, 1991

Frank moved in today. He is our dear 96-year-old friend whose wife recently died. He has no living family; we will be his family now. We will be his family until he moves on.

January 15, 1992

Today, I received a Reiki empowerment that enables me to teach Reiki. I felt my body start to shake, a vibrating that left me feeling exhilarated and confused. But I rode it out, understanding my body was adjusting to this new energy frequency. I love learning new ways to serve the body and spirit!

✻ ✻ ✻ ✻ ✻

Grandmother Spirit

Every religion, every spiritual philosophy has its own beliefs and teachings about death and the afterlife.

Sophia learned a great deal about these different beliefs when she traveled the world with Jahi and Raven. There are spiritual paths that teach of an omnipresent God who decides when you will be born and when you will die and whether you have been good enough to go to heaven or bad enough to go to hell. There are nature-based religions that teach how we are like a leaf on a tree that, when its time is over, drifts silent and unnoticed to the ground. There are ancient teachings that celebrate the movement of everlasting energy from body to body, life after life. As wise Raven taught, there are gems to be found in each tradition, and we can call upon them to help us through times of disaster.

* * * * *

Dear Anna,

Early on the evening of July 1, 1992, the phone rang. I had never heard my mom so upset. With a shaky voice and through her tears she told me that my beautiful goddaughter, Andrea, was dead.

I don't remember, Anna, if you ever met Andrea. She was my dear cousin Dolores's youngest daughter. She would have been ten years old on the 21st of July.

I flew immediately out to Arizona to be with

Dolores and her husband Dave. The whole family gathered to help search for Andrea's body, which would not be found for three agonizing weeks.
Love,
Sophia

* * * *

July 1, 1992

I am heartbroken, surrounded by people I love, and they are all heartbroken too. My plane to Phoenix got in late, and I rented a car to get to their vacation cabin. Everyone had gone to bed except Dolores who waited up for me. We sat and had tea together. She is a wreck. She told me what happened.

Andrea and Dave went for a hike up the Salt River canyon. It was a beautiful day. There wasn't a cloud in the sky. They had been hiking upstream for three hours on a trail that clung to the cliff above the river. Now and then, the trail wound down to the river and crossed to the other side. When Dave's hat was blown off and landed in the river below, Andrea scrambled down the bank to the water and waded in to retrieve it. She was 100 yards away when Dave first heard a roar in the distance and knew they could be in trouble. He yelled to Andrea to hurry, but it was too late. A six-foot wall of water came barreling down the canyon, pushing ahead of it rocks and boulders, tree limbs and whole trees. It swept Andrea away.

Dave ran down the trail above the river, trying in vain to keep up with the roaring wall of water, yelling, praying, frantic, screaming for help. But no one was there to help, and even if they had been, there would have been nothing they could do. He saw her once; then she was gone.

It's the middle of the night, but the house is restless. I can tell that no one else in this house is sleeping well tonight. I'm going to turn out the light and just let myself feel what I feel. Stop the thoughts. Stop creating more suffering.

July 15, 1992

We have been searching for Andrea for two weeks. This is torture. I am using my Reiki skills to help my family, grateful that I have this small comfort to offer. We are all shaken to the core. We also feel the deep love we have for one another. The bonds that hold us together are strong.

I asked Dolores if Andrea had behaved in any unusual way before the accident. She said yes, she did do some things that were out of character for her, things that created more intimacy and connection between all of them.

August 8, 1992

Andrea was buried in a beautiful old Catholic

cemetery. We laid her to rest under lovely, towering trees. Her best friend spoke and said that just a few days before she died, Andrea said she wanted to die near water.

After the service, we all were quiet. I went to Sebastian and gave him a sad, grateful hug. We held each other for a long time. He had been fond of Andrea too.

I am blessed to have had this time for my family and for my own grieving.

* * * * *

Anna

I am sitting on Perry's sofa sobbing. When I got here today for my appointment I wasn't feeling like this. Actually I was feeling excited to tell Perry about how, when I read about Sophia finding the amulet, I had felt something open up inside of me that was unlike anything I had ever felt before — something magical! Could it be true that magic is not just a part of Sophia's life, but I can be touched by the magical and the mystical too?

All this time I have been reading the journals, I have been feeling all of Sophia's torturous emotions. And then, for the first time, I felt her elation, her wonder, her gratitude for finding the amulet.

As I started to tell Perry about this, I was brought up

short. Here I was, talking about the possibility that the amulet, a simple physical object, might actually have power, when I looked up at the walls of Perry's office. They are covered with masks and strange paintings. His shelves are crowded with objects from his many travels and his dealings with indigenous medicine people. And I suddenly realized that these objects help him in his work. They give him power just as Sophia's amulet gives her power.

When I told Perry about Andrea's death it hit me hard. At first I just felt angry. Why did her father let her go in the water after his hat? How could God be so unfair as to take a ten-year-old girl, so full of life and promise? When I read the part in the journal about Andrea's accident I had felt sad for Andrea, for Sophia, for the whole family. But now, sitting here on Perry's sofa, I am not just feeling sad, I am wracked with grief, torn apart, shredded. Andrea's death was 20 years ago, but I am feeling this as if it were yesterday and as if she had been my own dear and precious goddaughter.

Perry has been working with me now for eight months since Sophia left, teaching me, in spite of my resistance, how to allow myself to feel what I am feeling and then how to use my breath to calm myself. But there is no calming myself right now. I am lost in my emotion. He just lets me sob and cry out in anguish and dissolve into grief until finally the emotion is spent and I am left lying on the carpet (how did I get there?) wrung out, raw, empty.

Perry is so gentle with me. He tells me over and over how I am doing great. He encourages me to keep going. He sends me home with a suggestion that I draw pictures of objects that are important to me and then write down the feelings that come to me. "Start with the amulet," he says.

* * * * *

Grandmother Spirit

Life sometimes throws us a shocking blow. Shiva and Kali, the masculine and feminine destroyers, reach into our lives and turn the world upside down, making it incomprehensible. Devastating, unanswerable questions arise like: Why would a child be taken when Frank, Sophia's 99-year-old friend, lives on?

Sophia was blessed with the ability to move into other realms and connect with Andrea. She would take shamanic journeys to dialogue with her and share the information with Dolores.

There were many clues to indicate Andrea had a premonition of her death. She had made efforts to communicate her love in special ways. A distant family friend, not knowing of Andrea's death, had been driving by that creek when, in his mind's eye, he saw a child under the water. Dolores, while driving to the grocery store at exactly the time when Andrea was struggling in the water, heard a voice say, 'What if you lost your Andrea?"

These are the things that remind us there is so much more to life than can be seen in the physical world around us. And if we turn our attention to that which is unseen, still there are worlds within worlds, layers of spirit.

We will always ask questions. And many of our questions will never be answered to our satisfaction. From here in this physical world, we can only see so far into the realms where all the answers are waiting for us. And when we finally get there? Perhaps by then we will have realized that having these questions answered is not really all that important.

Experiences come to us in this life. We live them in joy and in sorrow. We learn from them, or we don't. They reconstruct our lives. We move on. There is nothing else to be done.

Chapter Six

Grandmother Spirit

Have you noticed that spiritual teachers appear in our lives just when we are ready to take the next step in our evolution? Or perhaps they have already been in our lives, but their message is suddenly relevant and important. If their message is in alignment with our soul's journey, we will be attracted to their teachings.

Often we are not sure what the next step looks or feels like. Our teachers show us how to move forward on our spiritual journey — they show us by their very being; by the light of their energy; by demonstrating how to walk through the world with compassion and equanimity. By the way they feel, speak, think, and act, our teachers communicate their messages and their characters. The way they embody their teachings informs our souls. In them we see a mirror image of ourselves — the person we really are but have forgotten.

* * * * *

Dear Anna,

I am grateful that over the course of my life I have been exposed to so many different approaches to communion with the sacred energies of life.

Raven, of course, would always be a primary teacher for me. But her teachings were not constrictive or exclusive. She always encouraged me to explore any spiritual path that spoke to me and to learn all that I could from as many teachers as I wanted. She simply encouraged me to be sure their teachings rang true in my heart, their motivations were pure, and their characters honorable.

In the spring of 1993, I began to study with Rinsho, a renegade Vipassana teacher. The chants, images, and practices I learned from him transported me into other realms, and the truth of my experiences resonated in my body. I began to learn more about Buddhist philosophy. My Vipassana practice — also known as mindfulness practice — helped me stay focused and less attached to outcomes. I started doing daily practices and attending retreats where my desire to learn and grow was tested and tempered. I participated in my first sweat lodge.

I was driven to find the truth. I was committed to living a life unencumbered by false concepts. I longed for what I called "freedom of life" — a life where my choices would come from my heart and my soul and not from conditioned responses or cultural edicts. I *wanted to stand in my own truth freely, without hesitation and without the limitations of fear.*

When Karin moved away I felt abandoned, like I had when I thought The Center for Divine Union was moving away without me. But not long after she left, I met Mitch, a unique and special being who became an important teacher for me as well as a friend and an indispensable help in the challenging years to come.

I was relieved to once again have a healer in my life. Mitch was a chiropractor who understood the nuanced relationship between the body, mind, and spirit. He also had the skills to help me experience transformative states.

At the same time, I was meeting other healers, becoming a Reiki master, learning about new and interesting healing modalities and practices, and taking massage classes. Looking back on it, I think this was one of the most dynamic and expansive times of my life. I was 50 years old; I had found my calling; I was on fire!

Love,

Sophia

* * * * *

September 1, 1993

I'm on a plane, flying home from Washington. I

haven't written in my journal since before the Vipassana retreat. It's been 30 days, and it's hard for me to describe how I'm feeling. It was a challenge right from the beginning.

If, when I was younger, you had told me I would live in a cold little cabin with no heat for 30 days, where the damp and cold would sink into my bones, where the sheets on the bed never completely dried out, and that I would be doing this of my own free will — well, I wouldn't have believed it! But I did it.

I sat in silent meditation in that little cabin and in the cold meditation hall, day after day, until the silence magnified my fears and turned them into an anger so strong I didn't want to leave my bed for fear of acting out my rageful fantasies — like burning down the forest and everyone in it!

When I built up the courage to leave my bed, I marched through the forest directly to the teacher. When I told him what I was feeling, he chuckled and asked me if I had a hard time expressing anger! He told me if I had not already played out my raging delusions, chances were I never would. But I was still afraid of my rage, so he walked me through a guided meditation, which helped me to accept it and let it go.

September 15, 1993

Since I came home, I am noticing changes in myself. I don't react as much or as easily. I'm pretty blissed out.

Feeling lots of love for life and for Jahi. When I first got home, he asked how the retreat was for me. I told him it was heaven and hell wrapped in a beautiful bow.

* * * * *

Grandmother Spirit

Heaven and hell wrapped in a beautiful bow? What did Sophia mean? She experienced the Great Mother within herself — her immense divinity, her vastness, peace, and love. But Kali, with her deep, dark shadow of rage and fury also came forward. These two energies played together inside of Sophia, dancing with her, playing her like a flute and a drum. She danced through it all and came out holding both energies in a new and intimate way. She wrapped them in a blanket of love and tied them with a beautiful bow to seal in the beauty of the polarities whirling around, loving each other, dancing together.

* * * * *

October 1, 1993

Now that a month has passed since the retreat in Washington, I can start to get a sense of how it has changed me. Some of my experiences rattled my old imprints to the core.

One thing that really spun my head around was that the woman who had been sitting next to me in meditation was a Catholic nun! I didn't know this until the end of the retreat. It was a silent retreat, like all the Vipassana retreats I had been attending, so we did not speak to one another until the retreat was over. We were having lunch together, and she told me about her calling to the Church. I was stunned! She had been taught contemplative meditation from the very beginning of her service as a nun, and there was no conflict at all.

I had been taught that a good Catholic did not participate in another religion's practices. We were taught not to even attend services at a Christian church of another denomination, much less study and practice Buddhism. I had simply accepted that I was a bad Catholic, if indeed I was still a Catholic at all. Another preconception smashed; another limiting belief I can just let go of! How astoundingly liberating!

September 16, 1994

My friend is hosting a Tibetan Llama named Khempo Jinpa while he teaches at the college in town. She invited us to participate in a teaching on the Medicine Buddha at her home. I love these teachings! I love calling on the energy to heal, the practices of chanting in the Tibetan language, the wisdom of how I co-create my own energy field. It made me cry. I'm hooked! I am stepping into a rich realm of discovery and practice. I love Khempo's energy, his voice in prayer, his gentle way of reminding me of the value of this "precious human life."

January 18, 1995

For weeks I have been attending practices and teachings with Khempo. He was here today to do a fire ceremony at our center. People from our community were invited and received the profound blessing. We prepared special food for the fire gods and fed it to the fire as we chanted and prayed.

February 24, 1995

Khempo just told us about a very special llama named Tubten Rinpoche who is coming from Tibet. He will be teaching in the United States for the first time. Khempo told us this was a rare opportunity and we should do everything in our power to be there. I definitely want to go!

March 9, 1995

I am at a retreat in the Chimayo desert where I just met the highly venerated Tibetan llama, Tubten Rinpoche. He doesn't speak English, so Khempo is acting as his translator. I am honored and blessed to be here!

I have fallen in love with the landscape! We are all staying in an extraordinarily beautiful home with a spectacular view of the rolling hills that stretch off into the distance, striped and striated in rose- and rust-colored hues.

So many new sights, sounds, smells, and experiences are cracking me open, revealing what they call the Buddha Nature. I am soaring on this unencumbered pure nature of love and possibility. Then I descend again into old imprints and limiting beliefs and ego-centered actions.

One day there was a teaching about non-attachment. I practiced it all day then asked a question. I said, "When I apply non-attachment to situations, it feels like I don't care." Khempo immediately said with a laser-like energy in his body and words, "It sounds like self-importance to me." I was stunned by his response. His words pierced right through me. This truth struck squarely in my heart. My mind went into chaos — very hard for my ego. I felt shamed for not avoiding the pitfalls of this practice. But how do I expect to grow and evolve without facing my own weaknesses? I can do this. I want to do this.

I have met some amazing people at this retreat, like Kunchen, an American Buddhist nun from Virginia. She and I made a deep connection. She is also a Reiki master, and she told me about a Reiki lineage I had never heard of. It was fascinating! We spent hours today discussing healing, spirituality, and the possibility of jointly starting a Reiki school together. She would teach on the East

Coast; I would teach in the West. I am really excited about this idea!

I also met a man at this retreat. His name is Tom, and I am intrigued by him. I have to be honest — I find him really sexy. I am a married woman! I have no business feeling sexual about another man! But I do, and it is enlivening and thrilling in the way of secrets. Obviously, I won't do anything about or with these feelings. But they are there, and I can't deny they exist. We exchanged numbers.

* * * * *

Anna

Spring is in the air today! Actually it isn't here yet, but when I went walking this morning I could see tiny buds on the trees. I'm sitting on the porch swing, bundled up in a down quilt and sipping a hot mug of tea.

Page after page of Sophia's journal is filled with her spiritual awakenings and her practices. None of this really interests me much, but at least it doesn't leave me crumpled on the floor in tears.

Perry is always telling me to keep going, it will get better. Am I getting there? Any closer? Is that why I'm feeling better? Or is it only because, in this part of Sophia's story, she is fulfilled and happy?

* * * * *

Grandmother Spirit

Have you ever felt like you were on a roll — life was opening up for you; everything falling into alignment with your dreams and aspirations? Have you felt like that? Like you were on top of the world? These high points are like mountaintops we visit. But we cannot live there.

Life can't help but bring change; change is its very nature. Most of us are blessed to experience high points now and then during the course of our lives. We ride the wave on the thrilling upswing, and then...what? We cannot keep moving upward forever. Usually the turn to the descent is gradual; life changes slowly and evolves into a different life.

But sometimes the downturn is swift and brutal. And even if we don't understand why it sometimes happens this way, it's clear that intense, even life-threatening experiences bring us face to face with lessons we must ultimately learn one way or another if we are to progress on our spiritual journeys.

* * * * *

Dear Anna,

When something momentous and life changing enters our life, we often have no idea it is just a beginning. We have an experience, we get through it, and then we think, well, that was no fun, but thank God it's over. But maybe it isn't over. Maybe it's just taking a little time off, and it will be back with a vengeance.

I started having periods of time when I did not feel well. Then I would have weeks or even months when I felt okay. Just when I thought I was over whatever it was, I would get hit with it again. When my life began to fall apart, I didn't even realize what was happening.
Love,
Sophia

＊ ＊ ＊ ＊ ＊

January 25, 1996

The last few weeks have dragged by. I have been feeling horrible — agitated, restless, afraid. All I want to do is sleep, and I have indigestion. I just feel awful. And for some reason I can't explain, I feel afraid. I don't even know what I'm afraid of, I just feel afraid. I'm having memory lapses, times when I don't remember the last day or hours. So much of what is happening is unclear and unnerving.

I have been able to bring some mindfulness and equanimity to what I am going through. But this is like any other practice — I succeed for a while, then I completely lose it and the fear turns to terror. A couple of nights ago I actually woke myself up by screaming. My startle reflex is hyper sensitive, and I'm agitated and frightened by energy and sounds.

When I start to question why these things are happening to me, I just get lost in a fearful, mental quagmire. My equanimity and mindfulness slip away, and I'm caught again in the trap of identifying with thoughts and sensations. It's like my thoughts are bombs, each one causing an explosion of fear and panic. I'm being bombarded. I try to just let them go, but every time a thought passes, another arises. It's exhausting. I am tired of this. I have no energy to continue the effort of being mindful. It is as if I have no skill or ability to do anything but suffer.

February 12, 1996

Trying to figure out what is causing my fragmentation and disharmony is futile. It could be any of a hundred things. Is it the result of the last 10-day Vipassana retreat in Santa Barbara, where I was burning through old patterns? Where I sat with what is, and my fixated identities burned up in the furnace of awareness?

When I was in California I saw Karin in her new home. Before and after the retreat she did very deep emotionally-cathartic bodywork on me. Is that what stirred up all of this? Maybe it's the homeopathic constitutional I have been taking that's kicking up some deeper healing. And then there is the chiropractic and energy work I am receiving from Mitch several times a week. Not to mention, I was sick at the retreat — a cold or flu thing. Also, my hormones are out of whack. Menopause is upon me, and it's no piece of cake!

But to give what I am experiencing a name would simply support a particular identity I can associate myself with and point a finger at. So instead, I am choosing to see these experiences as just a passing of thoughts and sensations.

This works for a while, then the other side of the polarity shows up and I lose my equanimity and find myself at the mercy of my thoughts and sensations. I become my own jailer, locking myself in the prison of samsara's folly of suffering and endless repetition of patterns. It's a trap, and I fall into it over and over again.

March 5, 1996

Last night I had this dream:

I experience the energy patterns of my body and mind, and I start to play and experiment with how I feel when I merge with them. In the dream I know a shift is taking place. I see a clearing in the distance and feel a calming within.

I woke up this morning feeling confident I was beginning to re-establish my connection to the core place inside where I am calm and at peace.

* * * *

Dear Anna,

Everything changed on the evening of April 28, 1996. I had been having some health issues, but nothing that had slowed me down. My time was focused on the pursuit of enlightenment, going to retreat after retreat, empowerments, teachings, healing classes. If something was good for me, then more of it must be better.

I had just returned from Virginia, where I had been studying Reiki Jin Ki Do and making plans to collaborate with Kunchen to teach this powerful healing modality at our center in Utah. It was an exciting time, and I was inspired by visions of our center growing and flourishing, offering our abundant gifts of healing to the world.

I was studying the teachings I had just brought home with me from the retreat when I felt a hot burning fire rush up my spine. I was nauseous and disoriented. I made it to my bed. I felt like my spine was melting.

I asked Jahi to come and hold me. What was

happening to me? It was frightening. We lay together, my back snuggled against him, his arms tenderly enfolding me. He was my container, my witness. He comforted me. I managed to fall asleep.

When I woke up in the morning I lay in bed thinking through what had happened. My thoughts were clear, and I wasn't feeling emotionally reactive. But when I tried to get out of bed, I realized something was seriously wrong. My arms and legs were like wet noodles; I couldn't control them. I had never experienced anything like this before. I still felt calm and clear minded; in retrospect I realize I was dissociated. We called Mitch, who encouraged us to come in immediately. On our way to the car I heard Raven chanting in the temple. The 30-minute drive to town seemed to take forever.

When Mitch saw me, I could tell by the look on his face how concerned he was. I told him I felt crazed. I was doing everything I could to stay present. He and Jahi helped me through the door and up onto the treatment table.

Mitch asked me a lot of questions. What had I been doing? Where had I been? What had I eaten? What supplements and medications had I been taking? I answered all his questions and told him about the fumes on the airplane and the sushi I had eaten and the homeopathic remedy I had been taking for two years and how I had recently increased the dosage.

I lay on Mitch's table, and he worked on me, his competent hands searching, feeling, adjusting my energy. My body was totally placid, my wet-noodle limbs uncontrollable. Suddenly my muscles tightened and my body became completely rigid, frozen in a state of contraction.

I heard Mitch go in the other room and call his brother, also a chiropractor, and consult with him about my condition.

Just as I heard Mitch come back, I slipped into a catatonic state, staring into space, not moving. It felt like time stopped. I was conscious enough to register the severity of my condition. Now I was truly frightened.

After 30 minutes, Mitch was able to get me out of the catatonic state and to stabilize my body with acupuncture. I could stand and walk, and I felt fine at that point.

We were all mystified. What was happening to me? What had triggered it? Mitch instructed me to get blood work done, and he referred me to another acupuncturist and encouraged me to go as soon as possible. We went immediately, and while I was there I had another attack. Again, we did not know why. By late afternoon I was home, feeling tired from the ordeal but otherwise okay.

Was all of this happening because of a particularly high dosage of a homeopathic remedy?

Possibly, said my homeopathic therapist. We worked with the dosage, but nothing changed.

I had been on that remedy for two years, following the strictest protocol for homeopathics: don't take anything else. This is a very old pattern in me, a determination to do things the right way. I went so far as to suffer through a bladder infection with no medication. Anyway, I had never liked the idea of taking medications. I believed in the body's ability to heal itself. I still do, of course, only now I understand that sometimes it can take a long time to do so.

Anna, I have no idea how much of this you were aware of at the time. I had entered into a new phase of my life, a phase that was devoured by illness and shadowed by the hovering presence of death.
Love,
Sophia

✳ ✳ ✳ ✳ ✳

Anna

Just reading this letter made me afraid. Am I going to have to go through experiencing all of Sophia's feelings while she battles an illness she indicates goes on for a long, long time? I haven't even read the journal entries yet, and I'm feeling disoriented, even physically ill.

This morning, I decided I wasn't going to do this anymore

— no more journal reading, no more sessions with Perry, no more suffering through Sophia's emotions and ailments. I went to my appointment with Perry just to tell him I wouldn't be back.

"So," he said, "you are going to run away again?"

I snapped at him, "What do you mean by that?"

"Well, how much do you remember about that time in Sophia's life?"

I had to admit that I didn't remember anything at all. In fact, there are years, maybe as many as ten years, when I have no recollection of anything having to do with Sophia at all. So, is Perry right? Am I running away again?

I asked Perry today if he had been aware of Sophia's illness.

"Of course," he said. "It was a nightmare. Anna, did you just check out from Sophia's life during this time?"

"I must have because I can't find any memories of that time."

"Where do you go when you check out?"

I don't know what he meant. I have no way to answer that question.

I'm back home, standing in front of a mirror, staring at myself. I'm trying to, as Perry said, "find out where I go."

I knew Sophia had been sick. At least I think I knew. We weren't very connected during that time, and I honestly had no idea it was as bad as it was.

Also, I know this about myself: I don't like illness. And I don't like chaos, uncertainty, feeling out of control. I guess I'm not that good a friend. But Sophia, in her notes to me, doesn't seem to be upset with me for abandoning her when she was in crisis. She has just asked me to read about it. So I am doing that for her. And she asked me to keep seeing Perry. I'm doing that for her, too. And now I'm following Perry's instructions, standing in front of a mirror staring at myself. Where do I go? I don't know. I just go on with my life. When I stare at myself I just see me staring back.

✳ ✳ ✳ ✳ ✳

April 30, 1996

Tubten Rinpoche is staying with us this weekend. I asked him to help me understand what was happening to me. He is so kind. I feel compassion radiating off of him. He told me to relax and keep doing my practices. So that is what I'm doing. I meditate. I do mantras and prayers for all beings to be happy. I also include the prayer that my suffering might be enough so others do not have to suffer.

May 1, 1996

Last night the attacks started again and lasted all night. This morning I had the worst attack of all. It knocked me to my knees. I couldn't believe how much it hurt. It was like a gripping in my solar plexus — really frightening, wrenching and gnawing inside of me. I wondered if I was going insane or if I was dying. It kept getting worse until I actually felt my life force leaving my body! I had no connection to my legs and feet, and I could see my spirit moving across the room. I yelled for Jahi to grab my feet. As soon as he did, I felt my energy come back into me. Then I really fell apart.

Jahi called for Raven to come and help. As usual, she radiated calm as she came to my side, carrying her drum. She put one hand on my belly and with the other she drummed softly, calling on the goddesses, chanting their names. Each time she spoke a name I saw that goddess enter the room, surrounding me with love and healing energy. I was in the womb energy of Quan Yin, Pachamama, Spider Woman, Tara, Butterfly Maiden, Kali, the Great Mother. More and more of them kept appearing, the room filled up, the walls dissolved and were replaced with the goddess energy. Then Raven chanted an old Lakota song calling on the father energy for healing. She told me to sing along.

WANI WACHIYELO Wani wachiyelo ate omakiyayo.
Father help me, I want to live.

May 2, 1996

I saw two doctors today. What a polarity! At the offices of the first doctor, I was barely able to walk, and I couldn't hold my head up. I was shaking, bent over, moving very slowly. Jahi was holding me up. I don't know what I would do without him. I felt like I was sinking into the ground.

When I met the doctor, he seemed preoccupied. He

told me to lie down and then asked me why I was shaking like that. How should I know? He told me to wait while he took care of some computer business. I knew immediately that I was in the wrong place. So we left and went to Natalie's house to wait for an hour until it was time for my second appointment of the day with Dr. Dan.

As soon as Natalie saw me she put her arms around me. She and Jahi practically carried me into her living room. She sat down in a big overstuffed chair and had me sit between her legs with my back to her chest. I was really gone. I honestly didn't know if I was going to make it through this one. She held me and supported me. I could feel her love for me, and I felt really safe. Natalie is a wise and gifted healer herself. She just kept saying, "Breathe. You'll be okay. Breathe." Jahi sat on the floor watching us.

Dr. Dan brought me back with one adjustment to my neck. He believes I am having a radioactive reaction from my last airplane flight from Virginia, and he gave me a homeopathic remedy. I feel so much better tonight.

May 8, 1996

What makes all this chaos in my body? How is it that my mind just stops? It's like I am being thrown in and out of the normal world. Waves of rigidity grip me until I'm frozen in time and space. Then there are no boundaries, only my arms and legs flailing in rhythm with a vibration that is foreign and terrifying.

* * * * *

Dear Anna,

 It started in the spring of 1996, and it took over my life. Before it was over some four years later, I had sought help from allopathic, naturopathic, homeopathic, and osteopathic doctors; neurologists, acupuncturists, and chiropractors; Craniosacral, Bowen, Polarity, and massage therapists. I tried Reiki, Jin Shin Jyutsu, Lymphatic Drainage, and Colon Hydrotherapy. I also saw several medical intuitives. I traveled to the world-famous Mayo Clinic. For the most part, these consultations and treatments were useless or helpful only temporarily. The attacks persisted.

 Those who were able to help me were Mitch, Natalie, Dr. Dan, and later, my friend Nick whose Craniosacral treatments brought me relief. These healers could bring me out of an attack and help me back to a normal state, at least until my next attack.

 No one ever determined, in a medical sense, what was happening to me. It was suggested that I suffered from radiation poisoning or parasites or female hysteria, a misogynistic diagnosis I thought had been debunked in the 1950s. I was told I was just suffering a hormonal imbalance from menopause. One doctor told me it was all the result of a bladder infection. Were they crazy?

One thing became crystal clear: I could not expose myself to any toxic chemicals, even in minute amounts, without triggering an attack. Then there were the weirdly different things that seemed to trigger my attacks: walking into the living room when the TV was on; visiting with a friend in her home when someone in her kitchen sprinkled cleanser in the sink; fumes of any kind. There were so many unanswered questions.

I was fading away, my foundation unraveling. All the things I had relied upon as markers of who I was and how I related to other people were collapsing. Certainty was a thing of the past. I had lost control of my body and mind. I was completely helpless. I don't know what I would have done without Jahi's generous heart and constant support.

I heard the silent cries coming from deep inside me: Somebody please help me! I want this to stop! I want this to stop! I was catapulted into a new consciousness unlike anything I had known.

I found myself suspended in the realm of the in-between — not here, but not totally gone. I can't really explain this eerie place, even now. I couldn't imagine what was to come. Would I ever get better? Would I die? Everything was dissolving, disappearing, burning up. Was it possible I would emerge from these ashes reborn like a phoenix? Or would they gradually cover me completely,

smothering me, suffocating me, ultimately killing me?
Love,
Sophia

* * * * *

Anna

My heart is beating so fast, it feels like it's going to bump right out of my chest. I've been reading passage after passage about Sophia's struggle to maintain her equilibrium, to keep calm, to not let the fear of dying overtake her. I feel like I'm the one who might be dying. Do I feel like I want to run away? Yes! Am I running away? Not yet.

I'm getting better at remembering Perry's instructions when I'm in the middle of one of these reactions. So I breathe deep and slow. I stand in front of the mirror again, holding Sophia's healing stone. I stare at myself. I don't know what's supposed to happen. Then suddenly I'm watching Sophia struggle with her body; I can feel my own limbs going limp; I can feel how afraid she is. I don't want to see and feel this, but I can't tear my eyes away from the mirror. Then I feel myself withdrawing inside. Like falling down a rabbit hole. Inside it is dark and still, and I don't have to think or feel anything.

* * * * *

May 20, 1996

Last night I had this dream:

I was cleaning out a child's ear and I took about a cup of wax out. It was bleeding, so I wiped it clean. I realized I shouldn't leave it totally naked and raw, so I put some wax back in. Then the child told me he wanted to do the best he could and help people, but he had a problem of forgetting, of being confused and reversing things. I told him most all of the wax was gone now, and he would probably be getting better. Also, he would hear better since he had failed the hearing test.

So what is it I can hear now that I couldn't hear before? Obviously, I am being told I can't dig everything out at once. It becomes too raw. Were all my practices to remove obstacles in the way of my spiritual awakening too much, leaving me raw and bleeding?

June 1, 1996

Tarla told me she was so concerned about me that she went to Tubten Rinpoche to ask what to do to help me. She and some of my other friends from the Tubten Center were afraid I was dying.

When they asked Rinpoche, he went into a deep meditation, a divination. He traveled to me in his meditation and returned saying that there is nothing pathologically wrong with me. I will be fine. He said I was purifying my obscurations and I was to continue to do my practices. Yesterday Jahi returned from staying with Rinpoche. He told me that Rinpoche said, "I can hear Sophia doing mantra." When I heard this, a deep and profound awareness washed over me, an awareness of our inter-connectedness. He can hear me. Even when I am feeling totally isolated in this horrible frightening experience, I am not alone. This reminds me of my first profound spiritual experience when I visited The Center for Divine Union and saw the book I had seen in my dream. In the dream world and in other unseen realms, we are connected and we communicate.

* * * * *

Grandmother Spirit

Can we love ourselves in those times when we are wretched and weak, when we look horrible and can think only of ourselves and our own suffering? Can we learn how to release our attachment to how we want life to play out and simply be with what is in this moment? When we are lost in confusion and uncertainty, can we still hold the awareness that what we are experiencing is cultivating within us a deeper and richer humanity?

Sophia has entered a sacred time of challenge and discovery and deep, deep healing. Sisters, we all will live through turbulent and difficult times. When the challenges of life arise and emotions overtake me, I go to the water to pray. I pray for the waters to run through me; I pray that the emotions I am feeling might be washed away, leaving only their teachings, their inherent wisdom.

Chapter Seven

Grandmother Spirit

Living within us is an undercurrent, a breath of life which informs us on our journey. It is always there, always influencing us, but most of the time we are unaware of these subtle energies. However, sometimes its influence comes rushing to the forefront, especially at those moments when we stand at a turning point, a threshold that opens in a new direction.

These points of potential change are sometimes marked in our lives by ecstatic experiences — falling in love, exaltation, a moment of epiphany. Sometimes they hit us hard as illness, loss, or trauma. Our inner wisdom is pushing us hard to move in a new direction. If we are not paying attention, if we are not keenly aware, these moments can slip away, and we will be left with only the memory of our ephemeral happiness or the story of our suffering.

Why is one child born sick and another healthy? Why was one car on the freeway hit, and the car right beside it was not? Why did the tornado destroy this house, while the house next door is untouched? We cannot know the answers to these questions. We live in a huge, complex universe influenced by the laws of physics and the laws of attraction, working on layer upon layer of cause and effect, chaos and order.

Our life experiences are always guiding us in the direction of enlightenment, whether the experiences are blissful or wretched or mundane. If we choose to be open, if we practice being aware, we can grow and change and emerge into living a different way, a different life. There is grace to be found in every experience and every moment. We cannot control what will happen to us in our lives, but we can influence the direction our lives move by paying attention, making thoughtful choices, choosing to live a life of love and compassion, putting ourselves in the path of wisdom and understanding, in the hope we will encounter them there.

* * * * *

Dear Anna,

Raven always told me to trust my direct experiences. But it was unbelievably hard to do that when the experiences I was being told to trust were of pain and terror. Looking back, though, I guess I was able to follow her advice to some extent, because I always came back to knowing I was going through a transformation. And I always knew, deep inside, if I could trust in my direct experiences, ultimately it would help me on my spiritual path.

However, between these moments of clarity were times when I found myself lost in despair, sucked down into the always-present abyss of overwhelming confusion. One thing that made this whole experience so difficult was that my attacks seemed to come from every direction. I never in my life felt so vulnerable. It was a constant process of uncovering the next culprit. Sometimes I felt like the whole world was conspiring to kill me.

When I started having attacks every time I walked into the kitchen, we discovered a tiny propane gas leak. All the florescent lights in the house had to be turned off because they made my brain feel odd. The smell of onions and garlic sent me reeling. Gasoline fumes, cleaning agents, computers, fragrances, hair spray, and as you will soon learn, tiny little bloodsuckers! An unexpected sound or light could throw me into free-fall, tumbling down into uncontrolled fear. I would cry for hours. I was angry, and I was wounded. Everything was a potential enemy.

In my bedroom, which felt like my only sanctuary, I had to keep the door closed with a rolled-up towel along the door jamb to keep out any possible contaminants that could throw me into another attack. Even that place of relative safety would soon turn against me.

During the monsoons that year, Mother Nature outdid herself with the most spectacular thunderstorms we had ever seen. The lightning shot through my nervous system, making me sizzle. I would hide in bed with the blankets pulled over my head, even though I knew it wouldn't help.

The attacks were all similar in some ways, yet each had its own twist depending on what stimulant set me off. Sometimes I would go limp with no control over my arms and legs. Other times I would become stiff and rigid, unable to bend my limbs. My heart would pound. My breath would become rapid or labored. Sometimes I could hardly breathe — that was truly frightening! I would have coughing fits, panic attacks, periods of debilitating confusion. Always there was the question, what caused it this time?

One day, in the middle of a treatment with Dr. Dan, I felt my life force shut off like a light switch. The next thing I knew I was flying off the table with my arms and legs flailing. Dr. Dan and Jahi caught me in midair! My spirit had tried to leave but then slammed back into my body with such force it propelled me off the treatment table.

As you can imagine, things were pretty tense at home, all of us on pins and needles waiting for the next attack. When I wasn't being rushed to town in a crisis, I *hid under my covers and prayed. And I questioned everything. Why was this happening? Why me? What was this all about?*

As dreadful as my life had become, sometimes I was blessed with an awareness that a presence was holding me like a womb — I was safe; I was being transformed. My mantra was, "Getting better, getting worse, getting better, getting worse." I did get better sometimes, but overall I continued to decline.
Love,
Sophia

* * * * *

June 17, 1996

I am not really getting better, so this morning I called Rinsho. After I told him what has been happening to me and what I have been doing to help myself, he guided me through a new meditation practice. He is a genius with techniques and loves to work with people who are in crisis. This meditation practice is merging the inner and outer worlds through the senses. He directed me to first bring my attention to the outer sounds, then to the inner talk and then to watch the rhythm that takes place between them. Then we went on to the physical senses of inner and outer stimulus; then we explored the outer seeing and inner visions. I love this meditation. It leaves me feeling empowered and peaceful.

June 18, 1996

Raven and Jahi are amazing, so kind and supportive, day after day doing everything they can to help me. Even so, today has been a really hard day. My emotions are getting the best of me now. Lately it feels like my attacks are more intense and they last longer. I'm worn out. I have tried everything, and I am still suffering. I feel like my whole life is a cry for help. Please, someone, dear God, anyone, HELP ME!

June 21, 1996

Today Dr. Dan discovered an old hairline fracture on the left side of my skull. When he was adjusting my head I had a flashback: I was a little girl running to my grandmother for comfort. She held me and rocked me. When I got home I called my mom to find out if she remembered me hitting my head when I was young. She had no recollection.

June 22, 1996

Last night I had two dreams:

My head was being adjusted and a red demon jumped out and then turned into a scared little girl. It was me. I was looking for someone to comfort me, and I found my grandmother.

This was the second dream:

> *I saw a mark on my leg. It was like a large blackhead. I squeezed it and a lot of fluid squirted out. Then a colored tube like a worm without a head or tail came out. It was big enough to put on like a stocking that covered my calf. It was bright, vivid colors, striped like a rainbow. A little later, when I went to show my sister, more fluid came out and then the head of the worm-like thing. This time, it came alive and someone kicked it. I said, "Don't! It's alive!" Then a girl took it as a pet.*

* * * * *

Dear Anna,

> *It was weeks later when I saw a picture of the goddess Tara wearing rainbow socks on her legs. Then this dream made more sense to me. The inner me is the essence of Tara — pure love and compassion, embodying all human attributes and using them for the good of all beings.*

> *Shortly after this I had another attack while I was in bed. Jahi was sitting on the bed next to me, and I saw his face turn to light. I was fading away, sinking. But still I was present enough to know this was not a good thing, and I needed to do something to break this pattern. Jahi helped me as I tried to do some*

prostrations. With each attempt I would shake and cry, but by the end of the third one, the attack had stopped.

When I look back I can see there were many turning points and this was one of them. My journey through this illness was not over yet. But I woke up the next day feeling great.

Love,

Sophia

* * * * *

June 25, 1996

Rinpoche has told me to keep doing my practices. He encourages me to see everything as having no inherent or independent reality. Everything is impermanent and in constant change. Life is a continuum, a free flow of creation. No fixation. This is what keeps me from checking out.

There are three things that have become apparent to me. First, to heal or teach others about healing, I have to know what it is to heal. Second, ease is essential in life. And third, self-doubt and judgment are poison. These experiences are bringing out the part of me that doesn't know my Creator yet, the part of me that does not yet see the Divine in every experience.

June 26, 1996

I threw my neck out showing Jahi how I remember shaking my head as a child. I went to see Dr. Dan, and this time he found my atlas has a fracture from a hit to the head on the left side. This is what I saw in the dream with my grandmother.

June 27, 1996

Jahi left this morning to go to the summer teachings with Rinpoche in Chimayo. Of course, I wanted him to go, but when he left, I cried for a long time. I feel alone and abandoned by him. Raven is here, but she spends most of her time in prayer, and she doesn't drive anymore. Frank is here, but he can't help me — he needs me to help him. But Jahi and I had decided that I would be okay without him, so I guess that's a step in the right direction. And the land is here to support me as well. Is the worst over? Do I dare to hope?

June 30, 1996

It is really hard having Jahi gone. I don't feel supported. I tell myself to say good-bye to the way I think things should be — fantasy relationships, living happily ever after, always staying healthy. Growth is not for my ego's purpose to be happy, but to discover my divinity. If I become invisible, spirit shines through.

I called Tom, the man I met at the retreat two years ago. I could still feel the chemistry between us. I'm not sure why I called except I wanted to feel something different than this sense of being abandoned; I did, and it scared me.

July 4, 1996

Mom and Serena came from Albuquerque to stay with me for a week. This lifted my spirits! We had so much fun together, and I was feeling much better. Then, on the fifth day of their visit while they were shopping, I had another attack. Natalie was out of town, but I was at her house, resting on her sofa when it started. I called Dr. Dan's office, and they came and picked me up. I was back at Natalie's before Mom and Serena came back for me. It was wonderful to have them here, but now they've gone back to Albuquerque. I miss them. I'm feeling very alone again.

July 20, 1996

I have been seeing Nick for Craniosacral treatment, and I feel more alive than I have in a while. I have been having more insights into my healing process. Nick encourages me to examine how I have perceived life and is helping me to let go of old, limiting thoughts. The attacks feel different now. I seem to move in and out of them more easily. After one session, I saw a yellow light and a vision of my mother being very small with a twinkle in her eyes. This was a very healing vision.

July 30, 1996

Natalie showed up today and told me to get up because we were going for a hike. I told her I wasn't well enough, I didn't have the strength. She said, "Nonsense. You're going." I did, and it changed the way I looked at my body and my abilities. I am so grateful to Natalie for not accepting my objection.

August 18, 1996

Frank died today. These last few days I have been watching him slowly fade away. It has been an amazing experience, deeply revealing. Being with him has changed how I think about life and death.

One of the most profound things was the knowing that when he died, he would take all of his 99 years of experiences with him. All that unique knowledge — it feels like such a waste. He was fine three days ago. Now he is gone, his spirit vacated, his body lying motionless. I was blessed to be here with him, to witness his journey, just as I told him I would all those years ago.

* * * * *

Anna

Last night I had a vision. That sounds like something which would happen to Sophia, not to me. I'm not sure I even believe in visions! But I don't know what else to call it. I wasn't asleep, so it wasn't a dream. I was curled up on the sofa reading about Sophia's struggles with her illness. It's so much! She was really sick for almost five years, so there are quite a few journal volumes completely taken up with accounts of her weird symptoms and her many trips in to town to get help.

I'm in awe of her. How was she able, confused and suffering as she was, to keep bringing her focus back to interpreting what she was going through as a spiritual transformation?

Since I started reading her journals I've been going through this bizarre experience — I feel what she felt. Perry has given me an assignment. When I start to have these intense feelings, feeling what Sophia felt, I am to go stand at the mirror and look at myself and ask myself "where do I go?" A couple of times now, I have found myself sinking away into darkness, only to come to some time later, sitting on the floor. I don't know where I go, but it's obvious that I do go — I go somewhere.

But it didn't happen that way last night. I started to sink away, but then Sophia was standing in front of me, and she wouldn't let me go. She was kind but absolutely firm. "No. Go back. You must face this and live through it." She literally stood in my way blocking my path. She would not let me sink away even though I was feeling an almost-irresistible urge to allow the darkness to envelop me. I don't know how long this went on. I would start to fade away and Sophia would yell, "Hold on! Hold on, Anna! Hold on as if your life depends on it!" So I didn't sink away into darkness. Instead, after a while I became very still. And then, for a weird, brief moment, I couldn't tell if I was me or Sophia. It was like we were merging. Then she was gone, and I was alone, staring at myself in the mirror.

Oddly, I don't feel freaked out by what happened. I mean, it was weird! I felt kind of calm and peaceful afterward. But while it was going on, it was a raging battle inside of me between what I wanted to do, which was to disappear, and Sophia's insistence that I stay present. She yelled at me every time I started to fade away.

When I went back to the sofa and picked up the journal I had been reading, it was like holding something alive, as if every word inside was packed with energy and spirit. I had the thought again, *these books are sacred*. This is something Sophia might think or say, but now I could see it was true.

I told Perry about this experience today. Of course, he was very encouraging like he always is. He suggested that the next time I stand in front of the mirror, instead of asking myself where I go, I might try asking myself, "Why do I go?"

❃ ❃ ❃ ❃ ❃

August 26, 1996

What caused the attack to happen this time? How can I stop it? I don't know if there is anyone who can help me. We find something that calms the attacks, then very quickly it stops working. Everything is out of control. I feel so hopeless. Mitch or Nick works with me, and I am okay for a while. Then it, this unknown attacker, returns.

It's like I'm in a dark subterranean cavern, and I can't find my way out. I'm living in an unpredictable drama, and the chaos of everything I don't know keeps battering me, trying to push me down. I desperately want someone to help me, or maybe someone with a crystal ball who can reveal the truth of what this is and what I am supposed to do. I need encouragement, someone to remind me that there is light within this dark despair. My feelings of helplessness stimulate fantasies of an ideal place for healing. It's a place where I feel safe and supported. Where people understand what is happening to me and have the skills, intuition, and wisdom to help me.

If you are dying, you can get help from hospice. If you are having a baby, there are Lamaze classes and midwives to guide you. If you have a physical injury, there are physical therapists, and for emotional traumas, there are psychotherapists. But what about the process of — do I dare say it? — spiritual transmutation or spiritual crisis? Where do I get spiritual medicine? There has to be someone out there who understands, someone who has experienced this! Who can help me? I'm so fortunate to have my wonderful spiritual teachers. Even so, I feel there is an element missing. I need help, and I need it now!

Ultimately, I know I should trust more in the process and surrender my concepts of what healing is, what spirituality is, and how much time it should take to heal. Am I worth less because I am sick? Do I have to have the answers? How do I stand in this foundationless place? Over time my sense of myself, who I am and how I am valuable in the world, has come apart like a thousand-piece jigsaw puzzle scattered hopelessly across the floor. Remember, Sophia: trust, surrender, be patient.

August 28, 1996

Today, during a treatment with Nick, he suggested I go on a journey into my heart to find my inner physician, my inner healing wisdom. This is what I saw and experienced:

> *I find a full-bodied woman, rich and free, joyous, playful, and very wise. My feet are connected to the fire of the Earth and my hands are connected to the stars. I float into the sky with my Soul Whisperer below me. She supports and encourages me to see who I really am. I am part of the universe.*

This vision creates a big shift in my perspective.

August 30, 1996

I was referred to a Tai Chi master who I saw today, and after four hours, he said I have a chi disease. My energy went up my spine and got lodged at my brain stem and is causing the neurological problems. He gave me some exercises. I hope they work.

September 2, 1996

Alysia, Nick's partner, taught a gourd-art workshop last weekend, and she invited me to come. I really wanted to go, especially since I knew there would be a fabulous group of women gathered at her house. But I didn't feel like I had the strength to participate. Alysia suggested that I come anyway, just to be with the women. I decided I could do that, and I am so glad I did!

I received so much energy from the group and activities that I actually made my first gourd art. She is a magnificent piece! Her hands are connected to the stars and her feet are firmly embedded in the fire of the Earth. Just like my inner journey.

September 10, 1996

I am using the techniques given to me by the Tai Chi master. It's really hard to bring my energy down my body when I am having an attack. Sometimes I need Jahi to hold me while I do them. They do seem to help.

September 13, 1996

I found a book about kundalini, and when I read it I was astounded. The book describes everything I have been experiencing with this mysterious illness — from the moment I felt the heat go up my spine and I felt my spine was melting, to these states of confusion and physical discord and attacks. Kundalini is the energy held at the base of the spine which, when it is released, can bring us to a state of divine bliss. If you are not prepared for that much energy, it can short-circuit your body. This is what has happened to me. I have an answer that finally feels congruent.

October 22, 1996

I am on retreat in the forest where Tubten Rinpoche lives. I have embarked on this retreat to discover deeper wisdom and healing and to fill myself with the pure white nectar of union with the Buddha Nature. My heart is filled with gratitude for this opportunity.

This morning Tubten said, "Today is an auspicious day! The stars are right, and Tara needs her prayer flags put up." So Riva and Jampa and I collected tree branches. We anchored four of them in the ground and tied prayer flags to the tops while Tubten Rinpoche did the Tara practice.

July 9, 1997

What has been happening is so creepy I don't want to even think about it, much less write about it. But here goes: Something has been biting me in the night. The bites send me into anaphylactic shock.

So now falling asleep in my own bed, the one place I have felt relatively safe, is a traumatic experience. What am I supposed to do? Is the whole unseen world my enemy?

July 15, 1997

I called the poison control center at the university and asked them what kind of insect could do this. They told me I was probably being bitten by the nymph of a common insect on our land, the *reduviidae triatoma protracta*, also known as the conenose bloodsucker or the kissing bug. This makes me feel creepy just thinking about it. They are commonly found in mouse and pack rat nests. Now they are in my bed?

I found a small flea-sized insect on my bedspread and put it in a jar, and this afternoon we took it to have it examined. Sure enough, this is the bug they told me about. So Jahi and I looked under the mattress and there they were, five little ones.

July 28, 1997

Every night now before we go to bed, we tear the bed apart to ensure there are no creepy little bugs. The next step is to get rid of the mice that are living in the heating ducts. We have found a company to do the work. They are going to clean out all the heating ducts and seal all the crevices in the system. We tested the chemical compound that will be used to seal up the ducts to be sure I could tolerate it. It seems fine, so we are proceeding.

August 20, 1997

I left the house the day they did the work, but when I returned I couldn't be near the house. The fumes were so bad I got sick immediately, so I went and stayed with Natalie for a few days. When I returned, the fumes were still bad, so I have been sleeping in the temple, which is connected to the house by a deck and did not have any heating-duct work done on it. I have been living here for a couple of weeks, but I am getting worse. Every time I walk outside, the fumes get me. When I need to take a shower I make sure all the windows are open and run into the house and shower as quickly as I can. Things are not looking good.

October 30, 1997

This last year has been a trying time for all of us. Raven has been ill, Frank died, and Jahi is completely stressed out from my trauma. And I have been in and out of crisis, close to death many times.

Now I am thinking I may need to move away from my home, my spiritual community and Jahi in order to heal myself. The irony is that the repair on the heating system was made to keep me safe from the insects and to help me heal. Now it's the main reason I need to move away.

This morning I talked to Raven and asked her if she saw anything negative about me moving away. She did not. I spoke with Nick, and he sees this as a positive move for me energetically and emotionally as well. I am trying to look at this change as an opportunity to write my book about my illness and my healing process. And I have another hope — that Jahi will stay with me some of the time and we will have some badly needed time alone together. I am longing for an intimacy that has been lacking for several years. Now my challenge is to find a place where I will be safe.

* * * * *

Dear Anna,

The first time my inner wisdom, the Soul Whisperer, came to me she spoke to me of the ways of the elders and the power of being connected to our true nature. She encouraged me to help others awaken to their divine heritage, and she spoke to me about the wisdom fire and its healing power.

Fire as a method of purification is understood in religious and cultural contexts all around the world and throughout human history. There is a Tibetan Buddhist Tantric practice where the fire of wisdom blazes and your entire being is engulfed in flames. It signifies the burning of concepts of afflictive emotions. In the native Huichol tradition, fire, or Tai, is regarded as the most valuable gift of the gods. It burns away the dross. It purifies. It consumes. It transforms.

Do you remember reading about how I found the stone amulet — or maybe it is more accurate to say, how it found me? I had placed it on the Native American altar in our temple where it had been for many years. A few days before my 54th birthday, I was sitting alone and disillusioned in the dimly-lit temple where for several weeks I had been sleeping on the couch and cooking my meals in a wok.

I had been contemplating the move I was about to make, thinking about what I should take with me when I go. I found myself gazing at the Native American altar, drawn to the stone amulet hanging above it. The amulet was calling to me. I heard words, clear and distinct, but without sound. It was saying, "Take me with you."

"No," I said, "you belong here on this altar." But it would not stop calling to me. I went to the altar and knelt before it. I held the amulet in my hand. With sadness I told it, "You are part of The Center for Divine Union and this altar." Then out of the silence I heard, as clearly as if someone was in the temple with me, "I am yours. I belong with you."

In a flash I was back in the moment when I found this amazing, sacred object. I was crying, my tears falling on the stone. And I knew the truth of what it was telling me. This magical amulet was mine; it belonged to me lifetimes ago and had come back to me. It would not let me leave it behind.

That night my Soul Whisperer came to me for the second time. I was in a dream-like state, yet it was as real as any waking experience:

I walked down a path I have walked many times before. The sun was high in the sky. I stopped in the shade of a piñon pine and waited for something, though I wasn't sure what I was waiting for. I waited all day. Time passed quickly; the sun set, the stars appeared. I leaned against a granite boulder and watched the stars.

A tiny sound penetrated the night silence. I turned and saw a woman. She beckoned me to follow. She led me into a cave where I saw many women circling a glowing fire. Each woman held a ritual object: rattles, drums, sage, feathers, bowls of cornmeal, sacred pipes. The flickering flames made shadows dance on the walls. The cave smelled of damp earth and frankincense, sweetgrass and sage.

Out of the darkness, three women came toward me. One appeared to be a priestess or elder. She was holding a large amulet and motioned for me to enter the circle. Her essence was so powerful that her mere presence was an initiation. I was the link in this circle of fire dancers. I took my place in a lineage of women who carry the wisdom of initiation by fire.
My Soul Whisperer is the link, the lineage holder,

the guardian of the fire of time that burns away the obstacles that no longer serve us. The fire of time consumes everything that keeps the spirit from soaring. Its constant, relentless burning keeps everything in a state of transformation. Life itself is a cauldron for purification and transformation. It burns and glows with the light of wisdom.

Fire may burn me, but ultimately it is my ally.

Love,

Sophia

* * * * *

November 1, 1997

Bridget, my friend and Reiki initiate, came to visit me today. When she saw the condition I was in, she asked me, "Why don't you just let yourself die and stop this suffering? Why are you still here?" The question surprised me. But I knew right away what my answer was. I told her, "I'm here to do something more with my life. That's why I choose to live!"

November 4, 1997

The potency of my life has been flickering, and the veil between the worlds thins. I now walk this journey with my inner wisdom healer, my Soul Whisperer. My heart is full and spilling over with the abundance of light, love, and compassion so generously given. I feel the surging of an unbound force, which informs and animates my soul. At the same time I feel the weariness of this form that has been battered with illness, reorganizing and re-sculpting itself for so very long.

I know very soon my time of great change will come, leaving behind these tired, old patterns that have obscured my vision. My bones throb with this knowing. I feel compelled to share the journey of the healing fire that initiates and consumes me as it purifies my being. I pray for the strength to finish my journey and share the blessings.

November 9, 1997

Finally, something good has happened. A few days ago I was sitting in The Sacred Space bookstore with my friend Jane. She is a medical intuitive of Native American heritage — a great mother goddess, full and robust in her body and spirit, gentle and loving in her heart. While I was there receiving a session from her I looked out the window and saw a man walking toward a small house that I knew had been for rent six months ago.

I was moved to call the landlord, and I found out the little house is coming up for rent in a week. I asked if I could see it. It's perfect. I rented it. The landlord said he was going to have the house cleaned, but I asked him not to do so because I was concerned about toxic cleaning products. This is the perfect place for me to heal. It is nestled up against the red rocks where I started this journey in Utah, and it is right next to The Sacred Space bookstore where Jane does her healing work. I signed a six-month lease.

November 14, 1997

Now I have my own sanctuary, a safe place to heal in nature and work on my book. All of this has happened so fast. I have moved out of my home, away from the Center, Raven, and Jahi. Just two weeks ago I came close to death with another attack, and now here I am, living alone for the first time in my life.

November 28, 1997

And now, again, everything will change. I am a jumble of feelings. Jahi and I were sitting on the floor in my new living room, talking about our ongoing issues — the lack of passion in our marriage and the repeated attempts to resolve our problems. Again the force of something deep and unseen is shaping my life. The words I spoke came from a sacred place deep inside me. They entered the room like a rose petal floating into my heart. The words came through me like a soft whisper. Jahi and I were cradled in the energy of the transcendent as the words spoke through me, and I heard myself say, "It's time we set each other free." I was struck with the profundity and peril of this statement, and when he responded, "Yes, it is," we fell into each other's arms and cried.

Some thing, some truth, some force of wisdom came through me and spoke. This was not a predetermined conversation or decision. This was the only fruit that could have grown from our years of attempting to make our relationship work, our struggles to make it conform to our ideals. The same love and respect that has held us together all these years now gave us the strength and courage to do the unthinkable.

Our lives are so profoundly intertwined. We know we were lovers as Native Americans in the Escalante River canyon of Utah. We have been soul mates, and our bond has deepened through devotion to The Center for Divine Union and to Raven.

But all of that doesn't matter because my soul's journey must take this step to move on, to expand. This was another moment that I could not have chosen — would not have chosen. It's bigger than my limited sense of my life. It's time to step out of the old, familiar relationship with Jahi and step into the unknown.

❋ ❋ ❋ ❋ ❋

Dear Anna,

I realize nothing in my journals up to this point would suggest my marriage was in crisis. I never wrote specifically about the difficulties we had been having for a long time. I held my marital problems in

one compartment, while I lived and wrote about
my spiritual life in another compartment. I held an
image of what I wanted my marriage to be and tried
to give it reality by not writing anything down that
would shatter it. Writing it down would have made
it too real, too unavoidable. Writing it down would
have forced me to face the truth as my small
disappointments grew into a hollow realization
that Jahi was never going to be able to participate
in the kind of intimacy I craved.
Love,
Sophia

* * * * *

November 29, 1997

How did this happen? Why did this happen? The words and feelings keep filling my body and mind. I am so scared. How could I have gone from being so close to death, in total need of Jahi's care and then this — I am alone, really alone. I have to remind myself about the years of struggling around our sexual relationship. And, there was the time when I asked for us to live in our own space at the Center so we would have some privacy from Raven, and he said, "If you make me choose, I will choose my spiritual teacher." Those words went into my heart like a knife. That wound couldn't be healed. But it was also the medicine I needed to ultimately make this change. It prepared me for the words to come through when I said, "It's time we set each other free."

The only way to find my sense of purpose and reason now is to live a new story in hopes that I will discover where I am to go and what I am to do.

December 1, 1997

I miss Jahi. I miss his steady, consistent nature. I miss his warm body next to me in bed. I miss his sense of humor. He had a knack for saying something funny just when everything seemed dark and perilous.

I remember one time when I was having an attack and he was driving me in to town to see Dr. Dan. It was a hard ride. I was in acute distress, and I could tell he was really worried about me. When we drove around a bend and the sun suddenly hit my face, it was like being burned, searing into me. I screamed and threw my hands up to cover my eyes. "And now," he said, "you are turning into a vampire." We both cracked up! Priceless.

December 12, 1997

I received my first astrology reading today from Maryann. I didn't know her, and she didn't know anything about me. Jane had suggested Maryann because she was clear and connected to the divine feminine. She is a gentle and fluid being. Jane thought a reading might help me understand more about what has been happening to me.

I waited until Maryann was finished before I confirmed anything she told me. The whole time I was wondering how she could possibly know I had been so seriously ill. She was even able to pinpoint when it started based on the planets. This was only one of many things she would tell me about my life. I am stunned and in awe. I realize there is more to our relationship with the solar system than meets the eye.

December 19, 1997

There is no doubt a new life is unfolding before me. But I have no idea what it will look like or how it will feel. I loved all those years at the Center. I had my marriage, imperfect as it was. For all our problems, we were good friends, and I loved the easy, familiar companionship. And my spiritual work was the center of my life.

Now I have been torn away from the life I built with Jahi and Raven; it was the only life I ever wanted. I am lonely and sad, and I cry all the time. I'm grieving for all I have lost. Did I make a mistake when I decided to move out? Did Jahi and I make a mistake when we made our decision to separate? Why can't we heal together and grow together? Why?

* * * * *

Anna

After I read these journal entries and Sophia's note, I just put it all down and went for a walk. It really is spring now; the bulbs are out in force. Cheerful yellow daffodils and little purple crocuses decorate all the yards on my street.

I have never been married — never even tempted. But I can feel what it is to live with loss. I can feel how deeply loss cuts. I feel sad, Sophia's sadness, a kind of sweet melancholy. And I am also aware that tiptoeing around the edges is an excitement, a recognition of infinite potential. Sophia knew she was being given the gift of independence. For the first time in her life she was going to be truly autonomous. Here's what's interesting: I have been that way for as long as I can remember.

* * * * *

Dear Anna,

Living alone for the first time in my life was a shock. I found myself talking on the phone when I ate because I always ate with people. I was scared about what would happen if I choked and no one was there.

But I loved organizing my new home, decorating things the way I wanted. I settled into my own routines, going to sleep when I wanted, eating when I was hungry. I had no one to please but myself. I could dance around the house naked, sing very loud, and wail in misery without being seen or heard by anyone but me.

I loved it and hated it. I had loved being in a relationship, and I loved being alone, discovering who I was and how I liked to structure my life. I missed the daily hugs and discussions. I enjoyed the quiet. And when I settled in, I found my own rhythms, and I loved them.
Love,
Sophia

✳ ✳ ✳ ✳

December 20, 1997

I'm sitting at my window, like I do every morning, writing and watching the sun sparkle through the crystals in the window at The Sacred Space bookstore. I've been watching this light dance every morning for the last couple of weeks.

Just now though, while watching the shimmering light, I remembered a note Raven wrote to me last Christmas. I remember exactly what it said:

> *There is one who will sit at the window gazing at the light reflections of the crystal. She will see the many facets of life and listen to Great Spirit in the silence as she touches life anew.*

Suddenly I'm crying. I see how I have been looking at this the wrong way. I have been consumed with loss. But maybe this isn't about what I have lost. Maybe this is about what is to come next. Maybe I am here alone so I can heal and "touch life anew."

Ah, Raven. Once again, I am amazed by you.

* * * * *

Grandmother Spirit

There is work we must do alone. And there is work we cannot do alone because some lessons only come into play when we are relating to another. We humans — most of us anyway — have a desire to pair up, to witness another's life, and to have another bear witness to ours. This is fertile ground for the seeds of our imperfections and our wounds. They take root in our love relationships and they will grow — sometimes wildly out of control.

Most of us want our primary relationships to provide the complete experience of intimate connection with another. We want to feel loved and give love; we want full expression of our passion and sexuality; we want to know someone will always be there for us and understand our needs; we want to be the special one who will give the other all they need; we want to laugh and cry and play and sing together. We want to feel the depths of our spiritual awakenings and the intimacy of life unfolding as we discover more of who we are as human beings. We want to see and be seen with eyes that pierce through shadows and see beyond the illusions we live. We want to celebrate our divine natures. We want to support another to be the most divine expression of who they are, and we want the same. Doesn't it seem, Sisters, that we are asking a lot?

Usually relationships begin in a state of bliss. We are overwhelmed with optimism and energy. Over time, as we settle into life, our shiny ideals are often tarnished by our wounds and unmet desires. But my love was supposed to be a superhero! He or she is the god-like being who would always make everything right again!

And right there, right then, when confronted with the emptiness of that illusion, that is the moment when the alchemy can happen. That is the playground of our evolution. That is a moment when we can choose to expand into our divine nature where we learn compassion, generosity, patience. Our practice is to recognize those moments and be in them with no judgment, no preconceived ideas, only acceptance and love.

Relationships end, like everything else in this impermanent creation. And they end for a million reasons. Every day there are women around the world who find the courage to walk away from situations that are abusive or harmful to their hearts and minds. Relationships end by one trusted lover leaving or betraying the other. Relationships end when one partner dies. And sometimes a relationship ends, as Sophia's did, because it was time to go and do some of that other work, the work we can only do alone.

There is a sacred hoop, a medicine wheel that holds us in all directions as we navigate through life. The powers of this circle are love, forgiveness, unity of all elements, plant medicines, animal spirits, Mother Earth, and Father Sky. They do not worry about whether you have made wise choices or poor ones. They are far too rooted in the ever-changing present moment for that. Working together, they weave a blanket just for you. It will protect you and keep you warm as you walk your path wherever it may lead.

Chapter Eight

A mind that is stretched by new experiences
can never go back to its old dimensions.

~ Oliver Wendell Holmes

Grandmother Spirit

Learning to cultivate the heart is like learning to play
the piano; it requires patience, repetition. The good
news is when you learn a difficult passage, you have it!
It's yours to play whenever you wish. When you *get*
something, when you really understand it, it leaves its
imprint on you. It will always be there inside you, even
at times when other forces might obscure it. These
experiences, these lessons learned, weave the fabric of
who we are.

Our lives are steeped in mystery. What is unknown
is continually revealing itself, making itself known, yet
the well of mystery never runs dry.

Life itself is our greatest teacher, seeping into our
daily experiences the lessons we need most to learn. If
we can let go of how we think things are supposed to

be, if we can just be with what is, if we can rise above attachment and aversion, then we can learn. Then we can take into our hearts the wholeness of love that permeates the universe. This practice is the hardest of all. It's a dance between our two natures, our perfect divinity and our imperfect humanity.

So we take the time to meditate, to slow down, to sit quietly with a tree. We allow nature to come into us. We go on retreats and vision quests; we receive healing work; we spend time with people whose hearts and souls resonate with ours; we sing and dance. We do these things because they open us up and prepare us to receive the grace of understanding.

* * * * *

Dear Anna,

For the next couple of years I was absorbed in learning. It was one of the most amazing times of my life in terms of my growth and education. I was consumed by a drive to learn more, experience more, understand more. I went through rites of passage, initiations, Jungian analysis, vision quests, retreats, and classes. I studied Biodynamic Craniosacral Therapy (BioCranio), dream work, Birth Process workshops. I went to meditation retreats and empowerments. It was a wild ride!

I thought about calling Tom again, but decided this was my time to truly heal and find my own sense of self before entering into another relationship.
Love,
Sophia

* * * * *

January 21, 1998

Nick suggested I take a Craniosacral class on the treatment of shock and trauma. I told him I wasn't well enough, but he was adamant that I could do it. So I decided to take a chance on it, and I am so glad I did!

This class has given me direction. Chad, the instructor, talked about the brain — how shock and trauma affect us and how the resulting pattern distortions repeat themselves in our bodies and minds. I just sat there and cried. He was teaching about things I have experienced over and over again in my life, especially during my illness. The aggravating mystery, the question of why these things had been happening to me, was given a clear scientific explanation. This work helps me feel supported and understood. No one judges me for how I acted or reacted or for the decisions I made or did not make over the course of my illness. I found answers to lots of questions. I'm hooked! I want to take the four-year training.

The BioCranio work is centered in the concept of the

Breath of Life, a rhythm that permeates and transforms us. I have been given a new breath of life. I really want to learn more!

March 26, 1998

I am at a workshop with Chad and Perry, a Jungian analyst, exploring where the Breath of Life and the unconscious meet. Perry has thick, white hair and dark-rimmed glasses. He is lean, but strong. I find him intriguing. He seems to know something the rest of us haven't figured out yet. But his confidence is balanced by his gentleness.

I have never experienced Jungian dream analysis before. But all my life I have had vivid dreams, and I have been writing them down in my journal since I was 16. Now I'm learning how a dream can reveal the deep, unconscious workings of our minds and the essence of our nature and our personalities. Dreams lay bare the underlying patterns of our thoughts and feelings. I love how dreams make the unconscious conscious!

Carl Jung is recognized as one of the most influential psychiatrists of all time. He put forth the concept of a "collective unconscious," a universal cultural repository of archetypes and human experiences. Dream analysis is the interpretation of the symbols that show up in dreams, symbols that have their origin in the collective unconscious.

This is deep, life-changing — and I'm hooked again! I

can not be separated from these teachings. This work penetrates my soul and my psyche. It has awakened my passion for life...again!

How is it I have been blessed to be studying with two extraordinary teachers working on the leading edge of healing and awakening consciousness?

* * * * *

Dear Anna,

I was on a journey unlike anything I could have dreamed up. Everything I had done and experienced laid a strong foundation for the body of work I was now discovering.

When Frank died, he left me a small inheritance. I decided I would only spend it on my education and my spiritual development. I am so grateful to him. Because of his gift, I was able to attend all the retreats and take all the classes I wanted. What a blessing!

All the pieces of my life — my experiences and all the training in healing techniques and in spiritual development — everything came together. For the first time, I felt like my life was coherent. My inside was connected to my outside.

I reconnected to nature; I developed my mindfulness practice; I prayed; I meditated; I used ritual to build my strength; I evolved; I was held in the

embrace of discovery. The Mystery was showering her
wisdom down on me.
Love,
Sophia

* * * * *

July 14, 1998

For the next three years, every three months we will meet for a week for our BioCranio training. It's a concentrated time to learn, grow, and experience this profound work together. Between sessions we have study and practice to integrate what we are learning and to prepare for what will be presented in the next session. I just arrived home from our first class. I am astounded at the power of this healing work.

One woman in the class was shocked when she heard my story. She even asked Chad how he could have someone in the program who was dying. She saw me as a woman who would soon be dead! But I *know* how much stronger and healthier I am.

September 30, 1998

I'm at my second BioCranio training, and I am being transformed again. I am deeply committed to this work. I'm finding that I can connect to myself in the most intimate and profound ways. I am experiencing myself as an egg and a sperm, still not joined together, then as an embryo in the womb. I am getting in touch with the dynamics of my own birth. I am absorbing insights far beyond knowledge. I am a natural at this work. It's magical and magnificent. And I'm cultivating wonderful, new friendships in the process and discovering more intimacy with myself. Divine nature is dancing with me!

November 28, 1998

It has taken Jahi and me a full year to be absolutely certain about getting a divorce. We talked it through over and over again; each of us checking in on how the other feels. With all the love and respect we have for each other, it seems like a rash thing to do — to take the steps to formally end our marriage. But there is no denying we are finished with that part of our lives. So now we have taken the final steps, and I am a single woman. I'm ready to find out who I really am.

January 7, 1999

I've been in New Mexico for the last three weeks. What a whirlwind! A wedding, a funeral, and a ten-day Vipassana retreat in Chimayo. I am grateful I had the retreat to integrate after the intense concentration of family. Now I'm back home, and I find myself in a state of flux, back and forth between humility and empowerment.

* * * * *

Dear Anna,

Every retreat I attend changes me and alters my life. The lesson from this particular retreat was the understanding that desire is driven by an incomplete experience.

A meditation tool for the pain that comes from unfulfilled desires is to be in dispassionate observation, cultivating compassion and equanimity, emptying out the clinging to the desire. I would be using this tool a lot in the months to come as I came face to face with my insecurities and my own shadow.

At the Yaza (all-night meditation), we had a traditional Japanese Tea Ceremony at midnight. So simple, so elegant; all parts equal and valid.
Love,
Sophia

* * * * *

March 23, 1999

Every BioCranio training leaves me in awe, transformed and deeply rooted in this work. It's a rite of passage into the deeper work I will be doing in the world. I am discovering my true nature and how to connect to it in others. I am stretched and expanded, breaking through all the boundaries and diving deep into the unknown. I count my blessings every day for the teachings, experiences, and friends that have come from this journey.

July 8, 1999

I have been working with Perry for one amazing year! I arrived home late last night from the Sacred Fire and Dream retreat at his place in Moab, Utah. This was my third retreat at Perry's, each time going deeper, deeper, deeper into the true nature of my being. We do dream work and shamanic journeys; we tend the fire in the tepee and we pray. We participate in a sweat lodge at the end of each retreat.

At this retreat I had a profound dream:

I saw a shaft of light coming down from the heavens onto the pasture outside the room where we do our dream work every morning. The light called to me to approach. I could feel the shaft of light, rooted in the Earth and touching the heavens.

Perry referred to it as the *axis mundi*. For the first time I understand what that means! It's the very center of the world on all levels of existence, where Heaven and Earth meet, where the underworld and spiritual realms meet. It holds all the levels and manifestations of existence together from the lowest to the highest, with human existence at the center. This is what is called the midline in BioCranio language. Even now, days after I had the dream, I feel blessed and cradled by this magnificent energy.

August 12, 1999

Perry has invited me to attend a late-summer vision quest that he facilitates in northeastern Ontario, Canada. Is this pushing myself too far? After being sick for so long, how far do I really want to step out of my comfort zone?

But I know I need to — no, I *want* to, even though I have some fears working on me. I'm concerned about the food, the sleeping arrangements, being cold, whether I will have enough strength to go through with it.

And, I'm afraid of bears! I'm familiar with rattlesnake and scorpion, mountain lion and skunk, but I don't have a relationship with bear. What if I encounter one and it attacks me? I can think of lots of things to be afraid of. Every threat I can imagine is clamoring for my attention, and I can imagine some doozies.

According to Perry, the work of the vision quest begins at the moment when you decide you will go. Also, he says that the more arduous it is to get there, the more impactful it is because you are putting a lot of energy and effort into showing up for yourself.

To get there I will ride in a car, an airport bus, a commercial plane, a small plane, a cross-country bus, and a water plane — all to put my feet on an island in the middle of a lake in the middle of nowhere in the vast boreal forests of Canada. Really? Am I really going to do this?

August 28, 1999

I'm on the island. The water plane landed in Lake Temagami and let us off on a little dock. The island is small and truly beautiful. *Temagami* means "deep water" in Ojibway. The lake and land around me are the traditional territory of the Algonquin First Nations.

I am surrounded by old-growth pines and ancient boulders deposited here by melting glaciers in some far distant past.

There is no electricity except in the kitchen. The facilities consist of sleeping cabins and a lodge; we will sleep on bunk beds. These initial days are designed to prepare each of us for a solo vision quest.

Robert Johnson is here to facilitate one of the dream groups and to lead the men's time. Louise Carus Mahdi will facilitate another dream group and the women's time. They are both renowned Jungian analysts who personally knew Carl Jung.

This is extraordinary! How has it come to pass that I am here on this remote island with such amazing people tending to my vision quest, tending my soul?

August 29, 1999

We are being prepared. We have ceremonies and sweat lodges, group-process interactions, dream work — all to help us see ourselves more clearly. Well, the one we did today helped me see myself more clearly, that's for sure, and I was not very happy with what I saw.

We partnered up for the ropes course, and we were told to always consider our partner's safety, to make their safety a priority. We were told to keep in mind at all times where they are and how they are doing.

About two thirds of the way through the ropes course, we were 100 feet above the forest floor, my partner and I standing on wood planks that angled away from each other and continued to get farther and farther apart as we leaned into each other and worked our way along. I was so afraid I was shaking. Even though I was tethered, I was terrified. As soon as my partner and I reached the end of the planks, I scrambled to the platform where I felt secure. I left my partner behind.

Perry yelled at me to pay attention. But he was a thousand light years away. My fear consumed me. Survival was in charge of my body, and it acted to save itself.

I was embarrassed, humbled. With all the work I have done, shouldn't I be better at staying focused, at resisting the pull of primal emotions?

August 30, 1999

I entered the sweat lodge on my hands and knees, humbled and ready to be engulfed by the dark, moist, fertile womb of Great Mother Earth. I melted into the fire, and when I emerged I was wide open, deeply connected to the spirit world.

Someone put a life jacket on me and led me down to the lake. I floated in the dark waters, the light of the stars above. Time and space became a wave.

Sometime later we gathered around the fire to warm up. Then Robert Johnson, this scholarly, introverted, world-renowned analyst in his mid-eighties, went around the circle wiping each person's feet. This humble gesture was his way of blessing us and honoring us for our sacrifice and our prayers. I will never forget the moment he came to me and bent to wipe my feet. For as long as I live, I will hold that memory in my mind's eye and in my heart.

An Ojibwe elder met with us to tell us stories of this land and of the mountain where she did her vision quests. She said we had the tribe's blessing for our vision quest.

Tomorrow it begins. The dream analysis, ropes course, and social interplay are finished. I'm ready for the mystery to show me the way home to my real name, to my real self.

September 2, 1999

A traditional vision quest is without food or water and lasts for at least three days. I sat for two days. And because I am still healing, I took some nourishment for support. I took with me a small jar of water and some rice, a flashlight, some rain gear, and a warm coat.

After a short sweat lodge where we offered up our prayers, I got dressed quickly and found my canoe. I rowed where spirit guided me until I found a place that felt right.

I gathered stones to create my sacred closed circle. It will hold my energy and prayers. I am not to leave the circle except to relieve myself.

As night came and it began to rain I bundled up, sitting against a tree with my head on my knees. Later I lay down. At some point I heard the sound of footsteps in the darkness. Something very big and heavy was coming toward me. I froze and held my breath. Was it a bear? I didn't know, but my heart was beating fast and I was afraid. I waited, calculating distance, deciding what I would do if it came into the circle. I could hear it breathing. I decided if it took one more step closer I would get up and run. There was silence, and then it turned away. Gradually my heart slowed down. It was probably a moose.

I am back now in my warm house with all the conveniences and comforts of home. But it all looks different after my vision quest. It will take time to see how this experience has changed me. But this much I know: I did it! I am empowered; my dream world is rich and profoundly revealing.

October 1, 1999

I have lived through two divorces. I nearly died from an unknown disease. I have dedicated my life to understanding myself and my inner motivations. I have undertaken to find answers to the questions life has laid before me. Why do I do what I do? Why do I think the way I think? Why do emotions sometimes overwhelm me and take over my entire being, making me do, say, and think things that are not me — at least they are not the me I am striving to be. And when I am overwhelmed and lose focus, how do I regain my balance and find my way back to compassion and wisdom?

November 8, 1999

Perry just invited me to a week-long adventure on a schooner in New Zealand! We will be sailing and doing dream work. The magic is calling me! No question; I'm going!

He is also a presenter at a Jungian shamanic conference in Australia, just before he goes to New Zealand. Of course, I'm going to the shamanic conference as well!

February 9, 2000

After 20 hours of traveling, I am here in the land down under! Some of Perry's friends picked me up at the Melbourne airport and brought me to a small hotel near the ocean. I feel alive! And full of the energy of adventure!

* * * * *

Dear Anna,

Robert Johnson was also one of the presenters at the conference. I was taken to where he was staying, and we all went for lunch and then a swim.

Only many years later did I realize just how extraordinary this was — that I got to spend time with this amazing man who walked with Carl Jung in his garden. And to have had him wipe my feet? That is humbling.

Love,

Sophia

* * * * *

Grandmother Spirit

There are some magical moments in this grand mystery! There are seven billion of us, and each one is born unique. We come into family situations that will never be duplicated. We are born into a culture and a sense of place that others may share, but no two of us will experience them in the same way. We may live through an event together, but we will each interpret it in our unique way.

Each one of us is a unique reflection of God and Goddess, but we are more than that — we *are* God-Goddess. We are God-Goddess speaking, spinning, struggling, and filled with desire. We are God-Goddess needing to be heard and witnessed. This is the essence of living wisdom.

* * * * *

February 12, 2000

Recently, I had two dreams. In the first dream I chose Robert Johnson over the illusion of magic. I see this as an indication I choose my inner work over magic.

In another dream Robert was a threat, someone who would sexually molest young children. When the child was asked if he penetrated her, she said no, she had fought him off. I realize I am not yet ready to have this inner work fully penetrate and impregnate me.

* * * * *

Dear Anna,

On my trip to Australia, I met Beth, a new friend, but a timeless sister of my heart. She took me to the William Ricketts Sanctuary near Melbourne.

William Rickets was determined to preserve the integrity and wild nature of the aboriginal people. He created sculptures of aboriginal people and displayed them in nature. His work was designed to look as if the people are not just in nature but are nature, part and

parcel. I was deeply touched. I felt I could live their lives through his work. William Rickets said, "All things are wild life. It is our wild nature that is the creative source."
Love,
Sophia

* * * * *

February 16, 2000

Tomorrow I leave Australia and travel to New Zealand. I had just enough time to do a women's retreat with Paula M. Reeves, a Jungian Analyst who works with body movement and language to access our deep shadows, our deep wounds.

The retreat was about reclaiming the parts of ourselves we never fully embodied so we can move forward in life. We worked with the concept of the Virgin, the one who is unto herself whole and complete — all of her energies held within, no part of her lost or given away to others. She calls back our scattered essence.

It was amazing. I had a beautiful experience of being held tenderly by a woman and rocked gently in the warmth of the Great Mother.

February 17, 2000

By several quirks of fate, I was the only participant sailing with Perry and the crew on this journey into the dream world at sea. I was rocked by the great Grandmother Ocean; it was beautiful, exciting, fun, adventurous, challenging.

Every day we made offerings to Grandmother, worked on dreams, and explored. On the last morning, I found myself transparent and naked, not able to hide from myself. In my dream I was challenged to write my own name with my blood from a finger prick. What am I avoiding? I'm beginning to recognize my delusions. What a journey!

Now I am back home, back into my daily life, doing my cranial work, working at and managing Mitch's chiropractic office.

May 4, 2000

After sharing some of my experiences in Australia and New Zealand, Mitch said something really interesting. He said when you only deal with the mind and body you experience duality; when you add spirit, you get divinity!

May 5, 2000

The moment I saw her walking the grounds at the Tubten center yesterday, I knew it was Venerable Dhyani, holder of an ancestral lineage in the Cherokee tradition. She is also a well-respected teacher of Vajrayana Buddhism. And last night she came to me in a dream:

There was an initiation where we danced together like Vajrayogini, with a Native American prayer shawl over me. Then we entered a void — blackness, emptiness — where there was nothing but stillness. When we returned to the ceremonial ground, we were different.

When I met Dyhani and told her of my dream, she said, "Once you have experienced the emptiness you can never turn back again."

I showed her my amulet and told her how I found it on the property of our spiritual center. She said it was the making of the stars. She also said she knew I had put it there in a previous life so I would find it again in this lifetime. Raven also said my amulet was from the stars.

I listened to Dhyani's teachings until a voice inside said, "You have everything you need." At the break I left, knowing I needed nothing more from her.

* * * * *

Dear Anna,

I had a vision of two bodies. One was perfect in shape, appearance, strength, and abilities, full of joy, compassion, happiness, and intelligence. The other body was perfect in knowing fear, jealousy, anger, revenge, self-denigration.

When I put them together I have the perfect human being — one who knows and experiences all there is to experience as a human, not hiding from anything, not denying anything, not trying to be any more or less than what she is.
Love,
Sophia

* * * * *

May 16, 2000

I don't want to do any more of this tedious, unrewarding work. I just want to get to the end of it, to be done with it, to peel away the veils that hide my true nature. I get so tired of this never-ending, painful unfolding. Sometimes I feel like I am clawing my way up a mountain that never ends, never delivers me to the top where I can touch the sky, where I can see all around me and know who I am and where I am in relation to the world. Today I am discouraged beyond caring.

* * * * *

Anna

I read this in one of Sophia's journals. It's from Tilopa, and since I read it, it's been my constant companion:

No thought
No reflection
No analysis
No cultivation
No intention
Let it settle itself.

Something in this poem speaks to me. Maybe it's because I am starting to see how far I am from that ideal state of being. My mind is always thinking, figuring, deciding what to do and what not to do, always directed by my desire to have things go the way I want them to.

Accepting things just as they are makes me nervous. It's like the feeling of anxiety I have when I look in the mirror. I have never liked looking in mirrors. These exercises Perry has me doing, looking at myself in a mirror, are torture. Sometimes it's impossible, and I just can't do them.

Last night I woke up from a deep dream state, and as I started to fall back into the dream, I experienced a feeling of being absorbed into nothing. I felt myself being sucked up and breathed out into space — no longer Anna, the individual person, but just a mist of consciousness permeating everything but having no existence of my own. I was jolted back into my body like a slingshot.

Today, in my session with Perry, I told him about this dream. We starting from the beginning, methodically addressing each part so I could find the dream's message emerging from my unconscious. It took 40 minutes for me to uncover the meaning. The dream was showing me how I can merge with life beyond the physical. But my attachment to the way things are now is so strong I snapped back quickly from that dream state. I didn't take the time to explore what wisdom and grace was there for me. This dream was giving me a taste of what lies beyond the boundaries I create and perceive.

Perry told me to stand in front of the mirror again, and when I start to fade away, see if I can find my midline, that place inside where I am whole and complete even as I melt away. He said I should look for a way to be centered even when I have no fixed boundaries. I'm not sure I'm capable of that. And anyway, tonight I'm just too tired to even try.

* * * * *

Grandmother Spirit

I have learned many things in my long life. I have learned that I am expansive and contractive, expressive and introspective. I am full of my own power and goodness, and I am humbled by my weaknesses and my failings. I inhale and exhale and inhale. And I have learned that you also are all of those things and more — more than I could possibly imagine.

I am not here today as a teacher, though because of my age I am afforded the opportunity to speak, for which I am grateful. I am telling you the story of Sophia and Anna because I hope it will help you to understand yourself better. I hope this story will help you to see all that you are already and to glimpse the innumerable possibilities of your future. Most of all, I hope it will help you to understand the interplay between the blessed and joyful aspects of your life, and the grief, regret, and despair that not one of us will escape in this life. Everything leads us back here — here to this ever-changing now, here to the space between the in breath and the out breath.

I feel the energy of Heaven as I reach up through the vastness of the sky. My feet are deeply rooted in the Earth — deep, deep, down where the fires rage. The tension fields between Heaven and Earth create potency, creativity, change. Where they touch, in that liminal space between the inhalation and the exhalation, the forces ignite, sparking a new expression, patterned after all that came before but unique on the face of the Earth.

Chapter Nine

The wound is the place where the light enters you.

~ Rumi

There is a crack in everything, that's how the light gets in.

~ Leonard Cohen

Grandmother Spirit

We are perfection perfecting. We are discovering our true natures. We perform sacred rituals to create an environment inside ourselves that allows the Divine to reveal itself. We fall under its spell; it is deliriously enchanting. And once it has us hooked, it challenges us to recognize its presence in the profoundly difficult problems of everyday life.

It's challenging to simply be with what is. Equanimity is a wonderful concept and a blessed state of being. But it requires a lifetime of practice to sit with pain and misery and to embrace the moment as a privilege and a blessing. We try, and we usually fail. Even when we fail, the practice helps us develop compassion for others. Sometimes we succeed, and these are divine moments.

Don't be discouraged when these divine moments fade away and leave you struggling in what appears to be the same old place where you started. That is an illusion!

* * * * *

June 2, 2000

A nice thing is developing between me and Jahi. He picked me up at the airport and brought me flowers. Very sweet. We talk on the phone every day, and it feels like we are growing individually and collectively into something more again. There is a deep intimacy growing between us. We are working toward healing the old and moving forward toward each other.

June 19, 2000

I am shattered. Jahi is dating another woman. How could he do this? How could he have not even mentioned to me this was happening? I was totally blindsided when Mitch told me that Carol, a woman who comes regularly to our office, has been dating Jahi. My heart has been ripped out.

June 20, 2000

Of course, there must have been warning signs. But I ignored them because they didn't fit into the reality I chose to believe. I don't just have blind spots, I have blind boulders! Oh, God. Here I am, stuck in the consequences of my delusions again. Why do I keep doing this?

June 22, 2000

My pain feels more important and devastating than anyone else's right now. So now I am down on myself for being so self-important and self-involved. I feel hurt and angry, and I feel guilty because I feel hurt and angry. And I feel lost. I thought I still had an anchor in Jahi. I thought we were clear and honest with each other. I have been betrayed. I don't know what to do.

* * * * *

Dear Anna,

Knowing Jahi wanted to be with another woman was excruciating. I was angry at him and angry at myself for being so blind. Even when you believe you have healed a wound it can resurface over and over. It can open up and bleed and hurt more than it did the last time. But imaginary realities will always eventually collapse to reveal the vulnerability they were hiding.

Jahi and I were conscious people committed to our personal growth, committed to working hard to avoid being trapped in old patterns. Yet there they were: the blind spots, the complexes — samsara.

I had a life-long pattern of looking outside of myself for approval and acceptance, even to determine who I was. But the desire I have to be liberated was so big, the container of my neurosis could not hold it no matter how hard I tried. Lessons will come hard if that's what's needed. They will come with enough force to penetrate, to get inside where changes can happen.

If we choose to be whole, with all that implies, we have to be able to recognize our own blind spots and find a way to see around them. It takes courage and perseverance.

The way we see the world, blind spots and all, is comfortably familiar. Moving beyond them is stepping into an unknown future. But I can tell you, Anna, as someone who has made this my life's work, it is worth it!

I love you,
Sophia

* * * * *

Anna

Last night I had a strange dream:

> *I was sitting alone in the Escalante River*
> *canyon, feeling like something was supposed*
> *to be there but was not; there was something*
> *missing. It was afternoon, and the golden light*
> *created interesting shadows on the canyon walls.*
> *Then I heard something. I turned, but nothing was*
> *there. Suddenly a voice called out, "Remember! Go!*
> *Find what you have to remember!" I shouted, "No! If*
> *I find it I will die!" But I got up anyway and started to*
> *look for it, whatever it was. I looked under bushes*
> *and in side canyons. Finally, I found it lying in the*
> *bottom of the stream, obscured by the rushing*
> *water. Before I could really register what it was,*
> *I woke up.*

One strange thing about this dream, I have never been to the Escalante River. But I absolutely knew where I was, and I am as sure as I can be — what I saw in my dream was the river canyon.

Perry and I talked for a long time about this dream. As he sometimes does, he reflected the dream back to me. He said, "The Great Mother Earth surrounds you with her high walls and trees and water. It's familiar, and there are shadows flickering on the walls. The Great Mother is holding you; the shadows start to reveal themselves. We have talked a lot about our shadows being the unconscious patterns that hold our wounds and complexes. Then you hear, *remember*. What is it you are to remember while held by the Mother in the golden sun? Why will you die if you remember?"

I am blank. I have no answer to his questions. I will follow Perry's advice and let this dream continue to inform me. There must be something I have forgotten, maybe even something I chose to forget. What is it? And why would I choose to forget it?

* * * * *

July 31, 2000

For the last three weeks I have been tired, flooded with emotions, helpless, threatened. Sometimes I can't breathe. This morning I keep having thoughts that something is wrong with me. Mitch gave me a treatment, and five minutes later I was laughing, singing — I was alive again. Clearly my emotions and perceptions are ephemeral and insubstantial. Where did those feelings come from and where did they go?

September 1, 2000

I am at BioCranio training, and I'm being dis-membered and re-constructed. God, this is hard!

I have been living a lie, a masked version of myself. I see how my actions and words have been driven not by my soulful self, but by a pair of false identities — good girl, bad girl — in conflict with each other and each vying to control my psyche. As the real me is emerging, my past, as I remember it, is being revealed as illusory, deceptive, self-serving, and limiting.

Then there are times in a BioCranio session when I touch and feel the real me, the soulful me — times when I am held in the womb of the universe, and everything around me melts into grace. How did I live before I knew myself in this way?

* * * * *

Anna

I was feeling frustrated all morning, and when I marched into Perry's office this afternoon, I didn't even say hello before I blurted out, "Perry, I don't understand Sophia. What does she mean when she says she is being dismembered and annihilated? Those words really unnerve me. Why would she want to have an experience where she feels *dismembered*? It's creepy!"

Unruffled, as always, by my frustration, Perry smiled and said, "That, Anna, is a very good question! And, an important one.

"In every soulful culture's mythology you will find some form of this idea. In depth psychology, spiritual mysticism, shamanism, and in some healing modalities these terms, dismemberment and annihilation, are used to refer to a process of transformation that requires the destruction of some aspect of the psyche in order for a new construct to emerge.

"Our beliefs permeate our entire being. Here is a way to visualize this: Beliefs and limiting constructs can't just be cut off like a skin growth, with minimal invasiveness. They are deep in our cellular structure, spread throughout our psyches, our minds, and our bodies. In order for them to be released we have to be dismembered, taken apart, torn to pieces, annihilated.

"Seekers like Sophia choose to do the inner work of self- actualization or individuation to uncover the parts of themselves that are not truly theirs or have been taken on as adaptations or for protection. They invite the dragon to come and do its work. "Sophia did this by pursuing her different forms of healing and spiritual work. She chose to travel the path of soulful evolution and spiritual awakening. And somewhere along the way, she found herself at a turning point. A choice had to be made to either retreat back into her old way of being or to face that dragon and allow it to tear her illusions from her as if it were ripping off her arms and her legs. Of course, we know what choice Sophia made. She understood that something must be sacrificed for something new to emerge.

"In your case, Anna, you may not be consciously choosing to do this deep inner work, but the circumstances of your life, along with something deep in your soul and your psyche, are creating an undercurrent that is carrying you along. Sophia's hopes for you are a powerful influence, shaking things up, encouraging you to move in the direction of truth and away from illusion.

"You have told me several times in the last couple of months that you feel like you are being ripped apart, like you are losing yourself. You, Anna, are experiencing your own process of dismemberment and annihilation.

"I can tell you this: people who choose to surrender and allow the transformation to take place, generally emerge into a deeper and more fulfilling life — they feel free. It's a euphoria unlike anything they have felt before."

When Perry finished speaking, we were both silent for a long time. I understood something now about what I've been going through as I read Sophia's journals — how I have been being torn apart, my beliefs about myself and my life being shattered and re-formed.

I stood over by the window, looking out over the garden to the mountains beyond. The tears came, and then they came harder — a torrent of release from deep inside of me. I cried for Sophia and for her pain. I cried for myself and my pain. I cried with relief for finally having some idea of what was happening to me. When I could speak again my voice came out in a whisper. "I think I'm beginning to understand."

* * * * *

Grandmother Spirit

Just the words — dismemberment and annihilation — are frightening! In your quest for wholeness, you will encounter your demons, you will be ripped apart, you will be tested. You will be dismembered and re-membered, and it will be painful. You will endure your "dark night of the soul."

This part of the Heroine's evolutionary journey demands courage — the courage to face the illusions you have built your life around, the courage to let them disintegrate and dissolve into nothingness, taking a part of you with them. You should not undertake this journey without a clear vision of why you have chosen to walk this treacherous road to your own awakening.

* * * * *

September 3, 2000

This is what I dreamed last night:

The clutch went out on my car, and the part that was needed to fix it was not available anywhere in the world. The manufacturer was going to have to make it, and no one knew how long it would take.

The clutch, of course, is what disengages the motor and allows you to switch gears and move forward. There is no way to fix it; a new one needs to be made. I am disengaging from Jahi. There is no way to fix this. In my psyche, a new part has to be made.

September 4, 2000

Jahi just called to tell me that while he and Raven are away, Carol will be staying at the Center to care for the plants and animals. He didn't even ask me first.

When I hung up I was shaking all over. I felt like he had reached into my chest and grabbed my heart, twisted it, crushed it. I am being cut off, replaced. This is what jealousy feels like. It's awful.

September 6, 2000

Carol was stung by a scorpion and came to Mitch's office for help! All the angst and pain and the unkind thoughts about her, they all just melted away. Here was a person who needed help, and I wanted to help her. I drove her home and helped her with her children. I *wanted* to help. The rest was insignificant. My anger and my hurt, all just gone. This is what grace is.

As I was driving her home, I felt it wash over me and through me. In this state of grace, I set Jahi free. Three years ago I spoke the words that set it in motion. It took this long. I will no longer see myself as being wronged. Jahi will no longer hold this piece of my shadow. I am no longer bound and constrained by my self-importance. I feel so alive!

I remember these words pouring through me:

All my hopes and all my fears,
All my loves and all my hates,
All my gods and all my devils,
All my successes and all my failures,
Are the products of my own imagination,
And, therefore, they are temporary.
I invent me every day and because I create me
It is temporary.

September 21, 2000

Why are these feelings back? The intensity of this pain is overwhelming. Yes, we were separated, but I believed we had a covenant of the heart. What hurts the most is that he didn't even tell me. Didn't he know this would hurt? He wants to be with another woman. He is *sleeping* with another woman! I feel utterly betrayed. I have a knife in my heart.

I don't remember a time in my life when I did not feel hurt. It's a theme, a way I see myself. I am so tired.

October 17, 2000

I have had moments so complete I was in want or need of nothing. I am reclaiming my self, discovering who I am when I am not encumbered by energetic attachments. That said, I am becoming aware of a very troubled part of myself — a part that fills my head with stories that make me feel hurt and unloved.

I saw it coming, but I still fell in headfirst. I feel

drained and sad and angry. And I have had another of those lapses when I don't remember what I did yesterday or the day before.

October 23, 2000

I have been working on separating my energy body from Jahi's, slowly teasing apart and untangling the threads that have bound us together, cutting the cords, reclaiming the parts that are mine, sending him with blessings into the arms of Rinpoche and Raven.

November 4, 2000

Today Natalie asked me how I was doing. I told her about Jahi and my feeling of having been betrayed and how hard it is to know he is with another woman. She said, "This isn't about Jahi. You are addicted to futile striving."

What? These words were a sword whipping down and cutting right through to my pattern. I was looking at the naked core of this insidious demon which has permeated my existence and left its ugly stain on, well, everything! I saw how its tentacles wound into, around, and through every aspect of my relationship with men — first my father, then Kevin, then Jahi. I am addicted to futile striving.

Now that I understand, can I stop it? I can stop! None of this is about circumstance, nor about any other person. It's all mine. It's my attachment to the pattern of wanting what I can't have and feeling the wanting as if it is who I am.

This is huge.

November 5, 2000

Now I see it everywhere. In a BioCranio session today, I was asked about my birth. I told the story as my mother had told it to me: a long, hard forceps delivery — my first, pattern-setting experience of futile striving? I see how the pattern plays out over and over again in my life.

I knew I should leave Kevin, but I stayed and kept trying until Kevin did something I could use to justify ending the relationship. I kept futilely striving until then. I could have gotten myself killed.

With Jahi I didn't have this kind of ending, but even after we agreed to separate, I continued to futilely strive for something in the relationship — some vision of what it would become — until I was severed from that delusion by the ax of betrayal. It was my wakeup call.

November 9, 2000

I drove down to Page, Arizona, yesterday to be with Serena. I was thinking about the first time I drove through Page, on our way to St. George. So much has changed. I feel grief and sadness for all the dreams I have lost and the people who were so tightly woven into my life but are now gone. I sit here alone with my heartache.

And I am richly infused with grace. The channel remains open between spirit and form when you consciously experience the connection.

December 8, 2000

Sally died yesterday, and I am in and out of joyful remembrance and grief. Then I sit with the duality, holding both feelings at the same time with only a numinous, thin line between them. Each emotion is energy with an individual tone and vibration, and I relate to each one differently. When these polarities are this close, they create a precious joy.

Sally's death has illuminated my choice. I will live! I will never compromise myself or my spirit! I will not settle for less than my truth and my power. NEVER! NEVER! NEVER!

December 15, 2000

Another amazing BioCranio class. This process is remarkable; we are opening like flowers, with such grace, even as our identities are being annihilated.

I honor myself for the courage to walk this path. I am seeing my demons. I am opening and walking through doors where once I placed guardians to keep me from the fiery hell of my own fear and pain.

Again my compassion is growing. There is no room for judgment.

* * * * *

Grandmother Spirit

Sophia is beginning to learn about the numinous space created when you are able, without judgment or attachment, to hold two opposing thoughts or feelings. In their opposition, they create a tension field that is dynamically still — a midline, a transcendent field of potential.

These are divine moments, but they are not the absolute, even as they are perfect medicine for your enlightenment. They will come again and again, sprinkled in the soup of your delusion, scattered through the complications of your life. We do the best we can. We are perfection perfecting.

Chapter Ten

Anna

I'm sitting in the big comfortable chair in Perry's office, telling him about a long and complicated dream I had last night that he was in.

We were talking and walking along a path. Sophia was walking along a parallel path some distance away. The paths stretched ahead of us, coming together at a vanishing point on the horizon.

Then I was talking with you here, sitting in this room. And I started to fade away. Then suddenly Sophia was here and she called to me, "Getting closer! Remember? Getting closer!" Then she disappeared, and it was 1961, and I was at the church where Sophia got married. Only it wasn't really me. It was like I became someone else, or maybe like someone else became me. It scared me, and I woke up.

As I tell the dream to Perry, I remember something. When I was little, my Mom would hide a toy. As I searched for it, she would let me know if I was going in the right direction by calling, "Getting closer!"

"Anna, do you realize this is the first time you have ever said anything to me about your childhood?"

Suddenly, I am exhausted. I tell Perry I need to go

home. I'm not feeling well. He doesn't try to change my mind. He tells me to go home and rest.

* * * * *

Dear Anna,

For three years I only saw Raven on her brief visits to town. At the Center the chemical fumes were still more than I could stand. Raven's health was failing; it was time for us to sell the property and move her to town where I could help take care of her.

After months of discussion, Raven, Jahi, and I have agreed it is futile to try and keep the Center when we cannot care for it any longer. Within a day of our decision, we had two offers on the land. It really was time. I could see the winds of karma blowing across the top of the mountain and carrying us to new places and experiences — like a Tibetan sand mandala, created with love and devotion, scattered by the winds of change.

I Love you,
Sophia

* * * * *

January 24, 2001

It's too much! The demands on my time from the mail,

phone, newspaper, email, and studies fill my life with new information and data every day. I am helping with the temple packing, selling the property, looking for new property, negotiating the use of the funds and my mortgage refinance, cultivating my healing practice, studying for my classes, attending lectures and workshops, creating my project for BioCranio school. On top of everything else, I have a home to take care of. What about time to receive a healing session? What about taking care of me? What about just *being*?

February 22, 2001

Twenty-six years ago we moved to our land where we created our spiritual center from a dream and a vision. We created the mandala, and now it is being returned to the river of creative potential. Wow! What a magnificent expression of my futile striving! Still, I have learned so much.

All those years ago, I found this property, and now I sold it three days after we decided to put it on the market. When we manifested our dream, we could never have imagined what the end would look like. I knew the divine timing was right.

March 12, 2001

I have one more BioCranio training in June, and then I graduate. I can't believe it has been three years! Since the last class, something new opened up in me when I realized alienation itself was a midline, a center that holds the original pattern of feeling alienated. I see how my life has rotated and oriented around this midline. Feelings of alienation have permeated and seeped into the different crevices of my life, influencing the way I perceive and relate to my experiences. The stories I've lived were the way I danced with alienation in an attempt to come into relationship with this midline.

I am working on my final project for class and will use my new awareness of the Midline of Alienation to create an art mandala using gourds as an art representation of how we circle a midline in all our forms. My understanding and sense of this midline is that it comes into being at the moment the forces of nature engage and there is a flash of new life. At this moment, form and consciousness find each other, and the Breath of Life ignites the fire creating a new midline. In this moment, duality and infinite potential mutually arise within our consciousness.

Perhaps this midline is a recapitulation of cyclical experience, showing us the nature of our dualistic minds, urging us toward a non-dualistic experience. It does seem to be a double bind of sorts, to have a midline created from such magnificent power and creativity, holding such potential, and yet at the same time containing the experience of alienation from our non-dualistic nature.

I also have a significant final exam to take before June, and I am studying with Nick.

June 20, 2001

I did a long ritual last night. Nude in the moonlight with my cauldron and a candle, I reclaimed myself. I looked through old pictures, honoring the past. I selected one photo and carefully cut Jahi out of it and placed him in the hot embers. I burned him up — not with malice, but with the intent of cleansing, releasing, and accepting.

I circled the cauldron and swore allegiance to my inherent nature. I affirmed my promise to myself: I would no longer abide in the abyss of unconsciousness. I awoke this morning with a new sense of who I am and what I might become.

August 9, 2001

How does one stand in the light of grace and know it's not you, yet it is you? I have been to the Temple of God, been held in the arms of the beloved and fed the nectar of life. I am nourished. Today, I sang to my Guru, Tubten Rinpoche, at the end of the summer teachings. The greatest wisdom is kindness.

September 11, 2001

I don't have a TV, so I went to my neighbor's house where I watched in disbelief as the towers fell. I was in shock. I didn't want to watch it, but I couldn't look away as the images of the devastation replayed over and over again. The anguish on people's faces, their obvious fear, last calls to loved ones — I feel like I've been stabbed in my heart. I don't think I will be able to sleep tonight. I'm flooded with emotions — wild thoughts and intense feelings. How could this happen in our country? And what kind of knee-jerk, unconscious retaliation is bound to follow and carry us all into war?

September 12, 2001

Yesterday wasn't a dream. It really happened; we were attacked, and thousands of people are dead or injured. Everyone is in shock and fear. How do we hold such an atrocity in our minds and hearts? I am shaken to my core — physically, mentally, and emotionally. Now more than ever, people will need support to deal with this trauma. I want to help. In my BioCranio training, I learned treatments for shock and trauma. I'm grateful. I can be of service through my healing work.

September 21, 2001

Today I purchased Nick's stunning sculpture he calls *Emerging Woman*. He started to make this beautiful stone sculpture when I was leaving for Australia and New Zealand. I saw a photo of the finished piece when I read his graduation project report, and I got the message that I should buy it. I want to do this for Nick to acknowledge all he has done for me. But also, it is a stunning sculpture, and it touches me in a deep and sacred place. It speaks to me and of me. I *am* an Emerging Woman!

October 24, 2001

In my dream I was more powerful than in any other dream I can remember. This one is so rich and full of importance, I think I will be working on it for years!

I was a newborn baby, yearning to be held in sacred space. There was a wise old crone at my birth who knew the ways of spirit and understood the power of ritual and the significance of rites of passage. She was pulling hair from her head and bits of her clothing and throwing them into the fire. The crone was also me, unraveling myself even as I tended my newborn, perfect, emerging self. I was my own midwife.

And I was also the woman who sat on the sidelines and wept in divine, exquisite pain, observing my birth and my destruction, my destruction and my rebirth. Sorrow and Joy were also there. They were dancing all around us, singing their two oddly harmonic songs, while their pounding footfalls created a driving beat. All three of my forms were vibrating with the rhythm created by Sorrow and Joy.

I smile when I contemplate what Perry will make of this one!

January 1, 2002

I have been living an illusion. Before I was old enough to even know what I was doing, I had adopted my beliefs from others. And many of these beliefs were not congruent with my life force and my soul's purpose — like blaming others and projecting and spinning around in my own story instead of being fully connected to my center and my soul. I should have been listening to my heart and soul instead of listening to the voice of my delusion telling me I'm a victim, I am hurt, I have been shamed.

January 2, 2002

I wonder about my progress on my spiritual path. Am I really any closer to enlightenment? Am I more free? Sometimes it seems as if I haven't grown one bit. Have I gained any wisdom at all? Well, maybe a little. I know enough to recognize when my thoughts want to minimize my self-worth. I'm not second-guessing myself as much. I'm choosing my joy over my suffering. Even with two steps forward and one step back, I'm making some progress. I'm "getting closer" as Mom used to say.

January 3, 2002

In my childhood, I was taught, both overtly and covertly, that a woman is subordinate to a man. She stands behind him. She follows his lead. I remember my mother telling me to never let my father think I was smarter than he was. This concept was pervasive in our culture. It deeply penetrated my sensibility.

My life has fallen squarely into the era of women's awakening, women's liberation. But those early-childhood imprints — so pervasive, so primal, so welded to familial love and the security of belonging — are not easy to outgrow. There remains inside of me a little girl who feels vulnerable, helpless, victimized, and dependent. This severely compromises my feminine power!

January 4, 2002

Perry uses the word "complex" when he speaks of emotional patterns. I wanted a better understanding of what he means, so I looked it up. The Oxford Dictionary defines complex as:

> A related group of repressed or partly repressed emotionally significant ideas which cause psychic conflict leading to abnormal mental states or behavior.

Well, that's clear. I definitely have a complex! Then again, I suspect everyone does.

* * * * *

Dear Anna,

There is satisfaction when our complex finds justification for its existence by creating in our lives situations that affirm the truth of its skewed perspective. My complex continues to affirm that I am not good enough. My inner dialogue runs amok saying, "See? See?" it says. "I'm not important! See, see how I am bad?"

We often choose someone to share our life with simply because they neatly fit into our neurotic complex. They come tailor-made to push our buttons and arouse in us the justification of our complexes. We all do this until we are sick and tired of it and make the effort to change.

What a gift it is to haul it all out into the light where we can see it clearly and make different choices. A few of us lucky ones get a hard blow that shocks us out of our neurosis. Fewer still actually transform from the blow.

Anna, we are as good as dead if we remain a victim to our neurotic complexes. We always have choices.
Love,
Sophia

* * * * *

January 5, 2002

Today, after the teachings from Rinpoche, something extraordinary happened. I was able to see and experience my thoughts as clouds — ever-changing, no substance, empty. For years I have been hearing the words of my teachers; I have been absorbing their teachings. Today they fused and penetrated the veil of my illusion. I am graced and blessed — I felt it. For a moment, I was free from suffering.

* * * * *

Dear Anna,

Jahi and Raven moved to town. It was wonderful to have them closer so I could help take care of Raven. As the year went by, she needed more and more care. Her health declined several times to the point where we thought we might lose her. But then, for a time, she would rally. She was in and out of the hospital, sometimes in intensive care. She was diagnosed with diabetes and congestive heart failure. She had internal bleeding and several heart attacks. It was a hard year.

Each time I had a training or a retreat to attend, I was torn about whether to go or not, worried she might die while I was away. But I did go, and Raven hung on.

My life was an emotional rollercoaster. Sometimes my heart was open and clear; sometimes I fell into the old abyss of anger, shame, and fear. I was processing all the things I was learning in my BioCranio training. I was dealing with my feelings about Jahi and all I was learning from that situation. And then there were my complicated feelings about Raven, knowing she was dying.

Love,
Sophia

* * * * *

March 14, 2002

This is what I dreamed last night:

*There were women who came from all around the
world to celebrate women speaking their truth. And
there were men there who came because they valued
these women and wanted to deepen their relationships
and friendships with them. There were children
running around playing. They were treated
respectfully by the adults.*

*I was in charge of the group, along with one of
the men. But there was little for us to do because
the women knew their responsibilities and were
totally self-reliant. I was looking around for the
women who would be leaders. Then all the women
came into the lodge following a man. He had taken
them all for a morning journey. I walked up to him
and hugged and kissed him. It was a wonderful
embrace.*

I am still carrying the feeling of this dream deep
inside me — it's a peaceful feeling that naturally arises
when we honor and respect each other in such a
profound and loving way. This dream indicates a deep
healing of my masculine and feminine energies.

March 28, 2002

I am so blessed by my experiences; they have given

me understanding and sensitivity to others. I don't want to erase any of them: the pregnancy, the shame, the priest, the pink dress, being burned by hot coffee, being physically and emotionally abused, having a gun pointed at me, divorcing, leaving my children, leaving my home, nearly dying, being betrayed, divorcing again. So many lessons, so much I have learned.

April 17, 2002

I was going to the temple today to see Rinpoche one last time before he leaves for Tibet. He's being called to go back even though he knows that once he is there, the Chinese might not allow him to return to the USA. It's been seven years since I met him.

I badly wanted to be there today to express my immense appreciation for all he has given me. But I got a call from Jahi saying Raven wasn't doing well, and he had called the hospice nurse. I went to be with Raven. In my heart, I send my love and appreciation to Rinpoche. Both of my teachers are leaving.

May 5, 2002

Out to dinner last night at Nick and Alysia's house, I was talking to a past-life regression therapist. During the conversation she pointed out how often I mentioned stones as part of my healing process. She was right, of course.

I started to tell her about Raven's book — how she is

writing down the stories the stone has given to her. She has been working on the book for years. It isn't finished, but she can't write any more. In a flash I saw it so clearly! This is the karmic connection between Raven and me. I too receive messages from my stone amulet. I saw that I will finish Raven's book because I will be the holder of this stone lineage.

I told Raven about this conversation and asked her whether one stone holder had to be gone before another could hear. As usual, her answer was simple, "The stone will speak to the one who can hear." Then she said, "Truth is both relative and non-relative. The stone speaks the truth; how the receiver hears it and brings it to life is the relative truth." At that moment, I felt empowered to trust whatever the stone would give me.

What an incredible teaching! The stone has no preference, bias, judgment, or ego; it is just a transmitter of recorded experience.

May 27, 2002

Raven is very low today. I feel the quiet of her energy and the lack of vitality in her body. I'll stay with her tonight. It feels like when the Earth changes seasons, and everything is calm and serene.

May 31, 2002

I was longing to have the altar for The Center for Divine Union in Raven's room. I went through all the boxes in the garage and selected certain items to create the altar. It was sweet, handling these pieces again. I took the urn that holds the articles we collected from the sacred places we visited around the world. I found the rosewood box that holds the names of all those who are in need of prayer. I placed Raven's name in the box. I took the sand painting of Mother Earth and Father Sky, the candle holder with the Om stained glass, and the three small red ears of corn. I also took the stained glass window with The Center for Divine Union seal. I carried all these sacred pieces into the house, and I placed them in her room while she slept.

When she awoke it was overwhelming for her — too much! So I took everything out and created the altar in the spare room leaving only The Center for Divine Union seal, the corn and the candle holder. I realized that when you are preparing for your transition, you are letting go. I had just filled her room with the sacred altar pieces to sooth her. But in actuality, they were a distraction, creating attachment to her life and body, interfering with her transition, keeping her earthbound.

Then, I had a meltdown. Handling all those pieces filled with 29 years of memories and blessings pushed me right over the edge. How do I hold all of this in my heart? What will happen now? What will it be like with Raven gone? How will Jahi and I be with each other? What will happen to The Center for Divine Union?

June 1, 2002

Today I recognized how I find ways to comfort the uncomfortable part of myself — the part that feels needy and longs for appreciation, the part that wants desperately to be seen for who I am. I suspect we each find our own particular way to get what we think we need. For me, my particular way of getting what I want-is to be lovable, everything right so there is no reason for anyone not to love me. I see how my small self takes ownership of these qualities. I value them, and I believed others do too.

My inner need to be lovable and to do what I'm told was challenged when Raven wanted to get out of bed. She asked to get up; I told her she couldn't. She demanded I help her; I told her I wasn't strong enough. She was adamant that I do what she said, commanding me to listen and respond. Raven tried to get up by herself, pushing me as I blocked her efforts. I needed to physically restrain her.

My devotion and desire to do what she requested was deep and strong. But the reality was, for her own good, I couldn't let her. With an intense internal struggle, my love and compassion and concern for Raven's safety gave me the strength to ignore the voice in my mind scolding, "Do-what-you're-told!"

Then, like a lightning flash, I laughed at this folly. My small self believed these qualities belonged to *me* and made me special and loveable, when the truth is, these qualities of loving kindness, compassion, and generosity are the gifts of being human, the gifts of the universe. They don't belong to me.

June 2, 2002

I never want to forget what it is to live in harmony with nature. It is far too easy to be swept away by the business of life and forget the importance of being in communion and co-creating with the natural world. This is one of the most valuable things I have learned from Raven. I will remember this always.

June 4, 2002

Yesterday was hard. In the middle of the night I woke up thinking about Raven. She is in decline, in a state between consciousness and sleep. It was 1:30 am, and the moon was almost full. I stepped outside and, in the way she taught me, bathed in the glow of the moon.

June 8, 2002

I can hear the wind rustling through the trees outside. Raven always talks about the "whispering of the mystery through the pines." This is how she will pass. Her spirit will leave and rustle through the pines like a whisper of the divine mystery.

Today Raven made a comment about how the body has many moods. I answered that her mood was a very quiet one right now. I asked her how her meditations had been, and she said there is more to meditate on since meditation is awareness, and there is more to be aware of. I asked if she felt any anxiety about what was happening to her. She said, "You can only feel anxiety if you have something to lose, and there is nothing to lose." Death is a sacred process; I felt the sacredness permeate me.

This afternoon my deep pattern of unworthiness revealed itself once again. But this time I said, thank you, I am going to feel all of me including my unworthiness. It is all divine. And even as I was having this divine experience, I felt my lack of worthiness. Who did I think I was to deserve such sacredness? There it was again. But it didn't matter. I was held in a state of divine equilibrium. I was feeling both things at once: my divinity and my insignificance.

June 23, 2002

Life is dancing with death. Above it all the mystery hovers. Raven is still with us, very weak, sleeping most of the time.

June 30, 2002

Raven wasn't moving. We called hospice and asked if we were giving her too much morphine. They said no, it sounds like she is in her active dying stage. Before long an angel of a hospice nurse appeared. She has been to Raven's beloved Escalante River. She has read the *Tibetan*

Book of the Dead. She touched the top of Raven's head and said, "This is where you leave to go toward the light." She was perfect.

When the nurse left she told me, "Raven will die in the next two days." I went home to gather a few things. When I came back, Jahi went out to buy food for dinner.

While Jahi was gone I sat with Raven, wanting to be totally present for her. But my thoughts were wandering, so of course I was judging myself for that. Then I heard a voice say, "Your thoughts are just as divine as no thoughts." There is always a little Raven voice in my head telling me, "You don't have to do anything. Just be." Okay. I placed my hand over her head to feel her vital energy, and it was strong and potent.

When Jahi got home, we began to prepare dinner, checking on Raven now and then, listening to every sound from her room through a recently-installed monitor. We were prepared to sit vigil all night with her and for as long as it would take.

We poured a glass of wine and toasted Raven, her life, her wisdom. We were comfortable together in our joint sorrow. Jahi said he had run into one of the practitioners from the Tubten Temple at the store, and she said Traga Rinpoche was teaching the Phowa practice tonight. We both stopped. We looked at each other and together we said, "Phowa." We smiled. Phowa is the practice to help consciousness leave the body.

Just then I heard Raven call — not over the monitor,

a different kind of sound. I hurried in to check on her. Her eyes were open. I said, "Hi, Raven." She did not respond. She was not breathing. I called Jahi.

Raven took a big breath, and then another, and then another, each difficult and each taking a long time. Then, her journey in this form was over. In the rarified energy and the silence, we instinctively knew what to do. We laid her red shawl chetter over her with the talking stone and some flowers on her heart. We recited her favorite mantra: *Om Tare Tuttare Ture Soha.* We held each other and cried.

July 1, 2002

Last night I slept with the stone on my heart. It comforted me. In my sleep Raven spoke to me. She told me I was to carry on her lineage. And she released me from anything that kept me from being fully in my wisdom and strength as a spiritual teacher.

July 4, 2002

On July 4, 1974, I was in the Escalante River canyon, in Utah, where Raven was initiated into the Blue Bird clan of the Hopi. It was my first pilgrimage with Raven.

On July 4, 1975, I was ordained by Raven.

Today is July 4, 2002. I am celebrating her life and grieving her passing. It has been 28 years, a Saturn return, a complete cycle, a full circle.

Someone at the temple said, "In changing the place of her teachings, your teacher has opened up new realms of spiritual teaching for you; may you receive them fully, with clear eyes and an open heart." My heart is open, tender, and vulnerable in sorrow.

Mom called asking what she could do since there was no memorial service for Raven. This brought me to tears. What can anybody do? Just honor what a great and kind woman she was and how much she helped me.

Then a deeper understanding of what can be done came to me. To memorialize her was to live the truth she taught. Her teachings were simple and clear:

We are co-creators with life.
Start each day with a new face of God.
Never doubt and always trust in your direct
experience. Recognize your infinite human potential.
Let the mystery reveal itself.
Be the vehicle that is constantly opening to the
mystery of life.

✳ ✳ ✳ ✳ ✳

Dear Anna,
Raven understood the Divine Feminine and its
power to heal the wounds of both women and men
and even of Mother Earth herself, so abused by the
diminishment of feminine divinity.
She said women are the midwives of the spirit, the

alchemists and transformers. We are being breathed and lived by powers we don't understand but are constantly searching for. Living this search became my heritage.

I felt I was embodying what it is to be a priestess, to walk the cutting edge of evolution as an initiated woman. I was in deep relationship with nature, and I knew how to hold her paradoxes. I had learned to dance between the worlds of spirit and matter. I had been willing to dive deeply into my places of conflict. I had faced my demons and transmuted them into gifts.

Raven's death was an initiation — another rite of passage, another coming of age. A portal was opened, and what was being asked of me was nothing less than a willingness to lay my very identity on the altar of sacrifice. I was being asked if I was truly ready to take full and complete responsibility for my journey. The luxury of having a crutch was gone.

Anna, I can no longer be your crutch. This is your rite of passage.
I love you,
Sophia

* * * * *

Grandmother Spirit

When you look back on your personal tragedies, are you able to see the grace? Can you see how your feelings of devastation are the sacrifices you make in order to move forward? When Sophia left Sebastian behind and gave up her right to the daily joys of motherhood, she was sacrificing what was dearest to her heart in order to move forward on her spiritual path. Sometimes it takes a hurricane to catapult us out of our ignorance. There is grace in every disaster, every crisis, every death. That's why, in Hindu philosophy, Shiva the destroyer is honored every bit as much as Brahma, the creator, and Vishnu, the preserver. From Kali to Pele, grace is often gifted in the form of destruction.

We always want answers to our questions. But answers take us only to a dead end, a completion, a closed book. That is not life! There are no answers, because even as we are being created we are being sustained, and even as we are being sustained we are being destroyed, and even as we are being destroyed we are being re-formed, remade, recreated. That is life!

Chapter Eleven

Grandmother Spirit

Deep inside each of us is a wild woman — unharnessed, unbounded, unconstrained. The unobstructed forces within her are the same wild forces that weave the natural world. She doesn't care about cultural admonishments or family pressures. She talks to trees and understands their whispered messages. She dances with fairies in the garden and makes offerings to the earth and sky in gratitude for the abundance of life. She is at home with the ways of the shaman and the priestess — she plays in the territories of mystery. She understands how nature's extraordinary alchemy plays upon the energies of life, and she knows she is one with these energies and with the processes that keep them in constant flow. She sees through illusion to the authentic nature of all beings. Her wild nature plays with the circumstances of life with curiosity and wonder. She embraces intimacy.

And, here is the most important thing: no matter how we may have insulated ourselves from the muddy, bloody soil of our origins, our wild nature is still there, and it will awaken in us the moment we acknowledge its existence. Even if you are living a life constrained and overfilled with family duties, or if you are trapped in a life that keeps you bound and compliant in order to feed your children, still it is there inside you. Sisters, say it with me now:

> *I am a wild woman! Say it aloud!*
> *Wake her up! I am a wild woman!*

* * * * *

Anna

I had a confusing and disturbing dream.

My husband and I were taking care of a young woman. (In this dream I had a husband! Too bad I couldn't see what he looked like.) *The young woman had serious emotional issues, and her previous caregivers had given up on her. But we were sure, with our love and attention, she would be fine. Her father tried several times to take her away, but we kept finding ways to distract him. Then she attacked us. She was like a wild cat, biting our arms and legs!*

Her father came and took her outside where the rest of her family was waiting. While her father tied her up, the rest of them were pounding stakes into the ground. They nailed her feet and hands to the stakes! I yelled that she would die, and they said

*this was the only way they knew to stop the
madness. So she died.*

*They started to cover her in dirt, but then I
showed them how her blood was seeping up
from the earth. They frantically tried to contain
it because they believed the blood would spawn
new life and would keep her affliction alive.*

While Perry listened to me tell this dream, he had the
most intense look on his face. He looked just like the
Balinese mask hanging on the wall behind his head!
"Listen," he said, "I want to read you a quote from Carl
Jung: *There is no coming to consciousness without pain....
One does not become enlightened by imagining figures of
light, but by making the darkness conscious.*"

For the rest of my appointment we talked about the
dream. This is what Perry helped me to see: this dream is
bringing the darkness up and into my consciousness.
Perry says there are innumerable myths and stories about
how resisting the pull of truth leads to conflict. On the
journey of becoming, we have to be willing to face the
parts of ourselves that have been rejected, abandoned, or
ignored.

Also, the dream speaks to the part of me that is wild
and primal, my own life-giving blood. The family, led by the
father, calls this primal energy an affliction and wants to
contain it in order to destroy it forever. If the blood of my
wildness is allowed to flow freely, it will spawn more of
itself — more freedom, more wildness. I have to
remember that the father in the dream is a reflection of
me, the part of me that wants to keep something hidden.

This part wants to contain the complexes at all cost. By killing his own flesh and blood, he believes he can keep the family complexes hidden. Instead, the blood continues to flow freely, ready to spawn new life, filled with the potential of expressing wild, primal nature. Whatever is hidden is set free. This dream has stuck with me, lingering in my body and my mind. I told Perry I felt I would never be the same.

* * * * *

July 11, 2002

I put Raven's red chetter on, and my body started to freak out. I shook for at least a minute. This is another teaching: I must walk in my own footsteps. I am not Raven.

July 20, 2002

Jahi came back with a beautiful story. In spite of a washed-out road, he made it all the way to Paria, Utah. He mixed some of Raven's ashes with the sand at the spot where, so many years ago, Raven found the talking stone that became one of her most revered teachers.

July 28, 2002

I'm on an island in the Mediterranean. I'm here with Mitch and Terry, attending a chiropractic energy healing conference. Every now and then I have to stop and go through the mental equivalent of pinching myself. I am amazed, once again, at my good fortune.

I was down by the water at sunset when I saw the moon rising from behind the mountain. It was so bright I had to turn around to be sure it wasn't the sun! No, there was the sun setting, and over there the moon was rising. It shone bright orange on the sea.

It was magic time! There was something I needed to do! I ran to get Raven's ashes then waded out until the water lapped at my feet. Before I scattered her ashes in the water, I honored her one more time by taking a moon bath — a practice she taught me long ago. She taught me to reach out and gather the moonbeams in my hands and to bathe my body with them.

Then, under the golden moon, crying, grateful for all the gifts I was still receiving from her, I scattered Raven onto the ancient waters of the Mediterranean Sea. I had the thought: I will never be the same.

July 29, 2002

Today we stood in a hundred-year-old chapel singing, *"Be still and know you are loved."* I am feeling an indescribable peace.

Because of this healing workshop, I have found the words to express my soul's purpose: *I am a radiant fire of ancient feminine wisdom, igniting hearts and souls as I passionately dance between the worlds.*

Just writing these words excites my energy, and

my cells feel like they are dancing. As I move between the worlds of consciousness and unconsciousness, spirit and matter, the seen and unseen, I experience and weave their energies and soulfully evolve. So empowering!

* * * * *

Dear Anna,

In preparation for you reading all these journals, I have read them too, stopping here and there along the way to write you these notes, hoping to fill in some of the gaps and give you the benefit of my more mature thoughts. It has been fascinating and very educational!

I've noticed several recurring themes. Particularly, I have taken note of how many times I have written, "I will never be the same." Of course, this is true — even without extraordinary experiences we are constantly changing and will never be the same. But there is something important about the fact that I wrote this over and over again. Not only was I constantly changing, even as everything in the world is doing so, but I was becoming aware that I was constantly changing.

The other thing I see again and again is my awareness of how blessed I was (and still am!) — how grateful I am to come to this place of transformation

and grace over and over again!
Love,
Sophia

* * * * *

August 15, 2002

Just home from Italy and getting ready to leave for my second Temagami vision quest. I guess that's just the way I'm doing things right now. Italy changed me. I am swirling in a whole new sense of my self — everything is being reorganized in my body and my mind. I'm feeling strongly connected to the most blissful, grace-filled sacred energies!

August 29, 2002

It just dawned on me that in the last month I have spent two weeks on two different islands on two different continents. I arrived home from Temagami last night. Once again I find myself thinking I will never be the same.

Being in the forest, on the island, surrounded by the deep lake, connected to the spirits of Temagami has opened my heart and soul even more. This vision quest revealed my dark side, my shadows, with exquisite precision. I am so alive! I worked with Grandfather Fire and discovered a renewed sense of life. I was bitten by a spider on my third eye. My whole face swelled up. Spider Woman was spreading her magic.

Today Mitch said he sees the wolf in my eyes. He said I am a medicine woman. Spider and wolf reveal their medicine. They are seeing the world through my eyes.

August 29, 2002

I had this dream:

I was with a group of healers and teachers. It was a time of deep growth and connection. There was a Network Chiropractic doctor there and some children. I went outdoors and a black wolf appeared. It was elusive, staying in the shadows, looking at me but not coming close. Then a white wolf appeared. It was loving and caressing, slithering around my body. It brought me some beautiful clothing — gowns and jewels from the time of King Arthur. It was an enchanting time with the wolf. Everyone was in awe of how the white wolf was with me. Then, a second white wolf appeared. Three wolves!

Wolf energy is alive in me!

August 30, 2002

I am feeling the forces of nature working in me and through me. I am wolf woman! I am an enchantress! I have the ability to call in magic and the wildness of nature.

I am agitated and angry. I feel myself holding on, protecting myself from deep fears, keeping at bay a great grief. Dad is not doing well. I feel myself curl up, vulnerable, small, and scared. I don't want him to die. I love him so much.

This is what I mean by *heaven and hell wrapped up in a beautiful bow*. Heaven is my ever-growing feeling of empowerment, my recognition of my divinity — all of my blessed good fortune, the fruits of my hard work.

Hell is my fear for my beloved Dad, the fear that brings out my little-girl self, my insecurities. Hell is my descent into jealousy, my self-limiting thoughts, my pride that lacks compassion, and the crashing fall it will inevitably bring. Hell is made of my patterns, my complexes.

The bow that ties it all together is made of countless strands, each an experience of life on this spectacular planet, each one pulled up and out of this sacred ground. Black wolves, white wolves, they dance together weaving the joy and bliss with the grief and anger.

I realize I am only glimpsing the breadth and depth and importance of this lesson.

September 19, 2002

I'm getting to know my new, vulnerable, tender heart. I have found something, a small grief, a sadness that is a direct result of my pattern of always doing something. When I did my Womb Surround workshop, as I was going through my birth process, I found myself saying, "My mom never stops!" I must admit, I am just like my mom. I find myself caught in this so-familiar struggle.

I have more things to do than I can do. But I *want* to do all of them! Each one is beneficial and rewarding, enriching and nurturing, inspiring and creative. I think, in the past, I would have just pushed on, doing everything. Now, I am sitting with it, thinking about how I might make changes to my life to relieve this pressure. What should I do? What choices should I make?

I want to keep learning the Womb Surround work; I want to take all of Perry's programs. I want to deepen my abilities with BioCranio and develop my practice, to create art, and to write. And I want to take more classes. And I REALLY WANT A RELATIONSHIP WITH A MAN!!! I am full of desires!

* * * * *

Anna

I get tired just reading about all the things Sophia does and everything she wants to do. Doesn't she ever slow down? Wouldn't it be good for her to just stop and take a breath? How is it possible that one person's life is such an unending parade of difficulties and opportunities? With Sophia it never ends. But I have to admit, she rises to every challenge.

Perry told me today I am doing a great service for Sophia by witnessing her life in this unique way — by reading her past. He said, "To have someone who says, 'I will witness you each day and care about your joys and sorrows' — this is profound, and you are doing that for Sophia." Is that really what I'm doing? Am I truly being a witness to Sophia's life?

This much I know is true: I have come to care for Sophia in a way I never could before. When I consider my clinging need for Sophia's friendship, always wanting her to be accessible to me in order to validate my existence, I feel a little ashamed. I didn't really care about her. I just wanted to feel justified in my insistence that she be there for me.

Now, even though I have not seen her for months, I feel closer to her than ever before. And it's not just the notes and the journals. It's like she is inside of me.

Sophia's life is an ebb and flow of grace and sorrow. And it's true it will never stop because each step brings her more life, connection, and freedom. Sophia will always be Sophia — she will stretch the boundaries and reach for the stars.

I know how I have come to this place. Perry has been working with me for months to recognize my tendency to judge everything. Lately I have been embarrassed to realize how quickly I leap to judgment. I'm catching myself constantly. I can find fault in everything from the sloppy grammar in the morning paper to the behavior of my neighbors. As much as I have loved Sophia, I have judged her harshly. Perry has suggested that my freedom will come when I grow beyond judgment. I am not there yet, but at least now I am aware, I'm paying attention.

I told Perry about my dream:

> *There was a circle of wise elders. They were saying to me, "We don't want to know what you know; we want to know what you don't know and what you want to learn." They sent me out into a field. There were two deer walking toward me. As they walked they moved closer and closer together until there was only one of them. I watched this one deer for quite a while. Then it slowly separated, and there were two deer again.*

Perry asked what deer mean to me. I told him I love deer. They are regal and magical.

Then he read a long passage to me from Tagore about separation and duality and about how suffering is a gift for transformation and how even our feeling of alienation is a gift.

Those two deer in my dream, they were both beautiful, but they were different from each other. And when they came together, they became a deer that was not exactly like either of them.

* * * * *

Dear Anna,
   Like every person on Earth, I feel love and joy and

sorrow. I yearn to be happy. Someday I will die. But as long as I have a breath to take, I will aspire to conscious communion with the creative source of existence, and I will commit every ounce of my being to that end.

I am deeply moved by the Buddhist monks who were tortured by the Chinese but harbored no anger or animosity toward those who inflicted atrocities on them. This is such a profound expression of the interconnected nature of us all and of the unconditional compassionate hearts we have available within us. The monks see the Buddha nature within all human forms. And they see how ignorance veils the unity, the oneness of us all. The monks recognize the Buddha Nature in their torturers and understand the torturers too are deserving of compassion.

So, I have a question for you: If they can have compassion for their tormentors, Anna, what is holding you back from having compassion for yourself?
Love you,
Sophia

* * * * *

Anna

Last night I had this dream:

> *I dreamed I stepped out of my body and walked into our old home in the red rocks and became someone else. I was asking, is this real? Am I dreaming? No, it must not be real because I can walk through the walls. I thought, now I can make new choices. I stood in an empty room and yelled at the top of my lungs, "Who Am I? I am not bad!"*
> *I couldn't tell who I was.*

I had trouble telling Perry about this dream. I kept coughing and crying. I feel so stuck in my patterns — how I think; how I act; what I do or don't do; am I good or am I bad?   I've been seeing this pattern in myself for a while now, but I haven't been able to stop it. However much I might decide I want to change, my mind just comes up with the same old judgments.

Sophia has written about her complex, her unique pattern of self-defeating thoughts and emotions. This is my complex: everything is good or bad. Now that I am catching myself at this game, I am stunned to see it everywhere. I do it with the weather; I do it when I listen to the news; and I pass some form of judgment on everyone I meet. I'm always deciding if their actions are good or bad, if they should or shouldn't have done something or said something. I do it with everything!

I can see how my whole life would change if I could just get over my complex of judging everything! This way of thinking is familiar and comfortable like a well-worn pair of shoes. But those shoes don't walk me in the direction I want to go. And I have learned this at least from Sophia: there's no going backwards!

When the thought drifts through my head that I can't be happy living in this complex anymore, it comes with a touch of sadness. This pattern is deeply embedded. I have been avoiding life, snug and secure in my complex of judgment.

It's complicated and overwhelming. I have a pain behind my heart. I am more than my judgments; this is *not* the whole of who I am. Perry pointed out the irony to me: I feel bad about myself because I can't get over feeling bad about myself.

I'm getting ready for bed, not really thinking about anything in particular, when this thought drops into my head: When I was telling Perry about my dream, did I say, "I walked into our old home in the red rocks..."? But I never lived in that house. Sophia did.

* * * * *

January 4, 2003

Today is Raven's birthday. I woke up singing *Om Tara Tu Tara Tura Soha*! I miss her more than I can say. I still feel her presence. It's like she is hovering around me, light and free, unencumbered, encouraging me to be present and creative in every moment.

January 5, 2003

It's like an orgasm — you get to those few moments before it carries you away, and you feel the longing and all that tremendous pleasure with a knowing the best is yet to come. It's a feeling of opening, an expansion, a communion. Something bigger than this pleasure is awaiting! That is how I felt when my heart was opening. The day before I said, "How can it get any better?" I feel so much gratitude and love for life! Even in my pain, I can find the joy. I want to share this with everyone!

* * * * *

Dear Anna,

Now you know me better than anyone ever has. You have invested a lot of time reading my most intimate thoughts. You see how often I have failed, how quickly I bounce from joy and gratitude to failure and self-centered regret, and you are finding out how many times in my life I have failed to live up to my own ideals.

In spite of all my failures, this is the gift I have been given: In every moment, whether in despair or ecstasy, I have had a driving desire to do good in the world. I have pleaded with the power of my innate divinity, "Please, please, please help me to get out of my own way! Please don't let my self-limiting beliefs prevent me from being of benefit in the world! There is so much pain and suffering, and I have been so blessed. Please, I implore all that I am and all that gives me life, make it clear how I can help this world of precious beings."

My dear friend Mitch was an incredible doctor and a very wise man. He said, "Take everything that happens into the rhythm of your heart. Let the rhythm of the heart lead everything. If you are suffering, do something beneficial with it."

Raven said, "See and experience each moment with wonder and newness. Everything is divine. Always step into the mystery of perfection perfecting. Remember you are always held in the womb of the Great Mother."

One of the things I took with me from my chiropractic energy healing experience was, "If you are in hell, keep going; don't stop. Choose to do something that helps you transform and evolve into your soul's purpose."

Rinsho, one of my Vipassana meditation teachers, said, "The purpose of learning mindfulness meditation is to learn how to have a complete moment when all the senses are conscious and you are aware of all of your experiences at once. Then you will know the divinity of life."

Tubten Rinpoche says, "Use the energy of the emotions that are out of control, and give them something beneficial to do. Do some prayer, mantra,

*and offerings or practice to transform the energy and
to benefit others. Bring the energy to your heart where
the Deity resides."*

*I hope you are coming to understand why these
teachings are so important to me — why I have
structured my whole life around learning these lessons
and living up to these ideals. Are you beginning to
understand why I am the person I am?*

*Love is the greatest gift I can give. Everything pales
in the brilliance of love. When I can give nothing else, I
can give love.*
Love,
Sophia

* * * * *

Grandmother Spirit

You can live in the delusion of your thoughts, always trying to be acceptable to others, always striving to be in control. Or you can live each moment, open and creative, experiencing life unfolding in its mysterious way and being a part of the mystery. If you are lost in the maze of your own thinking, you will constantly be projecting your thinking and all its expectations onto the world. You are the creator of your life. How you perceive the world around you creates the world you live in and shapes the life you live.

One day when I was feeling tired and overwhelmed, I looked at a large water bottle I needed to refill. It felt like a monumental task — like it was more than I could do. I was tired. The bottle was going to be heavy. I was already overwhelmed with things to do.

Then I stopped and focused on my heart. I felt its rhythm and found my connection to my core and to the creative forces inside and all around me. I turned and looked at the bottle, and it was just a bottle. The Buddhists refer to "the bottle just being a bottle" as its emptiness. It has no inherent reality beyond the reality we give it.

We fortify our suffering when we feed our limiting patterns. We often do this by using every possible negative interpretation of circumstance to justify our limiting thoughts and perceptions. To see things as they are without any projection allows for life to unfold before us in its own magical way, uncolored by patterns of thought and our expectations. Seeing yourself in this way, with acceptance and curiosity, is the heart of compassion.

Chapter Twelve

February 19, 2003

I just watched the movie, *The Notebook*. I can only imagine the pain of losing a partner to Alzheimer's. But there was also the sweetness of commitment and deep love that stands strong no matter the circumstances. I feel sad for those who are living the nightmare of dementia, and I'm lonely living my life without a partner. I am so alive to love! I want to love and be loved, to feel tenderness and genuine appreciation and concern for another person. I am longing to connect with someone at the level of my soul. But intimacy of that kind is not part of my life right now.

February 23, 2003

I have created a very compressed and managed life again. I find myself in the grip of the same old feelings, listening to the same old voice. I want out of this!

As Nick said, all I do is avoid the void. But how can I undo what I've created? What if I let it all go? What if I walk away from my work and my activities and everything I'm doing? How will I support myself?

It really isn't any different than when I went non-stop to retreat after retreat saying, *this is good for me*. This comfortable, old pattern says there can be no empty space or I will die. Yet I am dying in this constrained and managed life! It is a catch-22. I have been fighting the river, this old, familiar river. My health is more important than anything. I almost died once from living with this much compression, and I am not going to do it again!

I feel an old energy pattern laughing at me as I write this, as if it has more power than my intention. I know this has been true in the past; I will not let it be true going forward. I see its distortions. I understand its motivation. I reject its premise.

I will not be a victim to the patterns of my past. I am stronger now. I will make a different choice.

April 5, 2003

Thirty years ago I met Raven at The Center for Divine Union and had my profound dream about the *Raja Yoga* book. This morning I had this dream:

I am in a government building with the political leaders, and I am invited into their inner chambers. My partner is not accepted. He feels threatened and sneaks out. I feel okay and stay. They accept me, it seems, but there is some unrest. They ask me to leave the room for a few minutes. One of the men comes out to talk with me. He is very pleasant and supportive of me, but I am not sure of his motives. When he leaves, I find my sacred bells have been taken. I see him and yell at him that they were taken and I want them back right now! He offers me something to replace them, two carved wooden figures made in Bali. There is a Garuda and a Saraswati. I am to pick one. I take Saraswati, of course. I wait in the lobby for my partner, hoping he will return. He does come, and I quickly run to put all my things in the car and tell him about how Saraswati was caught on the furniture.

In 1973, Raven gave me the spiritual name Keertana. It means, A Song in Praise. Now Saraswati comes to me. She is the goddess of wisdom, speech, and music; the daughter of Brahma; the female half of creation; and the feminine energy of the universe.

Perry says the Gods are always looking for form — the form of Saraswati; the form of music; the form of the vibrations on the air that carry the music. My individual self, my ego, has a conscious relationship with the Divine; my ego itself is divine. I am God-Goddess struck. I am in the world responding to the touch of the Divine. I am Keertana. I am Saraswati. We both were created from love, and we both stand in love. I am the song. I decide whether to sing the song of praise.

I can feel the winds of change lifting and carrying me out of the frustrations of managing my life and into a future I have already created for myself. It's exciting! I see and feel where I am heading. Right now it's a vision; in time I will grow into it, and as I do, it will take its physical form.

Of course, there is always the other side of this joyful

anticipation. It's frightening and unnerving, the uncertainties creating a windstorm, blowing me up into the sky and back down to Earth with a crash.

April 10, 2003

I had this dream last night:

I'm walking out my front door, and I stop in my tracks because what is ahead of me is different than what I expected. As I look back at the house I feel it tugging at me, pulling me back. But I have to keep going even though this familiar, comfortable place is pulling at me.

April 12, 2003

Change is quaking the foundations of my life, rattling up in the rafters. My old self has been suspended, stopped, put on hold. My new self has been created, but I have not yet walked into it. Everything feels disjointed. Everything is falling apart. I need to disentangle myself from everything and take some space to find my own rhythm. Things feel dry. I don't seem to fit anywhere.

September 17, 2003

Raven use to say the weeks leading up to your birthday are a time of potential, questioning, and rediscovery. Well, it sure is intense this time. I'm wondering what I will be doing for the next third of my life. Even more disconcerting is the ever-present question of whether I have lived the last 60 years in alignment with my soul.

The healing center where I have been working with Mitch is closing. He had emergency surgery and cannot work for at least three months. There is no way to predict if or when we might be able to open again.

I've been struggling to create a thriving healing practice for years now. Without a doubt, it's time to change my approach. I don't have a clue what that might look like, but I'm listening for new inspiration.

September 30, 2003

I went to Wolf Creek and had a wonderful day. I cried with delight at the frogs, the water, the rocks, and the butterflies. I cried with sadness for missing the Center and living in nature. I cried for Raven and all the gifts she gave me. I cried for Jahi and all he went through with me.

A few days ago he told me he had loved me very much when we were first together, but his deeply held patterns prevented him from trusting, so he turned away, abandoning me even while he was feeling abandoned.

October 3, 2003

My birthday is almost here, and I have been feeling something shifting in me. Yesterday I was on my way to the Temple to receive the Vajrakilaya Empowerment, a ritual and practice that helps remove all obstacles in the way of recognizing your pure nature. Suddenly, my confusion turned to clarity. I saw my future: I'm going on a pilgrimage, a migration, a vision quest.

This clarity has released a burst of energy and renewed inspiration! My issues around money just melted away. I'm going to take two months off to deepen into the truth of my nature, and I will let the truth inform me as to what I will do with my gifts. I don't know where I will go, but I'm telling everyone I will be gone by the first of December.

October 31, 2003

Today is my birthday. This morning I looked out the kitchen window and was inspired to write a poem reflecting on how these 60-year-old eyes see differently.

> **It's My Time**
> I awake beneath a turbulent sky
> Sweeping clouds and shifting light
> The rainbow colors shine, ignite
> I stand between the past and future
> With joy I laugh, with sorrow I cry
> Gratitude in my heart
> Grief for dreams undone
> Free to give my gifts
> Loving more! Loving more!
> It's my turn; it's my time.
> These sixty-year-old eyes see differently.

Natalie had a birthday party for me tonight, and she had arranged a big surprise for me: Mom and Dad and Serena came from Albuquerque! I spoke to them today, and they said they were out shopping. They really surprised me. When they walked through the door, I broke down in joyful tears. I felt so blessed. Mom brought my favorite dessert. I read my poem to everyone. I am alive in my soulfulness.

November 1, 2003

Living off of my savings is beginning to feel as if I'm digging a hole and not growing flowers. I want to flourish in my work. I know what gifts I have to give to the world. The question is: How do I bring them into the world in an effective way? How can I serve humanity?

I have been working with a coach to focus on my purpose and direction, and it's been helpful to see where my energy has been going. I have started to write a business and marketing plan for my healing practice.

However, something is calling me to step back out of my everyday life and go north. I want to dive into my inner world and my connection to nature. I can't see how I can do this with the responsibilities of everyday life. Besides, it's winter and cold up there.

November 2, 2003

I had this dream:

I enter a ceremonial area, and I go to the elder

grandmother who is leading the ceremony. I ask her what I will be wearing for the ceremony. She stares into my eyes for a long moment. Then she says, "You will be wearing the clothes of the white wolf."

I'm deeply affected by this dream. To wear the fur of the white wolf is to embody the medicine of the wolf.

November 5, 2003

I have been re-reading *Women Who Run with the Wolves* by Clarissa Pinkola Estes. This book touched me to the core when I was healing from my illness. Reading the stories again of the wild- woman archetype, I can feel myself reconnecting to my internal wild nature. I feel nourished by the energy I'm invoking. I still don't know how this will play out. I don't have a clear vision of the future. But I have a clear and certain belief it's out there for me, and I'm going to go out and find it!

November 7, 2003

Ideas are erupting inside me! I've been reading about the Ancient Native people and their migrations. What if I retrace the steps I took on my path of evolution and spiritual growth? What if I go to the places that changed me? What if I create a traveling ritual in honor of all the teachers who have facilitated my process? It will be a mandala I create both internally and externally. I will do an art project along each leg of the journey. Wow, I'm on fire! The creative thoughts and deep appreciation for all my teachers has begun this journey.

I am going to do this on my own. I will have no set plans. I will allow nature to unfold before me.

November 9, 2003

I am considering how cold it is up north and the fact that my astrocartography says Hawaii is where I will flourish and be honored for who I am. Should I go to Hawaii? I turned to the Soul Whisperer and sat in silence with her and the fire. She is my counsel and I trust her. When it was time, I asked, where should I go? I saw her put on a white fur wrap. This doesn't look like Hawaii to me! I check the Internet for the weather in Hawaii; it's 75 degrees. I look at Utah and Colorado; its 12 to 34 degrees. It's really cold up north. I turn to the Soul Whisperer again. This time she puts the white fur wrap on me.

I know I will be going north. I'm going to be at Perry's in Moab from December 1st through the 6th for a Sacred Fire and Dream retreat at his magical mountain home. In the cold and the snow, this will be a great place to begin my pilgrimage.

I still don't know where I will go when I leave there, but I know I will feel grounded and empowered. Still, the need to know where I will go is hanging over me.

* * * * *

Dear Anna,

Like you, I have just read the story of 45 years of my life. I see how many times the fire consumed me, and I recognize that over and over again I heard my soul calling to me. There were times when I could find and manifest wisdom and equanimity. There were other times when I just burned in the fires of my emotions and my physical pain. Only later, after the fires had burned down, could I pick through the ashes and find the undamaged, indestructible fragments of truth and wisdom.

I offer up these experiences in the hope that, as you read about my life, my troubles and my triumphs will shine a beam of hope on your uncertainties. Faced with a crisis, you can always choose to connect to a larger truth, a more profound reality. There is always a doorway, a way to move forward, and if you choose to pass through, you will be standing at the threshold of eternity, the endless expanse of infinite possibility stretching out before you.

I love you,

Sophia

* * * * *

November 15, 2003

It is Soyal Season, and I have set up the Soyal Ceremony altar in my home. Each article on the altar invokes memories of prior ceremonies, and the meaning behind each object becomes alive in me. It feels so good to place the Kachina Mudhead in the middle of the corn which is laid out in the four directions on the red sand from the Escalante, and to have the ladder up with a fresh evergreen twig on the fourth rung to signify the hope for the fifth world. This ceremony will send me off on my journey. This altar is my anchor, my axis mundi; it supports me as I live in my truth. Each night I make a paho (a prayer stick) and place it in the sand. My prayers are for the unfolding of my divine nature. May it bring forth my gifts to the world.

November 29, 2003

Tomorrow I leave for Moab. I've decided I will go to Hawaii after the retreat. Pele is calling to me! I've packed clothes for Moab, Hawaii, and Albuquerque for Christmas. I'll drive my car to Salt Lake City and leave the bags for the rest of the journey there. My plane for Hawaii leaves the morning after I return from Moab. Once I make a decision, I move fast.

November 30, 2003

My migration has begun! I am at Perry and Marcela's home and sanctuary. I feel so at home here! It's cold and snowy, and I'm filled with anticipation. There is a wonderful group gathered here for this retreat, beautiful souls ready to do some deep exploration and healing.

Marcela brings back Huichol art from a village in Mexico, which she sells in the US to support the village. This morning she showed me a strong-grounded figure of a woman, beaded in the traditional ways of the Huichol. When I picked her up and turned her over, I found the words, "Grandmother Growth." My heart skipped a beat. She will come with me along with the yarn art serpent and orb that was revealed to me in my vision quest.

Nestled in the red rocks and pine trees, we begin our sacred journey with dreams, feathers, and fire.

December 1, 2003

When I wake up here, the crisp air makes me feel alive! In the morning I go out into the snow to gather wood for the fire. At night the star-lit sky ignites my soul. With this state of wonder comes the clarity that I must and will live in the country again.

I'm not going to Hawaii. I'm listening to my soul and not my logic. I'm going to Utah, Colorado, and Wyoming. I'm going north.

December 2, 2003

Each day reveals more of my spirit and psyche. We are delving into the mysteries of life. This is hard. I'm unraveled, confused, broken, and vulnerable. The rituals and the fire are working me and melting down my defenses so I can see my true self. It's like digging into the dark, shadowy parts of myself — parts I have kept hidden in order to protect myself. I feel ugly. When I shared this feeling, Perry pointed out that in stories, fairy tales, and myths, ugly is always inherent in transformation. This gives me some hope and comfort.

December 6, 2003

After the retreat I was window-shopping in Moab when I saw a beautifully-made shamanic figure of a deer. I could tell that the person who made this figure is connected to the ways of nature. We went into the crowded little shop and wandered around looking. I came around a corner and found myself face to face with the figure of a wolf wrapped in a white blanket. I was stunned by it and excited. I knew it had to come home with me; it's been in my dreams and in the Soul Whisperer's teachings.

I want a home where I can hang my deer antlers and skulls on the walls, a place where I won't need to worry about scratches on the floor. I need to get myself to a more rustic place, more connected to the earthy aspects of life. Maybe I'll find a cabin to move into.

December 7, 2003

I cancelled my Hawaii flight with no problems. I made a few phone calls and found a little cabin in Escalante. It has a full kitchen and a wood-burning stove. It sounds perfect.

December 18, 2003

I had this dream:

I am running to catch an airplane with a baby in my arms, and they shut the door on me and say I have to wait for the next plane. I say, "I have a baby!" It didn't matter. I was told to wait.

When I spoke with Perry today he helped me understand that there are two themes here. First, this was the time I would have been leaving for Hawaii, and it was clear not to go. The other message was to wait. This one puzzles me because it feels so right to go to Escalante.

I am getting very clear messages. It's a time for me to disconnect from the busy life I have been leading, to cultivate my relationship to my instinctual nature. In the tradition of the Hopi, this is the time of Soyal and the Gathering of the Spruce, a time for ceremony, a time of solitude and silence, a time to live in harmony with nature.

Kopavi is the term used by the Hopi to refer to the place on the crown of your head that is an opening, a conduit for clear perception of the Divine. I am listening from this divine place, and the ancestors are talking to me. I am going to the Escalante. I am going to reconnect to my roots. The Escalante is where I first encountered the power of the land and the visions of the past and future.

January 3, 2004

I'm on my way! I packed my computer so I can write. I have my wolf and other significant altar pieces to support my journey. The drive is wondrous! Even in the dark I can feel the change in energy as I drive through the Utah mountain passes. The morning light reveals the majestic rock formations against a vast blue sky. When I drive into the Grand Staircase Escalante, I feel like I have come home. Mother Earth in all her splendor is holding me in her womb.

January 4, 2004

I stopped at the cabin in Escalante to check in before I headed out to the river. The owners are as charming as the cabin. They have put up a Christmas tree and decorated the cabin with ornaments. Of course the magic is here — on the mantel is a white wolf kachina.

There are elk, deer, and moose figures, a mountain lion skin on the wall, and elk antlers upstairs in the loft. Above the door is a painted cow skull with feathers hanging from it. All these pieces carry the energy and spirit of the animals, and I am blessed by their presence. Their energy medicine is teaching me how to be present to every thing that shows up in my life to support me on my journey. The cabin is perfect. It is exactly what I was hoping it would be. I will enjoy my time here. But right now, the river is calling me.

Today is January 4th, Raven's birthday. I have come

here to carry her remaining ashes to the Escalante River. It is Soyal Season, and this is my gift of thanksgiving.

January 5, 2004

It's a fifteen-mile trip to the river, and most of the way out there I cried with sheer joy and gratitude. My eyes could not get enough of the multi-colored canyons and the deep blue sky stretching as far as I could see.

My heart was beating fast; I was so happy to be there! The sound of the water rushing by stirred up memories of previous times in this canyon. When I reached the edge of the river, the banks were covered in ice. I found the place where the water was moving quickly. This felt like the right place. I stood quietly as prayer began to emerge from the silence. I made cornmeal offerings to all the directions. Kneeling on the damp earth covered in leaves, I held Raven's ashes to my heart. Then with great joy and appreciation, I gave her ashes to the river, and I heard the ancient ones sing, "*She wah nee la la la sha hee tee ya.*" I joined them and sang with every cell of my body. Then I stood in silence until I felt the call to move on. On the way back to the cabin, I felt solemn and joyful. In the sky in front of me, I saw Raven's face glowing, a big smile of joy. All is well.

January 6, 2004

For a long time I had known I needed a drum. I had been searching but hadn't found the right one — the one I resonate with. Yesterday, after scattering Raven's ashes in the river, I was on my way back from the canyon, and I saw a sign just at the edge of town that said Drums. In this land, where the heartbeat of Mother Earth spoke to me and where I learned the ways of the native people, this is where I found my drum. I had been told to look for a drum made with elk or deer hide, but my drum is made of buffalo hide. I can feel the power and steadfastness of the buffalo spirit in the drum. I met the man who made the drum, and it felt right.

When I returned to the cabin, I lit a fire and sat in the rocking chair. Right above me on the mantel was the white wolf kachina glowing in the firelight. I picked up the drum and began to play. I sang songs that came from some bone-deep place inside me. I rocked and rocked. I sang. I drummed. I started to know my new drum, and it started to know me. Together we created some magic in the cabin. I thought about the story of "The Three Golden Hairs."

* * * * *

Grandmother Spirit

The story of the "Three Golden Hairs" is from *Women Who Run With the Wolves* by Clarissa Pinkola Estes. It tells of an old man trying to find his way through the deepest, darkest night in the forest. He is very old with yellow teeth and yellow curved fingernails. He is hunched and furrowed. Every step is painful as his feet are on fire, and his joints screech like the owls. He sees a light coming from a cabin in the distance, and with the last of his strength, he struggles to the door. His lamp goes out just as he opens the door. He is so exhausted he collapses onto the floor.

The old woman inside gathers him into her arms and takes him to her rocking chair in front of a roaring fire. She rocks him through the night singing, "There, there. There, there. There, there."

The old man grows younger and younger. He is a man, then a youth, then a child. His hair turns from white to grey to light brown to golden blond. Just before dawn the old woman plucks three golden hairs from his head, and as she throws each one to the ground, it sings a tone, like a bell. The child crawls from her lap and runs to the door where he stops and looks back at her with a dazzling smile. Then he turns and flies up into the sky to become the brilliant morning sun.

This story is about the need to stop and get focused when we are in the dark night of the soul and our creative nature has become old and withered. When the old way of doing things has robbed us of our energy, it is not a time to do more, but a time to sit quietly, to heal, to restore our energies, to create the space from which new ideas and instinctual knowing can arise.

In my long life I have had trouble honoring the concept that taking time to rest is not a luxury, it is a necessity. When I feel overwhelmed, I need to stop; I need to be still and create the space for something new to arise. When the light in my lantern goes out, I know it's time for change, time for rest, rocking, drumming, getting my energy back. The hair thrown to the floor is the symbol of letting go of old ideas, and the sound they make awakens me to resonate once more with a lightness of spirit, a new way of being, a new story.

Chapter Thirteen

A Buddhist Prayer of Forgiveness

*If I have harmed anyone in any way either knowingly
or unknowingly through my own confusions,
I ask their forgiveness.*

*If anyone has harmed me in any way either knowingly
or unknowingly through their own confusions,
I forgive them.*

*And if there is a situation I am not yet ready to forgive,
I forgive myself for that.*

*For all the ways I harm myself, negate, doubt, belittle
or judge myself, for the ways I am unkind to myself
through my own confusions, I forgive myself.*

* * * * *

Grandmother Spirit

Expect the unexpected! No matter how much we plan, organize, intend, or pray, no matter how confident we are in our power to co-create our lives, everything can be turned upside down in an instant — a sudden death, your spouse has a stroke, you or someone close to you receives a cancer diagnosis. Your home may be destroyed by fire or flood. You may be betrayed by someone you love. In one moment you may make a choice that reverberates down the years of your life, echoing unintended and unforeseen consequences.

Each of us is a point of consciousness in a complex physical world. Hidden beneath this point of consciousness is a vast, complicated network of relationships, responses and reactions, memories and the residual effects of forgotten experiences.

Our life experiences and our interpretations of them weave themselves into our very psyches. Our DNA is a written record of our ancestors' lives — their joys and loves, their rage and pain. We add our own experiences to the record and pass it on to our children. We are pushed and pulled by impulses that come from a place so deep inside of us that, until we recognize they are there and make it a practice to observe them, will manifest in our lives over and over again, masquerading as truth and reality.

* * * * *

Dear Anna,

My pilgrimage was full of beauty. I renewed my deep connection with nature. I walked many miles through forest and canyon and desert and mountain. And I fulfilled my intention to create a mandala in gratitude for each of my teachers.

While walking in nature, I would feel a resonant energy specific to one of my teachers. There I stopped and created an altar, made offerings, and waited for the inspiration to speak the words of wisdom he or she had helped me to see, to learn, to understand, and to live.

Please take this letter and my healing stone, go sit in your special place in nature where you can be held by the energies of all that is and all that was, and I will share my pilgrimage with you.

These are the words that came to me from each of my teachers. May the blessings of my teachers fill your heart. May you experience the love and generosity they have given to me.

Standing in the Escalante River, I sang of Raven's blessings. When the Raja Yoga book appeared in my dream world many years ago, the night before I met Raven, it revealed a connection beyond time and space. From that moment forward, the fire of Great Spirit has continued to talk to me, often through Raven, my first teacher. From her I learned to feel each moment as a spark of new creation emerging from the mystery. Raven taught me how to trust my direct experience and to live in the cycles of life. She mirrored for me how to live in balance, how the Divine Feminine and the Divine Masculine integrate and create wholeness. For thirty years, she reminded me to be present in every moment.

In the high mountains of Colorado, deep in an aspen forest, I honored Khempo for his transmission of the profound nature of a precious human life. His pithy statement, "It sounds like self-importance to me," shocked me out of a life-long pattern of seeing myself as a "good girl," always doing things the "right way."

The desert energies were alive for Rinsho. I created an altar to him in Capitol Reef. His mindfulness techniques taught me to take my activated thoughts and feelings and love them to death. This was a radical concept for me! He said there are only three ways to experience life: thoughts, images, and the feeling sense. He taught me to divide and conquer by observing each way of experiencing life individually and watch their power diminish. He taught about what he called a "complete moment," when all three — thoughts, images and felt senses — are fully present and nothing is left unexperienced. When the moment is complete, there will be no lingering stress, trauma, or unresolved desire. His teachings are still emerging in me, and the practices he taught me are a part of my daily life.

Tubten Rinpoche was honored on the high plateau of Arizona where the winds carry his loving kindness and I feel connected to his vast mind stream, the continuum of all our experiences. I had seen his heart open as he guided me to the Buddha through the linage of countless ancient teachers. New realms of existence were revealed to me. When I was ill and he heard my mantra, I stopped having any lingering doubts that energies and consciousness are not bound by time and space.

I had a special ceremony in Page, Arizona, to honor my dear friends and extraordinary healers Mitch, Nick, and Natalie for their generosity of heart, wisdom, and persistence during my spiritual-healing crisis. I found a place of silence and stillness to honor the way they held space and brought me back to my stillness during my attacks.

My BioCranio training with Chad was an intimate transmission, bringing with it deep compassion for those whose prenatal traumas are played out for the rest of their lives. There is a mantra I love: Knowing what I know, how can I judge anyone? I honored Chad in the redwood forest.

I made Perry's altar by the sea. His dedication to service, his devotion to his work and to his clients, his skill and compassion are as deep as the vast ocean. He helped me to understand on a deeper level the power of ritual and prayer. With skill and *sensitivity, he encourages conscious awakening through the understanding of the dream world. From the oceanic depths of my psyche, he helped me to haul up my pain, my sorrow, and my shame. He guided me back to the safe shores of acceptance and forgiveness.*

Anna, continue to trust Perry as he guides you to trust yourself. You are opening up to a deeper sense of who you are, and now your freedom is within reach; it's only waiting for you to surrender.
I Love You More,
Sophia

* * * * *

Anna

I have been deeply affected by Sophia's last letter. I have an ache in my chest — a longing for the freedom she writes about, a knowing that it is close, but I still don't have a clue what it actually means or what I'm supposed to do next.

I'm gazing out Perry's office window, and I'm telling him about the letter. I read the last paragraph aloud to him, and when I get to the part where Sophia writes, "it's only waiting for you to surrender," I start to cry — great sobs from somewhere deep, deep inside. Perry hands me a box of tissues and patiently waits. Finally, I have no more tears.

I don't even know why I was crying, but it feels good to let it all out.

Perry gets up and comes to stand next to me at the window. Side by side we gaze out over fields and forests to the mountains in the distance. "Anna, how do you feel about surrendering?"

"Surrendering to what?" I know myself well enough to know there are many things I'm not about to surrender to. "Surrendering sounds to me like giving up, giving in to some big bully."

"That's the thing," he said. "You get to choose who or what you surrender to. I don't think Sophia is asking you to surrender to something that will harm you. I think she is wanting you to surrender to the wholeness of who you are. She wants you to enjoy your life to the fullest, to live fulfilled and complete within yourself."

"Perry, I still don't know how to do that. I don't even know if I have made any progress at all. Sometimes I feel like I'm just as confused and stuck as I was the first time I saw you."

There's a spider on the windowsill. Perry lets it crawl onto his hand. Then he opens the window and allows it to lower itself onto the shrubbery below. "Do you always feel that way?"

"No, sometimes I feel like I'm really different. I don't get as angry as I used to. I'm not as judgmental. I'm more open to learning about new things. When I read Sophia's letter about her teachers, I could really appreciate the gifts they've given her, and I feel like they have touched me too — that's different. Also, I understand Sophia so much better than I used to."

Perry smiles. "That sounds like progress to me."

When I get home, I sleep for hours.

* * * * *

April 9, 2004

I had this magical dream:

I saw a man reach out into the sky and touch a star that had a halo of energy. When he did this he was engulfed in the energy circle and was transported somewhere else. Later I was talking with friends, and I knew something had to change. I realized I needed to move. The story we were all part of was being rewritten and one of the main characters died. Then we saw the star with a halo of energy, and one of us reached out for it knowing it would take us. Somehow we knew we were to be transported to Wyoming. As the energy circle started to surround us, I said, "Quick! All who are coming, get over here!" Then I said, "This is how they have rewritten the story so this person is out of our lives and we will be able to start a new life in Wyoming with a new story and without any conflicting problems."

When I told Perry about the dream, the questions he asked took me into deep reflection. He asked what conflict will go away if I move, and why Wyoming? He asked how reaching into the light of the spirit world in the sky can change my life, and what is being rewritten? I really need to sit with all of this for a while.

May 3, 2004

I want to be in relationship with someone again. I want someone to love. All the inner reflection and transformation has brought me to a new place. I really want a man in my life. I have been told to try the dating groups online. How weird to look for someone to date on a computer! This idea really seems odd, but I'm going to give it a try.

* * * * *

Dear Anna,

In June of 2004, after six years of focusing on myself and my healing, I started to date. I met a man who lived in Wyoming, and I liked him. I even felt there was a possibility for a lasting relationship. I visited him and fell in love with Wyoming! For a while I had been feeling a wanderlust, and it was clear to me it was time to move on, time to stretch out into something new.

Anna, remember back in my April journal entry where I wrote about a dream Perry asked me so many questions about? In the dream, when I reached into the spirit world in the sky, I was transported to Wyoming. It said it was time for my life to be re-written. As much as I trust my dreams, it still amazes me when things like that happen. This life is filled with mysterious and profound moments.

My farewell party was bittersweet. More than 80 people came to celebrate our friendships and to say goodbye. With each hug my heart cracked open, overflowing with love and gratitude for all the memories we shared and a sweet, sad knowing this was the end of an era. Leaving all my friends and my home of 30 years stirred up a jumble of emotions.

I packed up my house and moved to Jackson Hole, Wyoming. My relationship with the man I met online opened me up to my sexuality again. I felt alive and free, full of passion and desire. I had been wondering if it had vanished! The relationship didn't last, but my love for Wyoming did! I reveled in the natural beauty that surrounded me —forests and rivers, mountains, canyons and lakes.

I bought a house. It was perfect for me. It overlooked two lakes and had a gorgeous view of the Grand Tetons. My friend, Bridget, said the lakes were two mirrors reflecting the full truth of my life. She called me the Lady of the Lakes, as referred to in the book, The Mists of Avalon. In the book, the Lady of the Lake is the one who has the power to separate the mists to reveal Avalon where women were taught the ways of the Divine Feminine. Big footsteps to walk in!

As you will read in the journals, the next two years were a flurry of productivity and joy. I met many like-

minded friends. I remodeled my home. I established
a healing practice and turned my home into my new
retreat center. I hosted and led retreats for women.
I wrote and created podcasts of my work. I created
healing sprays of essential oils and flower essences.
 I dug out a fire pit and performed ceremony and
blessed my essences with the moon and the stars, the
sun and the fire. I did all of this on my own, and I was
good at it. I loved my house. I loved Wyoming. Even
after eight feet of snow the first winter, I knew I had
landed where I was supposed to be, and I believed I
would spend the rest of my life there.
I love you,
Sophia

* * * * *

September 18, 2005

I have spent the last three days with the Dalai Lama in Tucson. There are no words to convey the refined energy that filled the air. He is so simple, so humble, so wise. His beautiful character has left its mark on me. I am carrying his teachings in my heart, bathing in his joy and grace.

May 17, 2006

It's just after Mother's Day, and I'm on a plane from Albuquerque back to Wyoming. I'm staring out the window, sadness creeping over me. Last night Mom and I were sitting together, talking about the things that need to be done around her house. And then Mom, the invincible one, broke down, "I can't do it anymore!" I had never heard my mom say anything like this before in my entire life. Then she started crying — something I had only seen twice before in my life. My 85-year-old Mom, who always took care of everyone and everything, is no longer able to keep up with it all. I know what this means for me, even as I try to not think the thought. I need to move back to Albuquerque.

May 18, 2006

As soon as my feet touched the ground in Wyoming, the magnitude of what I will be giving up hit me hard and fast, right off the plane. When I got home I wandered out into the backyard and felt the heart and silence of the land. I just stood out there and cried for all I had built here and all I would now be leaving behind. I could feel in my bones how hard this was going to be. And how was I, only now feeling healthy again, going to deal with the energy and toxicity of Albuquerque? I just stood there until I had cried myself out. For a very long time, I listened to the silence. I listened for the calling of the mists through the evergreen trees. Is this the right thing for me to do? I listened to the stillness and silence until I felt a calm knowing inside. Yes. My mother needs me.

I went inside to call Sebastian to tell him what I had

decided. He understood immediately. When I told him I was afraid of how the toxic environment might affect my health, he said he would help find me a place to rent in the mountains, maybe up around Tijeras. A place up there would put me within easy driving distance to Mom and Dad. I loved going to Tijeras as a child because it was so green and there were deer and rocks to climb.

June 5, 2006

I am kicking and screaming inside, even as I accept I have to make this move. I'm drowning in a sea of boxes, packing up what I will take and selling all the extra things I bought for the women's retreats — bedding, dishes, towels, beds, dressers — so much stuff. Will I be able to re-create all I built here? I hope someday, in the future, I will find my way back to my life in Jackson Hole.

October 15, 2006

I am in my little cabin just 20 minutes up above the Albuquerque basin in Tijeras. When I drive down the hill to work or to be with Mom and Dad, I can see the city sprawl out in all directions. It is massive and complex and filled with almost a million people, each with their own demons and fears, their unique dreams and joys. It's overwhelming. I miss Wyoming. Being in and around Albuquerque is difficult — so much pollution, so much driving. I travel to different ends of town to do my healing work.

I have connected with some old friends from our early days at The Center for Divine Union. It's wonderful! Also, I am making some new friends who are introducing me to new ways of looking at the world. They are opening my eyes to new ways to be in relationships too!

While I was in Wyoming, Serena had been doing more than I had realized to take care of Mom and Dad. Now that I'm closer, I do what I can to take care of Mom and to make things easier on Serena. Mom isn't doing well. We are having her examined to see if she has Alzheimer's. She's also in a lot of pain.

November 4, 2008

History was made today! Barack Obama is the first black man to be elected President of the United States. I am beyond happy. Someone with heart and consciousness will be leading the government, and I feel optimistic. This is a huge shift for our country, and I am grateful and excited.

I am feeling good today. Clear and strong. I still miss my beautiful house in Jackson Hole, but whether I am there or here, my commitment to awaken and live a soulful life is not dependent on circumstance or place.

* * * * *

Dear Anna,

Raven told me once that Mahatma Gandhi was able to look his assassin in the eye and say to him, "You are God" because Gandhi was "living his humanness." Raven told me Gandhi lived in the heart of truth to the extent that no one could move or sway him from that focal point. It was his midline, the pillar around which he oriented his life and his actions in the world. Gandhi was connected to his soul's purpose.

When I was blessed to have a personal conversation with Mother Teresa, I was stunned by the intense power radiating from that tiny woman. She would not be stopped in her quest to bring love to every being she touched. When I asked her what I could do to help, she said, "I don't need your help! Go home and do your part there. If each of us does our part where we live, we can make a difference. People in your country are so lonely." These words have lived on in my heart since 1979. Her love and compassion reached across the ocean, and she obviously understood what ails our country. She knew love would help. She understood her soul's purpose.

In the beginning of my process of awakening, each time I was blessed with an experience of grace — feeling free, feeling boundless, immersed in deep compassion — I foolishly believed this meant I was finished with that part of my healing. But as the years went by, I saw how I could be touched by grace in one moment only to find myself falling victim in the next moment to my old patterns of victimization and self-doubt, sliding once again down into the pit of my anger and hurt.

Each step I mastered on the path toward liberation felt like a gigantic accomplishment. But there are thousands of those steps, if not millions, each one lifting me a little higher, a little closer to my goal of personal enlightenment. I was so naive to think one or two experiences of the Divine would heal my wounds and reprogram all my emotional triggers.

Every time I am blessed with a moment of grace, every time I catch a fleeting understanding of my own divinity — it's the taste of that nectar that keeps me coming back. The memory of its sweetness is what compels me to keep learning, to keep exploring my life and my psyche and my place in the universe, in spite of how painful it sometimes can be.

This is my soul's purpose: to awaken and to share the process of my awakening so that others who may be struggling along this path can benefit from what I have learned.
I love you,
Sophia

* * * * *

July 18, 2009

I am getting ready to leave for my trip into the Escalante River canyon for another vision quest. I'm conflicted about leaving Mom. Serena assures me they will all be okay. Anyway, I am being compelled to listen to the voice that is calling me. I feel like something otherworldly is about to happen. I can't really explain it. I remember the Huichol yarn art I found years ago at Perry's with an orb and snake image. Looking at the image gave me a feeling of magic working inside me. Contemplating this upcoming vision quest gives me a similar feeling. It's like the pot is boiling and the magic is brewing.

August 3, 2009

My vision quest rocked my world. Something extraordinary has happened to me! There has been a voice from deep inside of me that has been crying out for a long, long time, but I couldn't hear it. During my vision quest my prayer was for the gifts of my soul to be revealed. I prayed to heal whatever has prevented me from fully embracing my true self.

Last night was the final night of my vision quest, and I had an amazing experience. Surrounded by the red rock canyon walls, listening to the water flowing down the river, I was sitting inside my sacred circle of rocks under a star-filled sky. I had just pleaded with the spirit world to reveal my true self. In the freedom of my solitude, I was crying out over and over again, "Who am I?"

Then I became still and was gazing through my tears into the night sky when an orb of light appeared. It moved toward me slowly like a plane in the distance moving directly at me. I listened for an airplane motor, but this was not an airplane. This was something much closer and silent. I wasn't afraid. Instead, I felt hypervigilant and very curious. I felt connected to my Soul Whisperer. When the light was almost upon me, I began having flashbacks of my life. Visions and instructions from the orb came pouring into my heart and soul with a brilliant clarity — a message that spoke to me in words, but the words were made out of light. Then the orb disappeared as quickly as it came.

The rest of the night went by in a timeless blur. I felt different. I still feel different, changed. Because now I know something about myself I could not see before; something that explains so many things about my life I could never figure out; something about Anna. It answers so many questions, but it also brings up a host of new ones.

This morning we all returned to the lodge. I did not share the essence of what I learned about myself. I am holding this close to my heart. But I did share what I had seen. One of the native elders was there. He looked at me in wonder and asked, "You say you saw the light of the orb?" I told him yes, I had seen it, and I asked him what it meant. Apparently, the native people have also seen the orbs, but are not sure what they are or what they mean.

The orbs are a mystery, even to the native elders. What does it mean that they came to me? The message they gave me has shaken me to the core. I was asking, who am I? And the answer was given to me, but I don't feel I can even write about it yet. It is still working inside me, sculpting a new sense of who I am.

August 5, 2009

This much I know: In order for me to live the truth of my soul, I need to get beyond some deeply held beliefs about myself and my life. This vision quest showed me Anna — who she is and how we are connected — the key to unlocking something inside myself that I have known is there but never understood. I need to get to know her and to find a way for us to understand each other— a way to get the two of us back on the same track. I'm going to make an appointment with Perry as soon as I get home. I'm counting on him to help me figure out a plan.

* * * * *

Anna

Okay, that's strange. I'm the key? That was the last entry in the last journal. There is one more note from Sophia.

This has been a long road, and it has led me back to . . .
what? Myself? I surprise myself by not feeling frustrated
by this somewhat abrupt ending.

Suddenly, I feel exhausted. I put the last journal down
on the coffee table, take the note with me and crawl into
bed. Just before I drift off to sleep, I read Sophia's final
note.

* * * * *

Dear Anna,

*Have you read the poem "The Journey" by Mary
Oliver? I have no words to express how much these
words mean to me. Do you feel it too?*

One day you finally knew
what you had to do . . .
Though the voices around you
kept shouting
their bad advice . . .
But you didn't stop.

*So, Anna, here is my question for you: Can you look
inside yourself and find the part of yourself that longs
to be free from the constraints of old patterns and bad
advice?*

*I know you are a good person. You always want
to do the right thing, and that is a worthy moral and
ethical goal. But not one of us on this Earth goes
through life without committing acts for which we*

need forgiveness. We all do things that are bad. And after doing them, if we are lucky, we bring together the pieces of what we have broken. We forgive ourselves, and we forgive others. We allow healing to happen, and we move on into life's next challenge.

I am ready to heal a deep wound. I am ready to bring together what broke apart many years ago. I am longing to reweave what has been unraveled. Anna, are you ready to do that too? Do you know what you have to do?
I love you!
Sophia

* * * * *

Grandmother Spirit

Sophia felt she had been given a great gift of understanding. And it is true she was given a gift. But it is more complex than just the giving of something desired by some unknown and unknowable entity. Sophia spent years on her spiritual practice. In a wild canyon in the Escalante, answers came to her. She had cultivated the environment, both inside and outside, that allowed her to see and to hear the guidance she was being given. Her thirst for knowledge and understanding took her far away from her normal environment in search of answers.

Do you want to open yourself to the wisdom of the ancient ones? You *can* cultivate your ability to receive wisdom and guidance. When you are able to become very still on the inside, the energies that you summon with your prayers and intentions can enter and inform you.

Learn to listen. Learn to be still! Let go of your thoughts. Do not identify with them. Allow them to flow through you and drift away. They have no reality. Emotions like guilt or shame or anger fill us up with their potent agitation. Don't fight them. They may be our demons, but they can become our allies. They show us the obstructions tripping us up. See if you can just let them be, let them drift through you.

It's a subtle practice. It takes patience, and it takes time. But if you try to bring this practice into your everyday life, if you "practice" it, then you will get better at it. Practice while you are grocery shopping, while you are washing dishes, or while you are dealing with a child's tantrum or an adolescent's intractability. Practice becoming still on the inside when the world around you is in chaos.

Then, when you take yourself away from your normal environment, when you go on retreat or on vision quest or into the woods or the desert, you will find amazing things will reveal themselves to you!

Chapter Fourteen

Grandmother Spirit

There is no shame without judgment. Shame emerges from deep inside of us when we believe, rightly or wrongly, we are being judged. But it will only come if we have bought into the value structure that deems us or our actions to be "bad." We don't feel ashamed of doing things we know to be right, even if others judge us and say we are "bad." So shame, you see, comes from inside of us. It comes from our personal beliefs.

Children are like little sponges, absorbing the values and judgments of the people and the culture around them. And if they dare to venture beyond the established moral boundaries, they are shamed — minimized, labeled, treated as if they are worth less than others. And if they believe it, if they accept this judgment, then they live in shame. Our culture has used shame as a teaching tool, with far-reaching and terrible consequences.

To set yourself free, learn the difference between judgment and discernment. If your outlook on the world is informed by judgment, you will constantly minimize the actions and beliefs of others. You will consider yourself to be superior, better in some way than others. Unless, of course, it is yourself you are judging. Then, you will find yourself caught in the net of shame.

If your outlook is informed by discernment, then you may observe the same propensities in others, and you will have the same experience of them and their actions, but discernment allows for compassion.

How can we not feel compassion when we know every one of us thinks and acts in response to our traumas and fears, our cultural imprints and unique life experiences? Learning to feel compassion for others is a step toward feeling compassion for ourselves.

We all play out the stories of our past. But there are ways to free yourself from the tyranny of these unconscious reactions. Some souls have been blessed to encounter wisdom somewhere along the way and, by a miracle of fate, been open to receive it.

＊ ＊ ＊ ＊ ＊

Anna

I have been lying low for the last two months, sleeping a lot. I haven't talked to Perry in quiet awhile. He comes to New Mexico twice a month to mentor some of the psych interns at the UNM Hospital. Then he sees clients in a little office near where I live. I hate to miss him when he comes, but I have needed time on my own. I can't believe it's already October. Sophia's been gone for a year.

I've been having intense dreams. Some of them have been disturbing, but others have been sweet, like the dream I had last night:

I was floating down a river. I was in a boat I couldn't steer, but it didn't matter because I knew I was safe. There were towering red rock canyon walls all around me, and I was feeling really happy because I knew that just around the next bend, the river would empty into the ocean, and when that happened, I would find my Mom and Dad waiting for me.

When I woke up I was feeling more peaceful than I can ever remember feeling. I have an appointment with Perry in two days. I really want to tell him about this dream.

I have finished reading the journals and all of Sophia's notes she stuck between the pages. I still have questions — I still don't know where Sophia has been all this time, and I still don't understand why she insisted I read all these journals. Why was it so important for me to learn about her entire life since she was 15 years old?

I have to admit, I am changed from this experience. I have come to understand Sophia so much better. I see why she made the choices she did. Through my work with Perry, I have learned to pay attention to my dreams. I have learned how to settle myself when I am overwhelmed. I am no longer anxious about where Sophia is and what she is doing or why she wanted me to do this. I have a sense my questions will be answered.

When I stand in front of a mirror, I still get the feeling I want to melt away and disappear, but I have learned how to resist that pull. And when I successfully hold on, looking at myself and keeping myself present, I am filled with a really amazing feeling of having accomplished something difficult.

Here is something else I have noticed: I never realized how judgmental I used to be, especially toward Sophia! Everything was good or bad, right or wrong, acceptable or unacceptable. Now things just are what they are. Why did I always think I needed to pass judgment on everything?

I just noticed something really weird. The journals I've had sitting on the coffee table for a couple of months have a new note on top of them from Sophia. How is this possible? Was it inside the journal with all the other notes and just fell out? How could it fall out and land on top of the journal?

* * * * *

Dear Anna,

For the last two months, Mom has been dying. I have been at her side, doing everything I can to ease her way out of this life. It has been a challenge and a blessing beyond words. The closer she gets to her transition, the less she speaks. She stares into space a lot, or into our faces.

Yesterday she was staring at me for a long time, and I asked her what she was thinking and feeling. She's very weak, and it's hard for her to talk. But she gathered her strength and said, "I did a good job." Anna, can you imagine how my heart broke open? In that moment I could see so clearly how all that transpires in our long and complicated lives, in the end, all comes down to love and appreciation. She has spoken hardly a word since.

I hope your journey of reading the journals has served you. I know it has been full of challenges, and I pray it has also been full of blessings.
Love,
Sophia

* * * * *

Anna

I had a session with Perry this morning. He told me Sophia had called him and told him her mother had died peacefully two days ago. I already knew this, though I wasn't sure how I knew. I think it had something to do with that dream. Perry told me Sophia had asked him if please, if he saw me today, would he take me down the mountain to the funeral? Of course I must go! I need to be there for Sophia!

We got into Perry's car and made a quick stop at my

house so I could change into my black dress. We headed down the mountain. I was grateful he was driving. I just looked out the window and cried most of the way. Perry just let me cry.

I was allowing myself to feel what I was feeling, using the raw emotion to dredge up something from deep inside. Of course I am feeling Sophia's grief. How could I not feel it? This is the feeling of life when it is messy and painful and doesn't just do what it's supposed to do. I was in Sophia's world. I needed to find her!

When we arrived at Sophia's parents' house, I ran inside calling out, "Sophia!" I ran from room to room. She wasn't in the kitchen or the living room. Her old room was empty. I ran down the hall to her Mom's room, and as I rounded the corner into the bedroom, there she was! I froze. Sophia was standing completely still, wearing my black dress, looking back at me from the ornate oval frame of Mom's dressing table mirror.

* * * * *

November 8, 2010

It's been two weeks now and almost every day I think of Mom's funeral and everything that happened that day — how Anna ran into the house frantically looking for Sophia. Again and again, I have gone over in my mind how I saw myself in Mom's mirror with a flood of recognition; how I sat down on the little bench in front of the mirror and stared at myself. I saw myself on that day long ago, a lovely but troubled young woman in a pink dress staring at herself in that very mirror. My whole life flashed before me, and in that moment I/we no longer existed as two entities. I felt the coming together of the two parts of myself like a thunderclap. But after that initial jolt, it was like I was standing in the eye of a hurricane — my reality unraveling, crashing, spinning out of control. But here in the center, after 50 years, I was whole again.

It was a good thing Perry was there to help me find my way in this new reality. But there wasn't much time for self-examination and processing. Everyone was gathering at the church, and there was no way I was going to be late for Mom's funeral!

The black dress seemed all wrong. Too somber. Too sad. I would honor Mom by wearing one of her dresses. I selected from her closet a beautiful one I had seen her wear many times. I looked at myself in Mom's mirror. The dress fit me perfectly. It was a lovely shade of pink. There was no shame now. This pink dress evoked in me only a sense of freedom and empowerment.

Mom's funeral was at the same church where I was married so many years ago in that other pink dress. In the entrance hall was the same window casting my reflection back at me. And in a flash I was back there, reliving the shame and terror felt by my eighteen-year-old self, walking down that aisle, knowing that as the congregation turned, they would see I was wearing a pink dress. And they would all know what that meant — I was not a virgin, I had been a bad girl. And I could hear again in my head my own voice screaming on the inside, *I'm not bad! I'm not bad! Please love me! I'm still the same person!*

I had walked down the aisle on Dad's arm, wearing the pink dress and feeling an unbearable shame — a shame so intense my psyche split. Anna came into being on my wedding day. I had always been a good girl, and a part of me could not live inside the psyche of a girl who was so shamed.

My father's cousin, my 90-year-old Godmother Teresa, brought me back to the present. I enfolded her in a long embrace. Teresa had baptized me, and I was her first godchild. I still remember the dress and tiara I wore as a four-year-old flower girl in her wedding. She holds a tender place in my heart.

"Tell me," she said, "what were you just thinking? I have been watching you for a few minutes, and I can tell you were lost in memories."

I said, "Do you remember 50 years ago when I got married?"

"Yes, of course I do!"

"Do you remember what you thought when you saw me walking down the aisle?"

She looked down for a moment, and when she raised her head, a tear spilled from her eye. "I remember it like it was yesterday. When the door to the church opened and I saw you on your father's arm, at first I just saw how beautiful you were. Then my heart dropped. You were wearing a pink dress." She paused. "I knew immediately what that meant, and all I could think was how hard this must be for you. Sophia Anna, I just kept sending you love and saying, 'You're okay. I love you. You're beautiful, and I love you!'"

I took a minute to let her words sink in. "Oh, Teresa, is that really what you were thinking? I was so sure you were all thinking, *She's not a virgin; she must be pregnant; we always thought she was such a good girl, but obviously she is not. She is not worthy of our love. She's bad!*"

Teresa grabbed my hand in her remarkably strong grip. "No!" she said. "That is not what I was thinking! I love you now, and I loved you then. And there was nothing you could have done for me not to love you. I have always known you are a good person with a good heart. A mistake made as a teenager doesn't change goodness. Never forget how much you are loved. And don't ever think like that again about yourself!"

We held each other for a moment. "And I love that you are wearing your mother's pink dress. What a beautiful symbol of your love for her and of your courage."

Under the archway into the sanctuary, Dad was waiting for me just as he had been 50 years ago. He smiled. "You're wearing your mama's dress. You look beautiful in it, just like your mom."

We stood together for a few minutes, thinking about

Mom, feeling the blessings of family and love. Then we walked arm in arm down the aisle. And the voice in my head was not crying out in the anguish of shame, but instead was filling me with songs of gratitude and love. My mom — ever the giver of care and affection — was, even here at her own funeral, touching me with her bounty of love.

November 18, 2010

Perry is helping me to find my way as an integrated woman. I've learned a lot from him over the years about the power of symbols and rituals. He suggested I do something tangible, ritualistic, to start the process of being grounded in my new reality. The ritual he suggested consisted of me weaving together two different-colored strands of yarn while speaking aloud the strengths and limitations, the qualities of Sophia and Anna.

Then I was instructed to go out into nature, find a straight wooden staff, ask and obtain permission of the tree, take the branch with reverence, and leave offerings of gratitude. I wrapped the staff with the woven yarn as a symbol of a new midline, a midline representing Sophia Anna as one being, integrated, whole unto myself.

December 25, 2010

It's Christmas, and Mom is gone. I am learning to live in the world as a motherless child. For the first time, we will celebrate Christmas without the amazing woman who always made it special. I miss her. I miss talking to her. There's a big empty space in my heart.

Yesterday, I needed to cut open a package, so I reached for a pair of scissors. When I picked them up, I was catapulted back in time. These were Mom's favorite scissors, the ones I took when I ran away with Kevin. I never gave them back to her. My legs just gave out from under me. I dropped to my knees on the kitchen floor, flooded with sorrow and remorse, howling, "Mom, I am so sorry! I'm so sorry!"

February 20, 2011

It's taking time for me to integrate all I have discovered about myself. I see Perry often. This is a journey of love and patience as I find my way. I have had to learn to be in the world as a different person than I was before — an integrated version of myself. Now I have all my memories, Sophia's and Anna's. Sophia found Anna at my vision quest, and Anna found Sophia in Mom's mirror.

I am Sophia Anna, a woman who has been fractured and mended — dismembered and reconfigured, healed and whole. But the Anna part of me still exists. She emerges as an individual voice when I am faced with a moral judgment, a problem of good or bad, right or wrong. She is not something separate from me. We are one person, standing in wholeness, able to see from more than one perspective, remembering all of myself.

* * * * *

Grandmother Spirit

Sisters, not a one of us is spared from life's upheavals. When something of huge significance happens in our lives, we tend to feel like the world should just stop for a moment — give us time to reconfigure, to resettle, to find our balance. But of course life doesn't usually give this to us. It is relentless in its ever-changing, ever-emerging now.

Sophia Anna's life moved on in ways that she could never have predicted. She found love again and moved to Oregon. She created another women's retreat center where she and her new love celebrated their holy-union ceremony under the Grandmother Tree. Sophia Anna wore a white dress with a pale pink rose at her heart.

A few weeks after the ceremony, she was deep in a medicine vision when a wisdom keeper came to her and said, "Do you remember the dream you created and lived? Do you understand its wisdom?" Sophia Anna said she did. The elder asked again, and again Sophia Anna said she remembered. The elder turned to walk away, then whirled around, her hand whipping up to point at Sophia Anna. "Your dream is over! Never forget your dream! Be grounded in the roots of your dream. Go now and create a new dream!"

The next day, while working in the garden, Sophia Anna received a phone call. The Grandmother Tree had fallen, snapped at her base, her roots still firmly in the ground. The old dream is over, and the new dream begins. Sophia Anna dusted the red dirt from her feet and turned, soul-centered and whole, to embrace a new dream.

I have only one more thing to say. If I had to point to one lesson from Sophia Anna's story, it would be this: the journey to freedom is not a straight line. There is a reason practices are called practices! If you are committed to your freedom, you will take each catastrophe that shatters your life, and you will use it to learn more about yourself.

Sisters, my prayer for you is that you come to know, as a deep and abiding truth, that there is no reason for shame. I pray Sophia Anna's story will inspire you to face your own shadows, to persevere in your spiritual awakening, to joyfully embrace the wild nature that lives in your heart.

The time will come when, with elation

you will greet yourself…

in your own mirror

and each will smile at the other's welcome.

~ Derek Walcott

Love After Love

Closing Ceremony

Grandmother Spirit

We sit together in the quiet. The wind coming down the canyon gently rustles the leaves. The setting sun casts dancing shadows on the canyon walls that rise above us, just like in Anna's dream. Above the rim of the canyon, a full moon is rising.

This story is complete, but just like Sophia Anna's vision, its completion only marks the beginning of the next story. For now, we bask in the quiet satisfaction of having completed together one leg of a long and magical journey. In thirteen moons we will meet again.

They are so lovely, these women! I watch them as they begin to stir, moving around, talking softly to one another, laughing, singing, preparing for the sweat lodge. They bring out their prayer bundles, filled with their intentions and prayers. In the beautiful way of women everywhere, they clean up the fire area, gather more wood, refresh the altar. They help with one another's small needs.

And now it is time for Inipi! We will enter the womb of the Mother and allow ourselves to be healed by the fires of transformation. We will sing our songs and pray our prayers as we dissolve and reform in the transformative heat and fire. When we emerge — changed, living a new dream — we will place our prayer bundles on the sacred fire, and as they burn, our prayers will be lifted up and carried to the spirit world.

Aho Mitakuye Oyasin. Thank you, all my relations.

Eve's Garden

Sweet silver moonlight awakens me tonight,

Through the open window, oh she shines so
bright.

Long barefoot shadows on the floor tiptoe
through the door,

Down the darkened hallway and down the
darkened stair,

Out into the garden where there's magic,
magic in the air.

Moon, sister moon, insistently you pull me
from my rest.

Moon, mother moon, a restlessness you touch
upon my breast

Moon, old auntie moon, you call me out into
the night,

Your voice so clear and bright, a song in magic
tones of light,

Heard in hearts that dance delight.

There never was a crime, no need for a pardon,

All the women in the world tonight

Are dancing to reclaim Eve's Garden.

No need for repentance, no suffering to grieve,

An end to the blame, no reason for shame,

We dance to reclaim the garden of Eve,

Moon, sister moon.

Moon, mother moon.

Moon, old auntie moon,

Moon, sweet daughter,

Queen of the waters

Grandmother moon.

> ~ *Alexa MacDonald*
> From the album *Compassionate Heart*

Heartfelt Appreciation

My heart smiles in gratitude. Thank you to all my friends, colleagues, teachers, and students who have supported the birthing of *Emerging Woman*.

The title for this book, *Emerging Woman*, was suggested by one of my content readers who mentioned that she liked the name of a sculpture I described in the book. My dear friend Neil Pinholster was the artist who created this amazing sculpture and named it Emerging Woman. Thank you, Neil, for your talented hands, your love, and the perfect title for this book.

I recognize my friend Pam Rousseau for her contribution to the creative process and her help finding a structure to ground and contain this story. Her consistent vision of women gathered around to hear the wisdom of the soul has inspired my journey.

My thanks to Brenda Littleton for holding the container in the beginning of my process and re-emerging later to support me through the final stages. With her Jungian wisdom and story-writing skills, she carefully crafted her questions to help me unearth what was missing and what needed clarification. She recognized the value of the prayers in the book and how they can benefit others. I am blessed and grateful.

My sister Kathleen Hannum has been there for me through each iteration of the story, encouraging every new spark of creativity. She listened from her heart with encouragement and love. She stood by my side in the hardest of times and continued to love me. From the Soulgazm of my heart, I thank you.

I appreciate my husband Jorg Rupf, who couldn't escape the reading of ideas and passages while on a road trip for 53 days. He is always there for me, championing my efforts and asking the hard questions. Thank you, sweetheart.

My gratitude goes out to the women who read drafts of the manuscript for clarity and continuity. Your wisdom, insights, and suggestions were invaluable. Thank you Carolyn Sell, Pam Rousseau, Marta Maria Marraccini, Brookelyn Sproviero, Kate Greer, Kimberly Reyes, Vicchi Oleski, Ashley Ciaglia Bodiford, Tina Root McBride, Brenda Littleton, and Tina Benson.

To Flora Aube and Ree Altavilla, who provided a sanctuary for the maturing of my creativity where the original cover painting for *Emerging Woman* was born.

To Tina Root McBride for the beautiful photos of my paintings and her encouragement to share my work. Your patience and follow-through are appreciated.

My life has been enriched by the love and support of my soul sisters. They held space, witnessed my journey, and shared their hearts and wisdom. Nancy Turcich, Mireya Marcet, Amanda Elo'esh Johnsen, Patty

Ebert, Lexi Fisher, Penny Neu, Jacki Elder, Beth Meyer, and many unnamed, I thank you.

Bill Georgevich and Melanie Pahlmann, friends and owners of Lucid Design Studios, have been unwavering in their commitment to service, integrity, and consistent quality. Their continuous support helped me through challenging times, and their consummate professional skills made *Emerging Woman* the beautiful book that it is. I value and appreciate both of you.

My editor, friend, and confidant Alexa MacDonald listened to what my heart wanted to communicate, guided my rewrites and stood in her integrity. Her devotion was unwavering as she walked with me through the crafting of *Emerging Woman*. She is the alchemist who turned the raw materials into gold. Alexa's heartfelt compassion, wisdom, and encouragement are deeply appreciated. Alexa was an essential part in the birthing of *Emerging Woman*.

Thank you for reading *Emerging Woman*.

Kerani Marie

About the Author

Kerani Marie is an inner-wisdom guide, the Soul's Muse for women on the sacred feminine journey.

With 40 years of immersion in multicultural spiritual teachings and healing practices, her wisdom is informed by direct experience with spiritual and healing crises. Kerani Marie's authentic heart inspires the conscious emergence of souls through her writings, art, ceremonies and rituals. She is a Craniosacral Practitioner and Reiki Master in 2 lineages.

Kerani Marie is the founder of The Center for Living Wisdom, Women Igniting Soulful Evolution W.I.S.E., SoWISE Creations, and The Soulgazm Rendezvous. She is author of *Cycle of Life Journey*, published in 1998, and *Emerging Woman*, releasing in Summer 2018.

SoWISE is an acronym for Stories of WoMen Igniting Soulful Evolution through their words of wisdom. SoWISE Creations accepts stories in service to humanity. Our books, art and poetry inspire, enrich, and transform lives.

Kerani currently lives in Sonoma County, CA with her husband. You can reach her via email at Kerani@KeraniMarie.com. Please visit her website at www.KeraniMarie.com.

AUDIOBOOKS

Emerging Woman:
A Rite of Passage from Shame to Freedom

Cycle of Life Journey:
52 Journeys of Self-Awareness
with 12 experiential exercises
and bonus material: 52 radio interviews
exploring each Cycle of Life Journey

SoWISE Creations offers a broad spectrum of author services including mentoring, book development, editing, publishing, audio recording, and web presence. Our mission is to assist woman (and men) who want to share the stories of their own soulful evolution.

For more information about bringing your book to life,
please visit www.SoWISEcreations.com

Made in the USA
Columbia, SC
03 October 2018